WHAT
REMAINS
OF HEAVEN

continued . . .

What Angels Fear

"Perfect reading.... Harris crafts her story with the threat of danger, hints of humor, vivid sex scenes, and a conclusion that will make your pulse race. Impressive." —*The New Orleans Times-Picayune*

"A stunning debut novel filled with suspense, intrigue, and plot twists galore. C. S. Harris artfully re-creates the contradictory world of Regency England as her marvelous characters move between the glittering ballrooms and the treacherous back alleys of London. Kat and Sebastian lead a cast of memorable characters you will want to meet again and again as they follow the twists and turns of the intricately woven plot to find justice for a young woman who was brutally murdered. Don't start this one in the evening—you'll be up all night! Start this one early in the day—you won't be able to put it down!" —Victoria Thompson, author of the Gaslight Mystery series

"Appealing characters, authentic historical details, and sound plotting make this an amazing debut historical." —*Library Journal* (Starred Review)

"An absorbing and accomplished debut that displays a mastery of the Regency period in all its elegance and barbarity.... [It] will grip the reader from its first pages and compel to the finish." —Stephanie Barron, author of the Jane Austen Mystery series

"A masterful blend of historical detail, page-turning suspense, and good old-fashioned romance." —Penelope Williamson, author of *Wages of Sin*

"The combined elements of historical fiction, romance, and mystery in this fog-enshrouded London puzzler will appeal to fans of Anne Perry." —*Booklist*

"A masterful blend of history and suspense, character and plot, imagination and classic mystery. A thoroughly intriguing, enjoyable read." —Laura Joh Rowland, author of the Sano Ichirō Mystery series

"Riveting ... a powerful blend of political intrigue and suspense.... This fresh, fast-paced historical is sure to be a hit." —*Publishers Weekly*

"Page-turning suspense, memorable characters, and an intricate chess game of a story drenched in period atmosphere." —Tracy Grant, author of *Beneath a Silent Moon*

"Harris cleverly blends fact and fiction into a haunting debut mystery. Though the Regency backdrop is familiar territory, the suspense and possible ramifications of the murder present a novel slant while introducing a strong new voice to the genre." —*Romantic Times*

WHAT
REMAINS
OF HEAVEN

A Sebastian St. Cyr Mystery

C. S. HARRIS

AN OBSIDIAN MYSTERY

OBSIDIAN

Published by New American Library, a division of
Penguin Group (USA) Inc., 375 Hudson Street,
New York, New York 10014, USA
Penguin Group (Canada), 90 Eglinton Avenue East, Suite 700, Toronto,
Ontario M4P 2Y3, Canada (a division of Pearson Penguin Canada Inc.)
Penguin Books Ltd., 80 Strand, London WC2R 0RL, England
Penguin Ireland, 25 St. Stephen's Green, Dublin 2,
Ireland (a division of Penguin Books Ltd.)
Penguin Group (Australia), 250 Camberwell Road, Camberwell, Victoria 3124,
Australia (a division of Pearson Australia Group Pty. Ltd.)
Penguin Books India Pvt. Ltd., 11 Community Centre, Panchsheel Park,
New Delhi - 110 017, India
Penguin Group (NZ), 67 Apollo Drive, Rosedale, Auckland 0632,
New Zealand (a division of Pearson New Zealand Ltd.)
Penguin Books (South Africa) (Pty.) Ltd., 24 Sturdee Avenue,
Rosebank, Johannesburg 2196, South Africa

Penguin Books Ltd., Registered Offices:
80 Strand, London WC2R 0RL, England

First published by Obsidian, an imprint of New American Library, a division of
Penguin Group (USA) Inc. Previously published in an Obsidian trade paperback
edition.

First Obsidian Mass Market Printing, August 2011
10   9   8   7   6   5   4   3   2

For my daughters,
Samantha and Danielle

ONE murder makes a Villain,
MILLIONS a Hero: Princes are privileged
To kill, and numbers sanctify the crime.
Ah! Why will Kings forget that they are men?
And men that they are brethren? Why delight
In HUMAN SACRIFICE? Why burst the ties
Of Nature, that should knit their souls together
In one soft bond of amity and love?
They yet still breathe destruction, still go on,
Inhumanly ingenious, to find out
New pain for life, new terrors for the grave,
Artificers of death! Still Monarchs dream
Of universal empire, growing up
From universal ruin. Blast the design
Great God of Hosts, nor let thy creatures fall
Unpitied Victims at Ambition's shrine!

    —From "Death: A Poetical Essay," by Dr. Beilby
      Porteous, Bishop of London 1789–1809,
      The Cambridge Intelligencer (September 14, 1793)

WHAT
REMAINS
OF HEAVEN

Chapter 1

*H*is breath coming in undignified gasps, the Reverend Malcolm Earnshaw abandoned the village high street and struck out through the lanky grass of the churchyard. He was a small, plump man, well into his middle years, his hair sparse and graying, his knees stiff. Looking up, he saw the belfry of the village church silhouetted dark against the white of the evening sky, and suppressed a groan.

"What have I done? What have I done?" he murmured to himself in a kind of chant. He never should have lingered so long with old Mrs. Cummings. Yes, the woman was dying, but he'd done what he could to ease her passing, and one did not keep the Bishop of London waiting—especially when one was a lowly churchman who owed the Bishop's family his living.

Hot and breathless now in his haste, the Reverend reached the sweep of gravel before the church. His step faltered, the small stones crunching beneath the leather soles of his shoes. "Merciful heavens," he whispered, his jaw sagging at the sight of the Bishop's carriage, its coachman dozing on the box. "He's *here*."

Swallowing hard, Earnshaw cast a searching glance around the ancient churchyard. Despite the lengthening shadows, the jagged piles of stones and aged timbers left from the demolition of the charnel house that had once stood against the north wall of the chancel were clearly visible. But Bishop Prescott was nowhere in sight.

The Reverend hesitated, the urge to rush forward warring with a craven desire to duck into the sacristy for a lantern. He pushed on, his heart thumping painfully in his chest as he neared the gaping hole before him. The workmen had accidentally broken through the thin brick wall that afternoon. The wall had concealed a forgotten staircase of worn stone steps that led down to an ancient crypt far older even than the venerable Norman nave above it.

During his ten years of service here at St. Margaret's, Malcolm Earnshaw had heard vague rumors of a crypt, sealed decades ago for health reasons. But nothing the Reverend had heard had prepared him for the workmen's gruesome discovery.

Tugging his handkerchief from his pocket, he pressed the linen folds against his mouth and nostrils as the foul air of the crypt wafted up to him. He was near enough now to see the glow of lantern light on the worn steps coming up from below. The Bishop had indeed gone before him.

Again Earnshaw hesitated, not from indecision this time but from revulsion at the horror of what lay below. The Bible taught that the trumpet shall sound, and the dead shall be raised incorruptible. And again in Ezekiel it was written that God shall put flesh on the bones of the dead and breathe life into them. Earnshaw knew that. Yet still he found himself trembling at the need to confront once again a sight that might have been conjured from the vilest visions of Dante's *Inferno*.

Grasping the rusted railing that ran along one side of the steps, he stumbled down the shadowy stairs toward the flickering light below. "I most humbly beg your pardon, Bishop Prescott," he began, his voice echoing back to him from that sepulchral vault. "I do hope I've not kept you waiting long?"

The oppressive silence of the crypt closed around him. Built of rough stone covered in limestone mortar and with a low vaulted ceiling supported by worn columns, the bays of the chamber stretched before him in shadowy phalanxes of death. Piles of coffins stacked five and six high were crammed into nearly every bay, their wood warped and split to reveal tomb-blackened remnants of tattered clothing and the occasional, unmistakable gleam of a skull or long bone.

But that clean scouring of time was rare. What truly horrified the Reverend and caused him to tighten his grip on the stair railing was the way the dry air had combined with the high concentration of lime to preserve most of the burials. All too often, what spilled from those crushed tombs was an arm or leg still recognizably human, or a hair-topped nightmare of a face, its flesh shriveled and tanned like that of a mummy brought back from Egypt.

"Bishop Prescott?" Earnshaw called again, his voice quavering. Misled by the gleam of lamplight, he'd obviously erred in choosing to come here directly. The Bishop must simply have abandoned his lantern in the crypt and returned to the sacristy to wait.

Devastated by his error, Earnshaw was turning back toward the stairs when his gaze fell on the far end of the chamber. A man lay facedown beside the last worn, spiraled column. Only this was not some ancient, desiccated corpse tumbled from its collapsed coffin.

"Bishop Prescott," said Earnshaw with a gasp, recognizing the man's tall, gaunt form, the distinctive purple cassock, the thinning white hair worn unusually long.

The Reverend staggered to where the Bishop lay with his head turned slightly to one side, his pale gray eyes open wide and blankly staring. From beneath the matted, crushed side of his head, a spreading stain of blood ran in a slow, dark rivulet across the ancient stone floor.

Chapter 2

*T*he Circular Room at Carlton House was an inner sanctum reserved for the most intimate friends of His Royal Highness George, Prince Regent. Here, amidst the glitter of crystal chandeliers and the glories of blue silk draped in imitation of a Roman tent, those with the privilege of entrée gathered late into the night to drink wine and listen to music and bask in all the benefits of being in the royal favor.

But tonight, the Prince was in a petulant mood, his full, almost feminine lower lip thrust out in a pout. "I hear the Bishop of London is set to give a speech against slavery before the Lords this Thursday," said the Regent, snapping his fingers for another bottle.

Once, the Prince had been a handsome man. Now, in his early fifties, a lifetime of overindulgence in the various delights of the flesh had taken their toll. His face was flushed, his features blurred, and not even the talents of London's best tailors—or the use of rigidly laced stays—could disguise the corpulence of his body.

His stays creaking perilously, the Regent turned to frown at his cousin Charles, Lord Jarvis, the acknowledged power behind the Prince's fragile regency. "What say you, Jarvis? Surely there's some way to stop him?"

His cousin Jarvis was also a big man, standing more than six feet tall and fleshy. Jarvis's size alone would have made him impressive. But it was his awe-inspiring intellect, his formidable ruthlessness, and a true dedication to King and country that had combined to make him the most powerful man in the kingdom. He took a slow sip of his own wine before answering. "I hardly see what, short of killing him."

A nervous titter spread amongst the men gathered near enough to hear. Everyone knew that those Jarvis considered his enemies—or even merely inconvenient— had a nasty habit of turning up dead.

The Prince's pout grew. One of his intimates—a slim, hawk-faced exquisite named Lord Quillian—raised one eyebrow and said, "The man's on a bloody crusade. You're not troubled by it, Jarvis?"

Jarvis flicked open a gold snuffbox with one careless finger. "You think I should be?"

"Considering the fact that Prescott was largely responsible for getting the Slave Trade Act passed five years ago, I'd say so, yes. There's a growing piety in this country, combined with a mawkish kind of sensibility that worries me."

"It's easy to support abolition in theory." Jarvis raised a pinch of snuff to his nostril. "In practice, things become considerably more complicated."

A movement near the door drew Jarvis's attention. A

tall, military-looking gentleman in a riding coat and top boots spoke in a low voice to the attendants, then strode across the room to whisper in Jarvis's ear.

"Excuse me, Your Highness," said the King's powerful cousin with a bow. "I shan't be but a moment."

Withdrawing to a secluded alcove, Jarvis snapped, "What is it?"

The tall, military-looking gentleman, a former captain in the 9th Foot, smiled. "The Bishop of London is dead."

In the cool light of early morning, father and son trotted their horses companionably side by side through Hyde Park. Faint wisps of mist still hovered here and there beneath the trees, although the strengthening sun was beginning to burn off the fog rising from the nearby river.

"It's been two months now since Perceval was shot," grumbled Alistair James St. Cyr, Fifth Earl of Hendon. Mounted on a big gray gelding, the Earl was a powerfully framed man of sixty-six with a barrel chest, a thick shock of white hair, and vivid blue eyes. "Two months!" he said again, when his son made no comment. "And Liverpool is still acting more like an incompetent backbencher than a prime minister. This situation can't continue. We're already at war with half of Europe. The next thing you know we're going to have the bloody Americans attacking Canada."

Mounted on the neat black Arab mare he'd acquired during his years as an Army officer, the Earl's only surviving son and heir, Sebastian, Viscount Devlin, ducked his head to hide a smile. Even taller than his father, the Viscount was built lean, with dark hair and strange, feral-looking yellow eyes. "You're the one who turned down the Regent's invitation to form a government," he said.

"I should rather think so," said the Earl, who for the past three years had held the position of Chancellor of the Exchequer. "Why should I spend my days fighting Jarvis for the loyalty of my own cabinet? Once, I might have been persuaded to do so. No longer."

"I should think you'd jump at the chance," said Sebastian, "if for no other reason than to spite Jarvis." The King's formidable, eerily omnipotent cousin intimidated most men, but not Hendon. The two had been at loggerheads for as long as Sebastian could remember. Yet as powerful as he was, Jarvis would never form a government himself. The big man preferred to exercise his authority discreetly—and more effectively—from the shadows.

Hendon blew out a long breath. "I must be getting old. I find I've better things to do with my time."

Sebastian raised one eyebrow.

"You heard me," said Hendon. "I'd like to spend my declining years surrounded by a passel of lusty grandsons. Unfortunately, my only surviving son has yet to condescend to give me any."

"You have a grandson. And a granddaughter."

"Bayard?" Hendon dismissed the children of his only legitimate daughter, Amanda, Lady Wilcox, with a wave of one hand. "Bayard's a Wilcox, and half as mad as his father besides. I'm talking about St. Cyr grandsons. The kind only you can give me. Heirs. You're nearly thirty years old now, Sebastian. It's high time you settled down and started a family."

Sebastian kept his gaze firmly fixed between his horse's ears and said nothing. The estrangement that had arisen between father and son the previous autumn had eased these past few weeks, but Hendon was straying into dangerous territory.

There was a moment of tense silence; then the Earl grunted, his eyes narrowing as he stared across the park. "I see you're still employing that impertinent pickpocket as a groom."

Sebastian followed his father's gaze to where a sharp-faced boy dressed in the Devlin livery and mounted on one of Sebastian's hacks pelted inelegantly toward them, one elbow cocked skyward to hold his hat in place. "What the devil?"

Tom, Sebastian's young tiger, reined in hard beside them. He was thirteen years old, although he looked younger, with his gap-toothed grin and slight frame. Bobbing his head to Hendon, he said breathlessly, "Beggin' yer pardon for the interruption, yer lordship." He turned to Sebastian. "Ye've visitors awaitin' ye at Brook Street, gov'nor. Yer aunt, the Duchess of Claiborne, and the Archbishop of Canterbury!"

Devlin said, "The Archbishop of Canterbury?"

"Henrietta?" said his father, eyes widening with incredulity. "At this hour?" The Duchess of Claiborne was famous for never leaving her bed before noon. Hendon sniffed the air. "The boy is obviously foxed."

"I ain't been drinkin'," said Tom, bridling. "It's 'Er Grace, all right, sittin' up there in the drawing room with the Archbishop 'isself."

Hendon's suspicious frown deepened. "The last I heard, Archbishop Moore was essentially at death's door. Why, Jarvis is already maneuvering to line up the man's replacement."

"Well, 'e don't look none too 'ale, that's fer sure,"

agreed Tom. "But I reckon that's to be expected, given what's 'appened."

"What has happened?" said Sebastian.

"Why, someone's done gone and murdered the Bishop of London. Last night, in the crypt o' some church near 'Ounslow 'Eath!"

Chapter 3

*I*n addition to a modest estate in Hampshire bequeathed him by a maiden great-aunt, Sebastian also kept an elegant little bow-fronted town house in Brook Street. His long-suffering majordomo, Morey, met him at the door with a grave bow. "The Archbishop of Canterbury and the Duchess of Claiborne are here to see you, my lord. In the drawing room."

"Good God." Sebastian handed the majordomo his riding crop, hat, and gloves. "It's true then."

Morey bowed again. "Yes, my lord. I took the liberty of offering to send up tea, but her ladyship refused."

Sebastian climbed the stairs to the first floor two at a time to find his aunt Henrietta—a vision in purple silk and a towering turban—ensconced in one of the delicate chairs beside the drawing room's bowed front window. A gray-haired, skeletally thin cleric with the pallid complexion of a man in the final stages of consumption sat opposite her. They were great old friends, his aunt and the Archbishop of Canterbury. Sebastian knew the Archbishop's long illness and approaching death had caused her considerable distress.

"My apologies for coming to you in all my dirt," said

Sebastian, "but I understand the reason for your visit is urgent."

Archbishop John Moore held out a thin, blue-veined hand that trembled visibly. "And I am sorry if we forced you to curtail your morning ride. You'll excuse me if I do not stand."

Sebastian bowed low over the Archbishop's frail hand, then turned to kiss his aunt's cheek. "Shall I ring for tea?"

"I've had all the tea I want this morning," said Aunt Henrietta with an inelegant grunt. "What I need is brandy."

Five years Hendon's senior, the Dowager Duchess of Claiborne was one of the grand old dames of society. As solidly built as her brother, she had Hendon's broad, fleshy face and the fiercely blue St. Cyr eyes. But she was looking decidedly drawn this morning, and it occurred to Sebastian that she was abroad so early because she'd yet to make it to her bed.

"You do have brandy, don't you?" she said sharply when he hesitated.

Sebastian cast an inquiring eye toward Archbishop Moore.

"Brandy sounds like a marvelous idea," said the Archbishop with a shaky smile.

Sebastian moved to the decanter kept on a side table near the hearth. "Brandy it is."

"I assume by now you've heard of the death of the Bishop of London?" said Henrietta.

"Only moments ago."

The Archbishop cleared his throat. "It appears someone bashed in his skull last night in the crypt of St. Margaret's, in Tanfield Hill."

Sebastian splashed brandy into three glasses and wondered what any of this had to do with him.

"The crypt has been shut up for decades," said the Archbishop as Sebastian handed him a glass. "I gather the odors from the place had begun to interfere with the use of the church and raised concerns about disease. The decision was made to wall it off."

Personally, Sebastian had always found the practice of stacking coffins in open crypts bizarre to the point of being barbaric, but he kept that observation to himself. He handed his aunt her brandy and said, "If the crypt was shut up, then what was the Bishop doing down there?"

"Some workmen accidentally broke through the bricked-up entrance yesterday and made an unpleasant discovery," said the Archbishop. "Due to the potential for scandal, the Reverend thought it best to involve Bishop Prescott right away."

Sebastian went to lean against the mantelpiece. "Scandal? Why?"

"Because of the body."

Sebastian paused with his glass raised halfway to his lips. "The body?"

"The dead body in the crypt," said his aunt, as if he were being deliberately obtuse.

Sebastian took a sip of his brandy and shuddered. He had something of a reputation for hard drinking and wild living, but half past seven in the morning was a little early to be drinking brandy, even for Sebastian. "I should imagine there are any number of dead bodies in the crypt of St. Margaret's. It dates from—what? The twelfth century?"

"Actually, the crypt is even older than the church,"

said the Archbishop. "It dates back to Anglo-Saxon times."

"So, hundreds of bodies," said Sebastian. "If not a thousand or more."

Henrietta leaned forward, her brandy held delicately aloft in one hand. "The body the workmen discovered was not one of the burials, Sebastian. The man was obviously murdered down there." She lowered her voice. "At some point before the crypt was sealed. He was found sprawled on the floor behind one of the columns. *With a knife in his back.*"

Sebastian glanced from his aunt to the Archbishop beside her. "Excuse me, Your Grace, but . . . why are you here, telling me this?"

"You know perfectly well why we're here, Sebastian," snapped his aunt. "We're here because the Archbishop wants you to solve the murders."

"Why?"

"Why?" she echoed indignantly. "What do you mean, why? Because you're good at it, of course."

Sebastian stood perfectly still. He'd been afraid this was coming. "I can understand that the local magistrate might find the matter overwhelming, but I should think Bow Street more than capable of dealing with the case."

The Archbishop cleared his throat again. "I have already discussed the situation with Bow Street. Sir Henry Lovejoy concurs with my decision to bring you into the investigation. Bow Street is all well and good when it comes to dealing with the murder of a shopkeeper or merchant. But they simply don't have the capability of handling an incident at this level of society, and they know it."

Pushing away from the hearth, Sebastian went to

stand beside the window overlooking the street below. It was true that in the last year and a half he'd found himself drawn into a number of murder investigations. Yet those murders had touched him personally in some way, or had involved victims who were otherwise unlikely to find justice. And each case had peeled another layer off his soul.

He said, "The last time I participated in a murder investigation, something like a dozen people ended up dead."

"I can understand your reluctance to be drawn into this," said the Archbishop in his soothing, father-confessor voice.

Did he? Sebastian wondered. Did he have any idea of the passions that swirled around murder? The secrets and lies, the rage and despair?

The Archbishop's watery gray eyes narrowed. The man might be old and ill, but no one rose to become the most powerful churchman in all of England without being both intelligent and very, very astute. "Yet I wonder if you understand how critical it is to the well-being of the nation that this murder be solved, and solved quickly?"

When Sebastian kept silent, Moore continued. "It's no secret that my days are numbered. The process is already under way to select my successor, which is as it should be. A lengthy hiatus in these situations is best avoided. As it happens, Bishop Prescott was a strong contender for the position. In fact, he was my personal favorite."

Sebastian frowned. "You think that might have something to do with his death?"

"It might. At this point we've no way of knowing."

Setting aside his brandy, the Archbishop leaned forward, his hands coming together as if in prayer. "But consider this: It's been just two months since the Prime Minister was killed. Now the Bishop of London has been murdered. If I die tomorrow . . ." He paused to spread his hands wide, as if inviting Sebastian to imagine a nation bereft of both spiritual and political leadership.

"This is a dangerous time in our nation's history," he continued solemnly, his hands coming together again when Sebastian still remained silent. "We've been at war virtually without pause for two decades. There is widespread suffering and much discontent among the people. And now the Americans are threatening to attack us."

Sebastian huffed a soft laugh. "I see. It's both my spiritual and my patriotic duty to solve this murder, is it?"

His aunt frowned at him.

Ignoring her, Sebastian said, "The other body—the one with the knife in his back. Who was he?"

The sudden direct question seemed to take the Archbishop by surprise. "That we do not know."

"But you say he was killed years ago?"

"So it would appear, yes. From his clothing, I'm told it's likely he died sometime in the last century."

The puzzle was undeniably intriguing—two men murdered in a crypt, their violent deaths separated by decades. Sebastian stared out the window, at a baker's boy making his rounds with the strap of a tray slung around his neck. "Hot buns," he called, "fresh hot buns!"

Aunt Henrietta could keep silent no longer. "Well?" she demanded. "Will you do it?"

Sebastian turned to meet his aunt's anxious stare. If the Archbishop had come alone to request Sebastian's assistance, Sebastian would have turned him down without hesitation. Exaggerated appeals to his patriotism inevitably fell flat, while the true nature of Sebastian's spiritual beliefs would doubtless give the old cleric a severe shock. Yet the wily old Archbishop was obviously shrewd enough to guess some of it, which was why he had brought his dear old friend the Duchess of Claiborne here with him.

She might be gruff and ruthlessly unsentimental, but of all the members of Sebastian's family she was the only one who had never let him down, whose love he'd always known was pure and unconditional. Sebastian could not refuse her.

He raised his brandy to his lips and drained the glass. "I'll do it."

Chapter 4

The village of Tanfield Hill lay about half a mile to the south of the main post road between London and the West Country, just beyond the notorious, highwayman-infested stretch of open land known as Hounslow Heath. Here, the scrub and gorse of the heath began to give way to open, rolling woodland of oak and silver birch. The village itself was a picturesque collection of thatched cottages and whitewashed stone shops strung out along a cobbled high street and a few flanking lanes.

Driving himself in his curricle, Sebastian rattled over a narrow stone bridge spanning the quiet millstream and into the village at around half past ten that morning. The sun was up strong now, bathing the old stone walls in a warm, bucolic glow and filling the air with the sweet scent of roses and honeysuckle tumbling over garden fences and scrambling up neat lattices. From here he could see the low, solid nave and single spire of the ancient Norman church of St. Margaret's crowning a gentle hill covered with daisy-strewn grass and a scattering of aged, moss-covered tombstones.

He turned his chestnuts up the slope, toward the gravel sweep before the church, where Sir Henry Lovejoy stood talking to a workman dressed in a rough smock. A diminutive, middle-aged man with a baldhead and a serious demeanor, Sir Henry was the newest of Bow Street's three stipendiary magistrates. At the sight of Sebastian, he dismissed the workman with a nod and started across the gravel toward the curricle.

"Find someplace to water and rest them," Sebastian told his tiger, handing the young groom the chestnuts' reins. "We'll be here awhile."

"I'll take care of 'em, gov'nor," said Tom, scrambling from his perch at the rear of the carriage. "Ne'er you fear."

"Oh, and Tom—ask around a bit while you're at it. I'd like to hear what the locals are saying about all this."

"Aye, gov'nor."

"Lord Devlin," called Sir Henry, coming up to him. "So the Archbishop convinced you to take an interest in the investigation after all, did he? I feared he might not succeed. This isn't exactly your normal type of murder."

Sebastian hopped down from the curricle's high seat. "I didn't know I had a normal type of murder." Once, this earnest little magistrate had sought Sebastian's own arrest. But over the past year and a half the sternly religious magistrate and the urbane, irreverent Viscount had built an odd friendship, founded on mutual respect and a strong, abiding sense of trust. Sebastian said, "Bow Street didn't object to the suggestion that I become involved?"

One corner of the magistrate's thin lips twitched with the faintest suggestion of a smile. "I wouldn't exactly describe Sir James's reaction as pleased. But when the Archbishop of Canterbury personally intervenes in an investigation, not even the Chief Magistrate would dare complain."

"And you?"

"Me?" Turning, Lovejoy led the way to the northern side of the ancient parish church, where scattered piles of building rubble lay deserted beneath the strengthening sun. "When it comes to murder in the upper reaches of society and government, I know our limits. A delicate business, this. And puzzling. Most puzzling."

Sebastian's head tipped back, his eyes narrowing as he scanned the worn, age-darkened stone walls of the church. The nave of St. Margaret's had the narrow, round-topped windows and heavy masonry typical of the early Norman period. Only the tower was noticeably lighter and more delicate, its spire probably added in early Tudor times.

He let his gaze fall to the rubble at their feet. Through the remnants of a broken wall he could see the upper reaches of a set of worn stone steps that disappeared down into a well of black. "How long ago was the crypt bricked up?" he asked, peering into the darkness. His voice echoed back at him from below.

"As near as anyone can remember, it was around the time of the revolt in America." The magistrate had an unnaturally high-pitched voice that had a tendency to squeak when he became excited or nervous. He was squeaking now.

"So, thirty or forty years ago."

"Something like that, yes." A lantern rested on a large, flat-topped stone near the broken wall. Stooping, Lovejoy flipped open the door and began to kindle his tinderbox. "According to the workmen, an old charnel house stood here. They were in the process of demolishing it when they stumbled upon the entrance to the crypt. It's been closed off for so long that people had forgotten the stairs were here. I gather it was a bit of a shock when the workmen broke through the wall. And even more of a shock when a couple of the lads decided to go exploring and tripped over the body of a man, dressed in the velvets and lace of the last century and with a knife sticking out his back. According to the workmen, the Reverend took one look at the body and left almost immediately for London."

Sebastian stared off down the hill, to where the millstream curled lazily around a stand of willows. "It seems a curious thing to have done. Why go to the Bishop? Why not the local magistrate?"

Lovejoy frowned over his task. "From what I understand, Reverend Earnshaw is of a somewhat, shall we say, excitable disposition."

Sebastian raised one eyebrow in surprise. "You haven't actually spoken to him?"

The magistrate was still struggling with his tinderbox. "Not yet, unfortunately. The discovery of the Bishop's body on top of the other horrors of the crypt seems to have been too much for the man. He managed to stagger over to the Manor and tell his tale to Douglas Pyle—that's the local magistrate, by the way: a typical village squire, far more interested in horses and hounds than in solving murders. Anyway, as soon as the Reverend told Pyle where to find the bodies, he simply went home and dosed himself with laudanum. Liberally." The magistrate's flame went out, and he had to try again. "He's still insensible."

Sebastian resisted the urge to take the tinderbox from Lovejoy's hands and light it for him. The magistrate was uncharacteristically shaken. "You say Earnshaw found the Bishop?"

"That's right."

"But if the Reverend himself went to London to get Prescott, then what was the Bishop doing down in the crypt alone?"

Lovejoy grunted with satisfaction as the lantern's wick finally caught. "According to what we've been able to ascertain, Reverend Earnshaw returned immediately to Tanfield Hill in his own gig, while the Bishop followed later in his coach."

"So where was the Bishop's coachman while the Bishop was getting his head bashed in?"

"He remained on his box, as per the Bishop's instructions. The man says he neither saw nor heard anything out of the ordinary." Lovejoy tucked away his tinderbox and flipped the lantern's small door closed. "Although if you ask me, he probably dozed off, and awakened only when the Reverend set up a shout. Seems the Reverend spotted the Bishop's light in the crypt and ventured down there again, alone, only to discover the Bishop lying nearly atop the earlier victim's body."

"*Body?* But surely if the other man had been dead for decades, he'd be reduced to a skeleton by now?"

A shadow of revulsion crossed the magistrate's pinched features. "Unfortunately, no. I understand it has something to do with the composition of the soil and perhaps the lime in the mortar. If there's no intrusion of water, the corpses in a crypt can essentially mummify, rather than decay."

Sebastian became aware of the putrefying stench of death wafting up from below. "I remember seeing something similar in Italy. In Palermo."

"Then you'll know what to expect," said the magistrate, turning toward the entrance to the crypt. Tightening his grip on the lantern's short handle, he stooped through the thin, broken remnant of the brick wall and started down the stairs. After a moment's hesitation, Sebastian followed.

Worn and cracked by time, the steps descended through a narrow stone stair vault, the light from the lantern playing over an arched roof plastered with limestone. The air was cold and dank, with an unpleasant, almost greasy quality that seemed to wrap itself around them as they reached the base of the steps.

They found themselves in an ancient central aisle, its low vaulted ceiling supported by thick spiral columns topped with crude pillow capitals. Dating back to Anglo-Saxon times, the crypt was larger than Sebastian had expected, with rows of bays opening to either side. Yet the bays seemed oddly dark. As his eyes quickly grew accustomed to the gloom, Sebastian realized the bays were dark because they were full of coffins. Hundreds and hundreds of wooden coffins, some left bare, some painted, but most upholstered in moldering woolen cloth or draped in tattered velvet. Stacked row upon row, floor to ceiling, and curtained with massive sheets of cobwebs, they reached as far as he could see in all directions.

"Good God," he whispered.

"The Bishop was found near the back end," said Lovejoy, his voice quavering as they walked between the towering walls of coffins. In the older sections of the crypt, the coffins at the bottom had begun to warp and split, their contents spilling out as the weight of the burials above slowly crushed the ancient wood below. Sebastian could see some bare bones, stained an odd brown. But most of the visble bodies were horribly whole, their skin shriveled and discolored but intact, their winding sheets and shrouds glowing white from the murky depths of the vaults.

"Here," said Lovejoy, his hand trembling as he paused to hold the lantern aloft. "Bishop Prescott was found here, just beside this last column. I've already sent the bodies to be autopsied, but everything else is exactly as it was."

Sebastian stared down at the long, rusty red stain of blood that had soaked into the uneven limestone paving blocks. "Where did you send them?"

"To Gibson."

Sebastian nodded with satisfaction. An Army doctor who'd lost the lower part of one leg to a French cannonball, Paul Gibson now kept a small surgery near Tower Hill. No one in London knew more about death and the human body than Paul Gibson. "I'll go see him as soon as I get back to London."

"Fortunately, the local magistrate had enough sense not to disturb anything," said Lovejoy. "I gather he took one look, posted guards at the entrance to the stairs, and sent for Bow Street."

Sebastian hunkered down to study the stained stones. There must have been a lot of blood. But then, there would have been, if the Bishop had been hit on the head. In Sebastian's experience, head wounds bled prodigiously.

Looking up, he studied the worn stone base of the nearby column. "Any chance he might simply have fainted and bashed in his own skull?"

Lovejoy shook his head. "We found an iron bar—possibly one of the tools left by the workmen—lying beside the body and covered in gore. I've sent it to Gibson along with the body, so he can make comparisons. But I've no doubt he'll agree it was the murder weapon."

Sebastian's gaze shifted to where the nearby paving stones showed a large, man-sized area of brown discoloration. "The other body was there?"

Lovejoy made an odd, strangled sound. "That's right. He must have been lying here in the shadows when the crypt was bricked up. They probably didn't even see him. The only reason Earnshaw spotted the Bishop was because Prescott had brought a lantern with him. It was still sitting on the floor beside him, lit."

Sebastian glanced over at the piles of cobweb-draped coffins stuffed into the nearest bay. The wood of one of the caskets had split, giving a grisly view of its desiccated contents, the corpse's head thrown back, its mouth wide-open as if in an endless, soundless scream. But the weight of the burials above kept the cadaver pinned down. Sebastian had thought at first, seeing the way some of the coffins had shifted and smashed, that the velvet-dressed body might simply have fallen out of one of the collapsed vaults and rolled here. Now he realized that was unlikely. Apart from which, who would bury a murder victim with the knife still in his back?

Sebastian pushed to his feet. "Any idea who the other man might have been?"

"None whatsoever. I'll be surprised if we ever know."

Sebastian studied the surrounding bays, each with its own towering, moldering cargo of splintered caskets and spilling contents. His eyes had completely adjusted to the gloom by now. There were times when he wished he were as blind in the dark as other men. "Could there be another way in here?"

Lovejoy nodded toward the far end of the crypt.

"There's a second flight of steps that once led up to the apse and was originally closed off with just an iron gate. Both entrances were walled off at the same time. No one's been down here for decades." The magistrate shivered, and by mutual consent the two men turned toward the stairwell.

"Sir James thinks the Bishop must have surprised a thief," said Lovejoy. "Someone who'd heard the crypt was open and seized the opportunity to sneak down here and look for jewelry or other valuables to steal from the dead."

"I suppose that's one explanation."

Something in his tone caused Lovejoy to pause at the base of the steps and turn to stare back at him. "Surely you don't think there's some connection between the two murders? How could there be? With decades between them?"

Sebastian had no explanation, of course, although he found it difficult to believe that two men could be murdered in almost exactly the same spot without there being some connection between them—even if their murders did take place decades apart. "It does seem unlikely," he agreed.

Lovejoy started up the steps, the crypt plunging into darkness again as the lantern light quivered over the old whitewashed stones of the stair vault. "Alternatively, someone could have been following the Bishop, intending to do him harm. He seized the opportunity offered by the Bishop's descent alone into the crypt, and killed him."

"You're aware that Prescott was a serious contender to be named the next Archbishop of Canterbury?" said Sebastian, following him.

Reaching the top of the stairs, the magistrate scrambled through the broken wall. "The Archbishop did mention it, yes. Although I received the impression that he was inclined to agree with Sir James's assessment—that the Bishop simply fell victim to a chance-met thief."

Sebastian followed him out of the rank chill of the stairwell into the clean, wholesome warmth of the sunny June day. "I suspect the Archbishop was being diplomatic."

Lovejoy snuffed out his lantern. "What makes you say that?"

Sebastian stared off down the hill toward the rambling, slate-roofed vicarage, where a middle-aged matron in a starched white cap and a high-necked black bombazine gown was standing on the back stoop, watching them. "Because if the Archbishop genuinely believes the Bishop of London was killed by a simple thief, then why did he come to me?"

Chapter 5

*W*hile Lovejoy set about organizing a party of constables to conduct a more thorough search of the crypt, Sebastian walked down the hill to the vicarage, to inquire after the Reverend Malcolm Earnshaw.

"He's still abed," said the matron in black bombazine, who proved to be the Reverend's wife. She was a hatchet-faced woman, her features as plain as her gown and just as no-nonsense. "He's received a terrible shock. Simply terrible. I've had Dr. Bliss in to see him, and he agrees it's best to keep the Reverend quiet for a time, lest the incident overset his mind."

She gave Sebastian a fierce, uncompromising scowl and refused to budge. The Reverend's wife was obviously made of sterner stuff than the Reverend. Sebastian had no choice but to admit defeat and withdraw.

His next stop was the small but graceful eighteenth-century brick manor house that stood on the edge of the village, near the millstream. He found the local magistrate, Douglas Pyle, behind the house, in his kennel.

He was a typical Middlesex squire, booted and spurred, full of jowl and wide of girth, with the ruddy, weathered face and squinting gray eyes of a man who spent his days tending his herds and fields, and riding to hounds. "You've no objection to talking to me while I supervise the feeding of the hounds?" said the Squire, his voice deep and rough. Sebastian took him to be somewhere in his early fifties, his brown hair mingled liberally with gray.

"Not at all," said Sebastian, stooping to tug the ears of a liver-colored bitch that loped up to sniff at him.

"She smells the crypt on you," said the Squire, watching the dog. "My wife swears she'll never get the reek of it out of the clothes I had on last night."

"It's a fine pack of hounds you've got here."

"They're Irish," said the Squire, nodding to the kennel boy. "And rogues, the lot of 'em. They'll bring down a cow if you turn your back on 'em. But they can't be beat on a hunt."

The two men watched as the kennel boy dumped boiled meat into the trough, the hounds jostling and scrabbling for position.

"I suppose you're here to talk about the murder," said the Squire, not looking around.

"Murders," said Sebastian. "There were two bodies, after all."

"Oh, aye. Two." The Squire grunted. "Which is two more than I've ever had to deal with. Believe me, I'm more than happy to turn the whole nasty business over to Bow Street. What do I know of murder?"

Sebastian studied the Squire's pack as they gulped eagerly at the trough. They were smaller than most fox-hounds, but strongly built, with broad heads. "I understand the Reverend Earnshaw came to you when he found the Bishop's body. What time was that?"

"About eight, I suppose. Maybe half past. At first I

thought the poor man had gone stark raving mad, babbling on the way he was about crypts and dead bishops and pools of blood. It took a bit of convincing before I finally agreed to go over to the church and have a look at the place. But there was the Bishop, all right. Dead as dead comes."

"You saw the older body as well, did you?"

"The fright in blue velvet and lace?" The Squire's ruddy cheeks sagged, and he pursed his lips to blow out a long breath. "I'll be seeing that face in my dreams for the rest of my life. Or rather, in my nightmares. He looked like a hog left too long in the smokehouse."

"You didn't recognize him?"

The Squire gave a laugh that jostled his belly up and down. "Never knew anyone looked like a dried hog. Did you?"

Sebastian smiled. "Point taken. Can you think of anyone in these parts who disappeared somewhere around the time of the revolt in the American Colonies?"

"Not off the top of my head. But then, I wasn't here myself for much of that time." He squared his shoulders with obvious pride. "The Sixteenth Light Dragoons. Cornet. We spent two years in the Colonies, fighting to put down the rebellion. We could have managed it, too, if the bloody government had been willing to let us do what was necessary. Now look where we find ourselves—dealing with a bunch of upstarts calling themselves the United States of America and threatening to declare war on us!"

"So you were in the Sixteenth, were you?" said Sebastian, encouraging him. "Where else did you see service?"

"India. And then Cape Town. We were headed for the West Indies when my father wrote to say my brother Ted'd died, and I was to sell out and come home." The trough was almost empty now. The Squire watched as the greedier hounds shifted from place to place, intent on scooping up the last morsels. "What makes you so sure it was someone from around here, anyway?" he asked. "We're but an hour's ride from London, after all. It could even have been someone who wandered over from West Wycombe. Thirty or forty years ago, that would've been back in the days of Sir Francis Dashwood and his Hellfire Club. I remember once when I was a lad, the priest caught Dashwood himself breaking into the crypt, looking to steal skulls and such for their blasphemous orgies."

"What about last night?" Sebastian asked. "Any strangers around?"

The Squire shook his head. "I did ask, you know. Before that squeaky-voiced magistrate showed up from Bow Street and took over. No one noticed anything out of the ordin'ry. The Reverend did think he saw the shadow of a man in the churchyard as he was leaving the crypt. But the truth is, Mr. Earnshaw's as blind as a bat. And the Bishop's own coachman was sitting right there on the box of his carriage just a few feet from the church door the whole time, and he never saw a thing." The trough was empty now, the hounds whining to be let out of the feeding yard. "If he'd been a different sort of man, I'd say Prescott probably just fainted and bashed his head on the edge of a coffin or some such thing. The Pyles have always been buried in the churchyard, thank God, but not the Prescotts. Can't be pleasant, seeing your own kith and kin reduced to grinning horrors. Not that it ever seemed to bother the Prescott brothers."

"Are you saying the Bishop was from around here?"

"Didn't you know? He grew up at Prescott Grange, between here and Hounslow. The Prescott brothers used to play in that crypt all the time when they were boys. All five of them."

"*Five?*"

"Aye. Five of 'em, God rest their souls. Some cousin or other had the living back then, and they used to steal the key to the gates off his belt when he was dozing in the sacristy." Turning to the kennel boy, Pyle said, "Open the door and let 'em have a run."

The kennel boy opened the door and called, "Come, hounds!"

Sebastian stepped back, his gaze on the Squire's full, weathered face. "You went down there with them, did you?"

A self-conscious grin crinkled the fleshy corners of the Squire's pale eyes. "Well, of course I did. Even played deerstalker and blindman's wand down there with them."

The Squire watched the hounds sweep through the open door, his smile fading as they raced off in joyous, fluid leaps. "But I never liked it," he said. Then he said it again, as if once weren't enough. "I never liked it."

"Learn anything?" Sebastian asked Tom when the tiger brought up the curricle.

"Nobody in the village seen or 'eard a thing last night," said Tom, scrambling onto his perch as Sebastian gave the horses the office to start. "Not till the Reverend started screeching, at any rate."

Sebastian nodded. "I gather the combination of a murdered Bishop and legions of old, half-decayed corpses was too much for the man's delicate sensi— What?" he said, breaking off when Tom leaned forward to give an audible sniff. "What is it?"

Tom's nose wrinkled. "What's that smell?"

"The crypt. I'm told the odor is rather pervasive."

"Per-what?"

"Pervasive. It sinks in and doesn't go away."

"I don't know about that, but there's no denying it stinks." He cast a wistful gaze over his shoulder as they started on the road back to London. "I'd like to 'ave seen it."

"Would you indeed? Frankly, I think it's the best argument in favor of cremation I've ever encountered."

"Cre-what?"

"Cremation. It's a method of body disposal practiced by the Hindus in India. The deceased is placed on a pile of wood, and burned."

"*Burned?* But that's 'orrible. Why, it's . . . it's unchristian, it is."

Sebastian laughed. "You think that's horrible, you should see what thirty or forty years in a crypt will do to you." As they reached the outskirts of the village, he dropped his hands and let the chestnuts spring forward. "I tell you what: When we get to Paul Gibson's surgery, you can have a look at the mummified body they brought out of that crypt. Make up your own mind."

Tom stared at him. "I can?"

"You can."

"Gor," said Tom, and gave a little shiver of anticipatory delight.

But by the time they reached the narrow winding lanes and ancient stone shops of Tower Hill, the sun was high in the sky and the coats of the horses gleamed dark with sweat.

"If you're gonna be 'ere long, I reckon I should take the chestnuts back to Brook Street," said Tom, unable to keep the disappointment out of his voice.

Sebastian hopped down to the lane's worn footpath. "Yes, take them home. They've had a good run. See them put up, and then bring the curricle back with the grays."

Tom's face cleared. "And then can I see the mummy?"

"And then you can see the mummy."

"Thank you, my lord!"

Sebastian stood for a moment, watching the former street urchin negotiate his way through the lane's traffic with admirable skill. Then Sebastian turned to cut through the noisome alley that ran along one side of the surgery to a neglected rear garden and the low stone building where Paul Gibson performed his autopsies. It was also here where the surgeon expanded his understanding of the human body with surreptitious dissections performed on a covert supply of cadavers, culled from the city's churchyards and sold by masked, dangerous men who did their best work on dark and moonless nights.

Chapter 6

Charles, Lord Jarvis, was in the library of his house on Berkeley Square, perusing the latest report from one of his French agents, when his daughter, Hero, came to stand in the doorway and said without preamble, "Did you kill the Bishop of London?"

He looked up at her. Since the death of his son, David, at sea several years before, she was his only surviving child. In some ways she was a handsome woman, with a Junoesque build and strong features. But she looked too much like Jarvis himself—and had far too forceful a personality—to ever be considered *pretty*. He said, "I won't deny I'm glad Prescott's dead. But it's not my work."

She met his gaze and held it. "Would you lie to me?"

"I might. But not in this instance."

At that, she gave a soft laugh. "I must say, I am glad to hear it."

Jarvis settled back in his chair. "The Bishop was something of a favorite of yours, was he not?"

"We were friends, yes. We worked on several projects together."

Jarvis made a face. "*Projects*. You're five-and-twenty,

Hero. Isn't it time you gave up this unnatural penchant for good works and found yourself a husband?"

"I might." She came to lean over the back of his chair. "If English law didn't grant a man the powers of a despot over his wife."

"A *despot*, Hero?"

"A despot." She placed an affectionate hand on his shoulder. "But as for good works, you must be thinking of Mama. She's always been far better at that sort of thing than I."

At the mention of his wife, Jarvis turned down the ends of his mouth in a grimace. He had no patience for Annabelle, a silly, half-mad imbecile who belonged in Bedlam. He grunted. "Women like Annabelle dispense soup to the poor and shed tears over the plight of orphans in the streets because it's an easy sop to their consciences. Nauseating, perhaps, yet ultimately harmless. But you—you spend your days with your nose stuck in books, researching theories and advocating schemes that could almost be described as radical."

Hero's fine gray eyes narrowed with a hint of a smile. "Oh, believe me, some of my schemes are most definitely radical."

Jarvis pushed to his feet and turned to face her. "The most powerful men in London quake in terror at the thought of annoying me. Yet my own daughter openly behaves in ways she knows full well displease me. Why is that?"

"Because I'm too much like you."

He grunted. If she were a son, he would be proud of her intellect and her force of character—if not her political notions. But she was not a son; she was a woman, and lately she'd been looking strained. He studied her pale, unusually thin face. "You've not been looking your best these past few weeks, Hero."

"Dear Papa." She leaned forward to kiss his cheek. She was tall enough to do it without standing on tiptoe. "Surely you know better than to tell a woman she's off her looks?"

He allowed himself to be coaxed into a smile, and pressed her shoulder in a rare gesture of affection. But all he said was, "I didn't kill your meddlesome bishop."

"Then who did?"

"That, I don't know. And neither, to be frank, do I care."

Leaving her father in the library, Hero hurried up the stairs to her bedroom, yanked her chamber pot from its cupboard, and was wretchedly sick.

She'd learned the sickness normally came upon her first thing in the morning, although it could strike unexpectedly at any time. She was not a woman accustomed to feeling either fear or vulnerability. But as she settled on the floor, her eyes squeezed shut, her damp forehead pressed against the cupboard door, Hero found herself perilously close to succumbing to both.

For a young Englishwoman of her station to bear a child out of wedlock was the ultimate, unforgivable disgrace. It mattered not how powerful or wealthy her family, or how bizarre the circumstances that had led to such a fate; the result could only be social ostracism, complete and everlasting. Hero had always considered herself an independent-minded woman. But even she could not contemplate such a fate with equanimity.

Her options were depressing, and limited. She could contract a quick, convenient marriage; she could give birth in secret and give the child away; or she could eliminate herself in a decorous act of self-destruction. Since Hero had no patience with suicides and refused under any circumstances to submit herself to the power of a husband, she was left with only one real option: a secret birth.

The results of such births were typically dumped, anonymously, on the parish or some desperate peasant family, either of which could generally be relied upon to kill the unwanted infant within a year. But Hero had no intention of abandoning the child growing within her to such a short, brutal life. And so she had approached her friend Bishop Prescott for his assistance in locating a good, loving family. Such arrangements were dangerous, since they could be difficult to keep hidden. But she had found Prescott both supportive and blessedly nonjudgmental.

Now Prescott was dead, and all her plans were in disarray.

At the thought, she felt a new surge of nausea, but suppressed it resolutely. Pushing to her feet, she smoothed her gown, washed her face, and walked down the hall to her mother's chambers.

She found Lady Jarvis stretched out upon the daybed in her dressing room with the drapes closed. She still wore her wrapper, and the left side of her face drooped in that way it had when she was tired.

"Didn't you sleep well, Mama?" asked Hero, bending to kiss her mother's cheek. Her hand dropped to Lady Jarvis's shoulder, and she felt so thin and frail that Hero experienced a new leap of fear.

Never well, Lady Jarvis had been especially listless lately. She was nearing fifty, a fading shadow of the beautiful, vivacious woman she had once been. Worn-out by an endless series of miscarriages and stillbirths, she had succeeded in presenting her lord with only one sickly son and a hale daughter before suffering a seizure that put an end to her childbearing days and left her weak of mind and body.

Now, she gripped her daughter's hand and said, "Troublesome dreams. Always troublesome dreams." Her soft blue eyes came into focus on Hero's face. "You've been looking tired yourself, Hero; is something wrong? Are you ill?"

Hero felt an unexpected lump in her throat. She had no doubt of her mother's love and devotion. But Lady Jarvis lacked the mental or emotional strength to deal with her own problems, let alone her daughter's. Hero forced a smile. "You know I'm never ill. It's such a lovely day; shall we go for a walk around the square?"

"I don't know if I can, dear."

"Of course you can. Let me ring for your woman to help you dress." Disengaging her hand from her mother's grasp, Hero went to open the curtains and give the bell a sharp tug. "It will do you good. I've a quick errand to run, but I should be back by the time you're ready."

Lady Jarvis frowned and struggled to sit up. "An errand? What type of errand?"

"Oh, nothing of importance," said Hero, who was in fact bound on a very important errand, to the official chambers of the late Bishop Francis Prescott, in St. James's Square.

Chapter 7

*P*ale and naked, the body of the Bishop of London lay stretched out upon the slab table in Paul Gibson's secluded outbuilding. Thanks to the thickness of the stone walls, the atmosphere in the low-ceilinged, windowless space was cold and dark and thickly scented with death. Sebastian paused in the open doorway and took one last gulp of fresh air.

"Ah, there you are," said the surgeon, laying aside a bloody scalpel. "I knew you wouldn't be able to resist this one."

Of medium height, with the dark hair and ready smile of an Irishman, Paul Gibson had known Sebastian for years. Once, they'd worn the King's colors and fought together from the mountains of Italy and the Peninsula to the West Indies. They might come from different worlds and speak the King's English with markedly different accents, but theirs was a friendship forged in blood and guts and fear.

"Nice to be predictable," said Sebastian, eyes blinking at the room's rank air. After only some fourteen to sixteen hours of death—and most of that during the cool hours of the night—the Bishop's corpse was still relatively fresh. The sheet-covered form that rested on a stretcher in the room's far corner was anything but fresh.

Limping over to where a chipped enamel basin and pitcher stood on the wooden shelf that ran across the room's back wall, the surgeon splashed water into the basin and rinsed his hands. "There's no denying it's an interesting puzzle. Two men murdered decades apart in the same place? Not often we see that."

"Judging from the smell, I'd say that's fortunate. Have you found anything yet that might link the two?"

"Not yet. But then, I've only just started on the Bishop. It's definitely the blow to his head that killed him . . . not that that'll come as a surprise to anyone who's had a good look at him."

Sebastian studied the corpse before them. The Bishop of London had been a tall man, and thin, with long, sinewy arms and legs. In his late fifties or early sixties, he had a high forehead and a strong nose, his cheekbones prominent and knifelike beneath the flesh of his face. His hair was completely white, worn straight and unusually long. Even in death, something both scholarly and gentle lingered in his expression.

"Did you know him?" said Gibson.

"I met him once or twice." Sebastian examined the gash that disfigured the left side of the Bishop's head. "Sir Henry said they found an iron bar near the body. Do you think it was the murder weapon?"

Gibson nodded to a stout bar, one end gently curved and notched, that lay on the nearby bench. "I'd say so, yes. It fits the size and shape of the wound very neatly. The blow shattered his skull, tearing the lining of the brain and leaving it exposed. He probably died almost immediately, although it is possible he lived as much as half an hour after he was hit. I doubt he ever regained consciousness, though."

Sebastian glanced up in surprise. "So he might still have been alive when Reverend Earnshaw found him?"

"Possibly. Not that it matters. Even if the Reverend had gone for a doctor rather than the magistrate, there's nothing anyone could have done for him."

Sebastian studied the Bishop's long fingers, the nails meticulously manicured and unbroken. "No sign of a struggle?"

"None." Gibson tossed aside the rough towel he'd been holding. "The papers are saying the Bishop surprised a thief who'd taken advantage of the crypt being opened to rob the burials."

"I suppose it's a more reassuring tale than the alternative—that someone deliberately bludgeoned the Bishop of London to death."

Gibson looked over at him. "Any idea who?"

"Not a clue. Not even a suspect." Sebastian hunkered down to study the dead man's bloodied head. "What can you tell me about his murderer?"

"Very little, I'm afraid. Judging from the position of the wound, I'd say the Bishop was hit from the front, by someone who was right-handed. The assailant was either extraordinarily tall, or the Bishop was positioned below him—as if sitting, or at least crouching."

"What makes you say that?"

"If you look closely, you'll notice that the wound isn't exactly on the side of his head. It's up toward the crown. The only way anyone could strike at that angle is if he were standing above the Bishop, or if he were considerably taller than the Bishop—which is unlikely, given that Bishop Prescott was an unusually tall man himself."

"You think the Bishop could have been crouched down beside *him*?" said Sebastian, nodding toward the shrouded form on the stretcher behind them.

"From the way I understand the two men were found, I'd say that's highly probable. The Bishop was lying virtually on top of the earlier victim."

Reluctantly, Sebastian went to draw back the covering from the eighteenth-century corpse, and let out his breath in a sharp hiss. "Good God."

"Fascinating, isn't it?" said Gibson, limping over to stand beside him.

"That's one word for it."

"I'm afraid I haven't had much of a chance to examine this one yet, but I'm looking forward to it."

"Really?" Sebastian studied his friend's rapt expression. "You'd love the crypt of St. Margaret's, then."

"I would indeed. What an opportunity!"

Sebastian ducked his head to hide a smile.

Beneath the froth of lace, the once fine blue velvet coat, and the satin waistcoat, the body's sinew had shriveled and sunk. Yet it was obvious that the corpse had belonged to an unusually large man, robust of frame and full of flesh. Time and the action of the chemicals in the crypt had withered and distorted the features of his face and darkened the skin until he looked like an aged Moor from the mountains of Morocco. Without the chin strap that normally held a burial's jaw closed, his mouth had fallen open in a gaping, hideous yowl, but where once had been eyes were now strange, paperlike wisps.

"Old fly pupae," said Gibson, when Sebastian looked up in question.

Sebastian cleared his throat and overcame the urge to

draw the covering back up over that horror. "I understand this one was stabbed in the back with a dagger?"

"That's right." Gibson limped over to retrieve an object from the bench and held it out. "This."

The blacked blade was long and thin, cast in one piece with the handle, then hammer-forged to produce a diamond blade cross-sectioned without any sharpened edges. A stabbing weapon, it was designed not to cut, but to penetrate deeply.

"A fine weapon," said Sebastian, running his thumb along the delicate floral scroll of acanthus leaves and flowers that decorated the handle. "Renaissance, perhaps?"

"I'd say so, yes. Italian."

Sebastian brought his gaze back to the withered cadaver at their feet. "What I want to know is, what the hell was our gentleman in velvet and lace doing down in that crypt in the first place?"

"I don't know. But whatever it was, he obviously wasn't alone."

Chapter 8

*A*fter allowing his awed tiger a suitable amount of time to gape at the mummified corpse in Gibson's dissection room, Sebastian drove to St. James's Square, where a vast mansion known as London House served as both the London residence and the official chambers of the Bishop of London. A thick layer of straw had already been laid on the street outside of Number 32; the blinds were drawn at all the windows, and every opening had been hung with black crepe. When Sebastian rang the heavy iron bell, a sepulchral-looking servant ushered him into a darkened entry.

A hushed voice behind him said, "Lord Devlin, I take it?"

Sebastian turned to find a lean, flaxen-haired cleric regarding him from the doorway of the small chapel that lay just to the right of the entrance. "Yes."

The cleric stepped forward in a waft of incense. "I am Dr. Simon Ashley, the Bishop's chaplain. The Archbishop has asked me to render you whatever assistance is necessary to expedite your endeavors to make sense of this dreadful tragedy."

"Thank you," said Sebastian.

The Chaplain laced his fingers together and bowed. Somewhere in his late thirties or early forties, he had a fine-boned, delicate face and the pale complexion of a man whose life was lived indoors. To the uninitiated, the position of chaplain might seem a lowly office. It was not. Bishop Prescott had once served as chaplain to the Bishop of Winchester, while the current Archbishop of Canterbury had been chaplain to the Bishop of Durham. Serving as a Bishop's chaplain was an important step up the ecclesiastical ladder.

"I assume you'll wish to begin with—" The Chaplain broke off, his thin nose twitching.

"It's the crypt," said Sebastian, letting his gaze drift around the entry with its gleaming marble floors, its soaring wall panels, its rows of heavy oils framed in gilt and hung with more black crepe. Yards and yards of black crepe. "I'm told the odor lingers."

"Yes, well . . ." The Chaplain cleared his throat and gestured with one hand toward the stairs. "The Bishop's official chambers are this way. If you'll come with me?"

Sebastian followed the black-robed man up the grand staircase, their footsteps echoing in the stillness of the vast house. "The Bishop was here yesterday?"

"Most of the day, yes," said the Chaplain, pausing on the first floor to throw open the doors to a set of apartments to the left of the stairs. "He had a number of appointments. We weren't scheduled to move to Lambeth Palace—the Bishop's summer residence—for another fortnight."

These rooms, like those below, were in shadow, the blinds drawn fast. But Sebastian's eyes were unusually well adapted to the dark. Pausing just inside the entrance, he let his gaze wander over the wainscoted ante-

room, its gilded, velvet-covered benches and unlit
branches of wax candles in gleaming brass sconces. Beyond the anteroom lay a second, smaller chamber with a
broad desk. Sebastian had taken two steps toward it
when the Chaplain cleared his throat again.

"You'll understand, of course, that ecclesiastical affairs are often of a, shall we say, *delicate* nature?"

Sebastian looked around. "Meaning?"

"Meaning, the Archbishop has delegated to me the
task of going through the Bishop's papers. I can assure
you that if I find anything that appears relevant to his
death, I will of course pass it on to you."

"In other words, the Archbishop would rather I re-
frain from rifling through the Bishop's drawers? Is that
what you're saying?"

The Chaplain gave a nervous titter, but didn't contra-
dict him.

Sebastian wandered the rooms, his hands clasped behind his back. The Chaplain trailed at a distance of six or
seven feet, a handkerchief pressed surreptitiously to his
nose. But there was little enough for Sebastian to see. As
an administrator, Prescott had obviously possessed a
passion for neatness; the surface of his desk was clean
and polished, every drawer carefully closed. If the
Bishop had any skeletons in his life, he'd kept them
tucked away, out of sight.

"What about the Bishop's private apartments?" said
Sebastian.

"They're upstairs. This way."

The Bishop's private chambers on the second floor
were more relaxed and informal, for it was here that
Prescott had passed his leisure hours. A riding quirt and
a pair of gloves rested beside a snuffbox on the gleaming

surface of the inlaid round table at the center of the room, as if their owner had just stepped out and would return in a moment. Near the hearth, a book lay open across the arm of an overstuffed chair. Sebastian glanced at the title. *The Libation Bearers*, by Aeschylus.

He turned in a slow circle. Most of the walls not taken up with windows were covered by vast floor-to-ceiling bookshelves. Running his gaze over the titles, he was surprised to see the works of Cicero and Aristotle, Plato and Seneca, nestled beside the more predictable volumes on Aquinas and Augustine.

"An interesting collection," said Sebastian.

"The Bishop began his career as a classics scholar at Christ's College, in Cambridge."

"He had no family?"

"A nephew only. His wife passed away some eight or nine years ago. There were never any children."

"Was he close to his nephew?"

"Very. Sir Peter was like a son to him."

Sebastian swung around to look back at the Chaplain. "The Bishop's nephew is Sir Peter Prescott?"

"That's right. You know him?"

"We were at Eton together." Sebastian remembered Sir Peter Prescott as an ebullient, good-natured boy with ruddy cheeks and a ready laugh that hid a quiet streak of mule-headed obstinacy. Aloud, he said, "At exactly what time did Reverend Earnshaw reach London with news of the discovery in the crypt?"

"Reverend Earnshaw arrived shortly after five. But as he was closeted with the Bishop in private, the details of his conversation with the Bishop were unknown to us." The Chaplain's thin nose quivered with indignation at what he obviously considered a personal slight. "Even when the Bishop ordered his carriage for later that evening, he remained uncharacteristically secretive as to the exact nature of his errand."

Sebastian frowned. "When did Earnshaw leave?"

"Some twenty minutes after his arrival."

"Yet the Bishop himself didn't set out for Tanfield Hill until—what? Seven?" Tanfield Hill lay an hour's drive to the west of London. "Why the delay?"

The Chaplain sniffed. "Again, the Bishop did not take me into his confidence. I do know he had an important appointment scheduled for six. Presumably, he was reluctant to cancel it."

There was a simple opening cut into the wall beside the hearth. Going to stand in the doorway, Sebastian saw that it led to a small bedchamber, unexpectedly plain, almost Spartan, the bed narrow and hard. He said, "It seems a strange thing for Earnshaw to have done, to involve the Bishop of London, personally, in the discovery of a decades-old murder in a rural parish church."

The Chaplain cleared his throat. "Unfortunately, the Bishop provided us with little information before his departure. Only that there was an incident in Tanfield Hill requiring his attention, and that he might not return before midnight."

"He didn't mention the murder?"

"No."

Sebastian cast one last glance around the rooms, then turned toward the stairs, the Chaplain following at a noticeable distance. As they reached the first floor, Sebastian said, "How long have you served as Prescott's chaplain?"

"Four years now."

"So you knew him well."

The Chaplain gave a slight bow. "Quite well, yes."

"Did he have many enemies?"

Sebastian expected a quick, automatic denial. Instead, the Chaplain said, "The Bishop was not a man to back away from taking an unpopular stance. Unfortunately, such men do make enemies. Many enemies."

"What kind of unpopular stances are we talking about?"

"Catholic emancipation. The need for child labor laws. Slavery . . ."

"Prescott was an abolitionist?"

"It was his principal cause. The Bishop of London is responsible for the spiritual welfare of the Colonies, and Bishop Prescott took that aspect of his duties very seriously. As far as he was concerned, seeing the Slave Trade Act passed a few years ago was only the beginning. He was determined to get a Slavery Abolition Act through Parliament."

"That's definitely a good way to make enemies," said Sebastian. Some very powerful men in England had fortunes sunk in the West Indies; the loss of the islands' slave labor would ruin them. "Ever hear anyone wish the Bishop harm?"

"You mean, threaten him?" The Chaplain paused at the base of the staircase, his brow furrowing as if he were in thought. But he only shook his head and said, "No. I don't think so."

Sebastian studied the cleric's lean, acerbic face. The man was a terrible liar. "I'd be interested to see a list of the Bishop's appointments for the past several weeks."

The Chaplain sniffed. "I will check with the Archbishop. If he has no objection, I'll direct the diary secretary to make you a copy of the Bishop's schedule." He nodded to a hovering footman to open the front door. "You're actually the second person today to ask for that information."

"Oh? Who was the first?" said Sebastian, pausing at the top of the front steps to look back. "One of the Bow Street magistrates?"

"No. Miss Hero Jarvis." The Chaplain raised his handkerchief to his nose. "Good day, my lord." He threw a speaking glance at the footman, who quietly shut the door between them.

Sebastian stood for a moment, staring out over the wide square, with its vast central reflecting pool and statue of King Charles. Then he raised the cuff of his coat to his nose and sniffed.

Chapter 9

*H*is face crinkled in a pantomime of distaste, Sebastian's valet lifted the discarded coat of dark superfine on one carefully curled finger and held it at arm's length.

"I know," said Sebastian, not looking up from the serious business of tying a fresh cravat. "Do what you can to get the smell out. But if it doesn't work, burn it."

Jules Calhoun drew back in mock astonishment. "What? You mean to say you don't fancy walking around London smelling like a hundred-year-old cadaver?"

"A hundred years might be all right. It's the in-between stages that are the smelliest."

The valet gave a soft laugh. A small, slim gentleman's gentleman in his thirties, Calhoun had started life in one of the most notorious flash houses in London—a beginning that had left him with an undeniable flair and a variety of useful connections to the city's underworld.

Assembling the rest of Sebastian's discarded raiment, Calhoun bundled the offending clothes together and said, "Are you likely to be returning to St. Margaret's?"

"Possibly."

"Then I suggest we keep these."

Sebastian smoothed the folds of his cravat. "Good point."

The valet watched Sebastian slide a slim dagger into the sheath hidden inside his right boot. "Expecting trouble?"

Sebastian straightened his cuffs. "When I'm dealing with the Jarvises? Always."

Most daughters of the Upper Ten Thousand spent their days shopping on Bond Street, or attending a dizzying round of picnics, Venetian breakfasts, and morning visits. Not Miss Hero Jarvis.

When Sebastian tracked her down, she was at the Royal Hospital in Chelsea. A vast redbrick complex designed by Sir Christopher Wren and clustered around several wide courtyards, the hospital had been established by Charles II for the relief of the nation's wounded and aged war veterans back in the seventeenth century. But after decades of continuous war, the facility was now grossly underfunded and overcrowded.

He'd heard that Miss Jarvis had made the improvement of the hospital one of her projects. As he crossed the sun-drenched main courtyard, he saw her step out of the chapel in the company of a stout gentleman with a swooping auburn mustache and the officious air of a physician. She was dressed in an emerald green walking gown ruched at the hem and finished with darker piping at the neck and sleeves, and carried a delicate silk parasol in a matching shade of green that she tipped at just the right angle to shade her face. A gray-gowned maid, fists clutching the strings of her reticule, hovered at a respectable distance.

"Ah, there you are, Miss Jarvis," said Sebastian, walking up to her. "If I might have a word with you?"

She swung her head to look at him, her lips parting on a quickly indrawn breath. She was a striking woman, with her father's aquiline nose and intelligent gray stare. Now in her twenty-fifth year, she had medium brown hair she usually wore scraped back in an unbecoming fashion better suited to a governess. But lately she'd taken to having a few wisps cut so that they fell artfully about her forehead. The effect was one of unexpected, misleading softness. None knew better than Sebastian that there was little that was soft about Hero Jarvis.

She might be disconcerted to see him, but she recovered almost immediately. "I'm sorry, my lord," she said, "but Dr. McCain here has most graciously offered to escort me on a tour of the facilities, and I wouldn't want to inconvenience—"

"I'm convinced the good doctor will excuse us for a moment," said Sebastian, giving the stout physician a smile that bared his teeth.

"Of course," said the doctor, withdrawing immediately with a polite bow.

"My efforts here are important," she told Sebastian in a low voice as they turned to stroll together across the paved courtyard. "It is beyond shameful for a nation of our wealth and grandeur to ask men to risk life and limb in war, and then abandon them to poverty and neglect when they return home wounded and infirm."

"Believe me, Miss Jarvis, I have nothing but admiration for what you're trying to accomplish. I won't delay you long." He studied her classical profile. She looked thinner and paler than he remembered. Once, just two months before, Sebastian had held this woman in his arms, tasted the salt of her tears, felt the shudders rack her unexpectedly yielding body. But that had been a moment out of time, when they'd thought they faced certain death together.

Instead, they had survived. Now, those shared moments of weakness had become a source of embarrassment and regret that could have profound repercussions for them both. He'd known her to shoot a highwayman at point-blank range, to confront certain death with a rare and clearheaded fortitude. But for a young gentlewoman to face the potential shame and ostracism of an unwed birth was something else entirely, and he had no intention of allowing her to suffer alone for what they had done together. The problem was, he wasn't convinced she would tell him if there were, in fact, repercussions from that fateful afternoon.

"Are you well?" he asked.

She knew precisely what he meant. "I am quite well, thank you." She kept her gaze fixed straight ahead, her step never faltering. "You've no need to concern yourself."

He wanted to believe her, but couldn't. She'd already given him her forthright opinion of marriage; when he'd offered her the protection of his name after their rescue that day, her answer had been swift and unequivocal. Studying the self-possessed features of the woman beside him now, he could find no trace of the vulnerable creature who'd given herself to him in the cold, dark vaults beneath Somerset House. Yet it had happened.

He said, "The Archbishop of Canterbury has asked me to look into the murder of Bishop Prescott."

For an instant, the hand holding the parasol clenched so hard Sebastian heard the delicate bamboo crack. But the calm self-control of her voice never slipped. "Bishop Prescott?" she said airily. "And what, pray tell, does his death have to do with me?"

"I don't know. Which is why I was curious when I heard you had requested a copy of Prescott's most recent appointments."

She stared off across the courtyard, to where an emaciated man with one leg hobbled on a single crutch. "Ah," she said softly. "And now you're wondering why, are you?"

"Yes."

She kept her gaze on the wounded soldier in his gay, old-fashioned uniform. "In point of fact, it's my belief the Bishop was being blackmailed."

"Blackmailed?" Whatever Sebastian had been expecting her to say, it wasn't that.

"Yes."

"And precisely what, Miss Jarvis, led you to this conclusion?"

"When I met with the Bishop yesterday evening, I found him quite disturbed."

"You had a meeting with Prescott?"

She glanced sideways at him. "You hadn't discovered that yet?"

"No, I had not. At what time did you meet with him?"

"Six."

"So you were the important appointment the Bishop was reluctant to cancel. Do you mind if I ask why you were meeting with the Bishop of London?"

She twitched her parasol back and forth in short, sharp jerks. "You may ask, if you wish, my lord. But I have no intention of answering your question. Believe me, it is not at all relevant to your investigation."

"Perhaps," he said quietly. "But I will find out, you know."

She swung to face him, her jaw set, her eyes icy with dislike. "Very well, if you insist. The Bishop asked for my assistance in preparing the speech he was to give before the House of Lords this Thursday."

Sebastian studied the smooth line of her cheek, the dark sweep of lashes that half hid her eyes as she looked away. She was a very good liar. But not quite good enough. He said, "The speech on abolition."

"That's right."

Sebastian shifted his gaze to the statue of Charles II, decked out like a Roman emperor, that stood in the center of the court. If his understanding of the events of that evening were correct, then Miss Jarvis would have arrived at London House not long after the Reverend Malcolm Earnshaw's meeting with the Bishop. But Sebastian found it difficult to understand how there could have been anything in the discovery of a decades-old corpse in a small village church to rattle a man as powerful and worldly as the Bishop of London.

He said, "Did Prescott tell you he was being blackmailed?"

"Not in so many words."

"So what precisely did he say that led you to such an unlikely conclusion?"

"I'm sorry, but I can't tell you that."

"You—" He caught himself up short, took a deep breath, and said more calmly, "Miss Jarvis, do I need to remind you that a man is dead?"

She held herself very still. "Obviously not, my lord Devlin. But Francis Prescott was my friend. He told me what he did in strictest confidence, and I do not believe that a man's death relieves his friends of their responsibility to respect his desire for privacy."

He stared at her. "You would respect the Bishop's confidence even if it meant letting his killer go free?"

Her nostrils flared on a quickly indrawn breath. "No. But if I can preserve the Bishop's confidence by making some preliminary inquiries myself, then would you not agree that it is incumbent upon me to do so? If I should discover that the information I have is relevant to his death, then I shall of course disclose it to you."

"Hence your request for the list of the Bishop's appointments?"

"Yes."

He watched her glance away again. She might be telling him the truth, but he had a nasty suspicion it was only a half-truth. He said, "Blackmailers don't necessarily make appointments, you know."

Her nostrils flared. "That had occurred to me."

"And were you looking for anyone's name in particular on that list?"

"In point of fact, I have not yet received the list."

Sebastian tightened his jaw. "And when you do receive the list, Miss Jarvis, whose name do you anticipate finding upon it?"

He didn't expect her to answer him. But to his surprise, a faint, unpleasant smile curled her lips, and she said, "Lord Quillian's."

"*Quillian?* Surely you don't suspect Lord Quillian of murdering the Bishop?"

One eyebrow arched. "You find that so improbable?"

"The man is a fop. He wears his shirt points so high he can barely turn his head, and his coats are so tight I

swear the seams would split if he tried to bludgeon anyone to death."

"You might think so. Yet he has fought two duels—"

"Twenty years ago."

"—and he is an outspoken opponent of abolition."

"As are any number of other men in London."

"True. Yet how many of those men went so far as to
actually threaten the Bishop?"

Sebastian frowned. "Quillian threatened the Bishop?
Did Prescott tell you so?"

She shook her head. "He had no need. I was walking
with the Bishop in Hyde Park on Saturday when Lord
Quillian accosted him."

"Accosted?"

"Yes, accosted. He warned the Bishop specifically to
give up his support of the Slavery Abolition Act, saying
that men who lived in glass houses shouldn't throw
stones."

"That might not necessarily have been a threat."

"Perhaps. Except he followed it up by saying, 'Beware
lest your own house should shatter, my lord Bishop.'"

Sebastian glanced over to where Tom was walking the
grays up and down the lane near the overgrown entrance
to the old Ranelagh Gardens. "You know, of course, that
I shall now accost Lord Quillian."

"I should sincerely hope so. Why else do you suppose
I told you?"

He grunted. "You don't actually believe that aging
exquisite has anything to do with the Bishop's death, do
you?"

"On the contrary, I do," she said, and turned to walk
back toward the chapel.

He fell into step beside her again. "You say the Bishop was your friend?"

"He was."

"So tell me about him."

She stared off across the court, to where the stout, mustachioed physician waited patiently with his hands clasped behind his back. Studying her face, Sebastian saw her features contort with an unmistakable pinch of grief. "How do you reduce such a vital, complex man to just a few words? He was . . . he was the most intensely compassionate, caring man I have ever known."

"I've heard he was an advocate for reform."

A strange, sad smile hovered about her lips. "I am an advocate for reform. Francis Prescott was that, and so much more. I've seen him give his own coat to a woman he found freezing in the street, and stop his carriage to personally take into his arms the filthy, starving child someone had abandoned at the side of the road."

"He sounds like a veritable saint."

"A saint?" She thought about it. "No, not a saint. He was a man, like anyone else."

"So he had faults."

"We all have faults, my lord Devlin."

"And what were Bishop Prescott's faults?"

She looked vaguely troubled. "I suppose he could at times be accused of behaving uncharitably toward those of French or American origins."

He looked at her in surprise. "Because of those two countries' revolutions? But . . . I thought Prescott was an advocate of reform?"

"Reform, yes; revolution, no. The violence of the French and American revolutions horrified him. Although I think there was more to it than that. He lost three of his own brothers in the wars of the last century—one fighting the French in Canada, one fighting the French in India, and the third fighting the American rebels."

"A very martial family, for a bishop."

She glanced over at him. "It's what younger sons do, is it not? Take the cloth, or buy a pair of colors."

Sebastian gave a wry smile. As the youngest of three sons born to the Earl of Hendon, Sebastian himself had been destined for a career in the Army, before the deaths of his two older brothers thrust him into the position of heir. Once he became Viscount Devlin, there'd been no more talk of his making a career of the military. Hendon had been furious—and terrified—when Sebastian went off to spend some six years fighting the French anyway.

He said, "Did you know Prescott was planning to drive out to Tanfield Hill last night, after your meeting with him?"

She shook her head. "He never mentioned it." They were almost back to where Dr. McCain and Hero's maid waited patiently beside the doors to the chapel. She slowed and swung to face him. "Now you really must excuse me, my lord. There is nothing more I can tell you."

"Can't? Or won't?"

She raised one eyebrow in an expression that was disconcertingly evocative of her father. "Does it matter?" she said, and brushed past him, her parasol tilted at just the right angle, her chin held high, her back uncompromisingly straight and rigid.

Chapter 10

Sebastian had no doubt Miss Jarvis was more than capable of tossing the Prince Regent's well-dressed friend Lord Quillian to the proverbial lions if that was what it took to distract attention from whatever she herself was trying to hide. But on the off chance the middle-aged exquisite might indeed have been involved in the Bishop of London's untimely demise, Sebastian spent the better part of the afternoon tracking the dandy through the fashionable male shopping precincts of Bond Street, Jermyn Street, and Savile Row.

He finally ran Quillian to ground in the discreet premises of Schweitzer and Davison on Cork Street. A slim man of medium height with lean cheeks, an aquiline nose, and heavily lidded green eyes, Lord Quillian was of the same generation as the Prince. Born a second son, he had come into his inheritance late in his twenties, on the death of his older brother. Like so many of the Prince's cohorts, the Baron was addicted to games of chance, to free-flowing wine and free-spirited women. But his ruling passion was fashion, the vast majority of his time—as well as much of his considerable fortune—being expended on the arrayment of his person.

When Sebastian came upon him, Quillian was dressed in fawn-colored breeches of the finest doeskin and a flawlessly tailored coat with silver buttons. He had a silver-headed ebony walking stick tucked up under one arm, and was pensively debating with his tailor the rival merits of superfine and Bath coating.

"I hear the Beau swears by the Bath coating," said Sebastian.

"True," said Quillian. "But then, Brummell began his career as a Hussar. Once a military man, always a military man." Glancing sideways, the Baron frowned at Sebastian's own well-tailored but nonchalant rig. "I daresay you order your coats from Meyer's on Conduit Street, and always in Bath coating."

"Frequently, yes."

"Well, there; you see?" He nodded to the tailor. "Let's say the superfine, shall we?"

Mr. Schweitzer gave an obsequious bow, and withdrew.

"Walk with me a ways," said Sebastian, falling into step beside the exquisite as they left the shop.

The aging roué cast a dubious eye at the sun shining brightly from the clear sky. "Well, I can walk with you to the end of the street, I suppose. But then I fear I really must call a chair. I'm frightfully susceptible to the sun, you know; if I'm not careful, I quickly turn as brown as a savage."

Sebastian blinked at the exquisite's creamy white complexion. "Just so." He waited while the dandy paused to inspect the tray of buttons displayed in a nearby shop window, then added, "I assume you've heard of the death of the Bishop of London?"

The Baron gave a delicate shudder and moved on.

"Who, pray tell, has not? The description in the *Morning Post* nearly brought on my spasms—not that I ever had anything but the utmost contempt for the man himself, but still. Violence of any sort is so . . . crude."

"Yet I've heard it said you fought two duels yourself, when you were younger."

Quillian gave a tight smile, the sleepy eyes suddenly looking considerably less lazy. "Surely you don't mean to conflate what happened to Prescott with a duel conducted under the gentleman's code? I mean, to have one's head bashed in is so, well, *plebeian*, wouldn't you say?"

"Not to mention fatal."

"I suppose." Quillian sniffed. "Although it's Prescott's own fault, really. He should have thought of the consequences before."

"Before . . . what?"

"Why, before he set about putting up the backs of half the men in town, of course."

"I hear you quarreled rather publicly with the Bishop yourself. Last Saturday, was it not? In Hyde Park," Sebastian added, when the exquisite continued to stare at him blankly.

"Oh, that." Quillian waved the incident away with the flap of one slim hand gloved in snowy white kid.

"Yes, that. Over abolition, I assume?"

Quillian sniffed. "The bloody, righteous idiot was trying to push a Slavery Abolition Act through Parliament. If you ask me, even to suggest such a measure in time of war is tantamount to treason. The financial repercussions from that kind of foolishness would be ruinous."

"For you."

"For *England*."

"I suppose the Bishop believed he labored in the service of a higher power."

"The man was a fool."

Sebastian watched the Baron's hand tighten around the silver head of his walking stick. Sebastian owned a similar piece; the ornate handle unscrewed to reveal a long, slim dagger.

He said, "I've heard speculation that someone may have been trying to blackmail Prescott. You wouldn't happen to know anything about that, would you?"

"Blackmail? Truly?" Quillian's lips stretched into a thin, tight smile, but his eyes were hard. "Are you suggesting there was something in His Righteousness's past that could have left the man open to blackmail? How very . . . entertaining. If only one had known of this sooner, one might have made use of it."

Sebastian studied the exquisite's carefully powdered face. "You're saying you don't know of anything in the Bishop's past that might have made him vulnerable to blackmail?"

"Blackmail is so . . . sordid. Don't you agree?"

"Like murder," said Sebastian.

"Exactly. If you want my opinion—and I take it you must, since you have obviously sought me out to discuss this dreadful matter—the authorities could do worse than to look into the movements of that horrid Colonial."

"Colonial? You mean an American?"

"That's right. Franklin, I believe his name is. I understand he used to be governor of New Jersey or some such place, before the recent unpleasantness."

"You mean *William* Franklin? Benjamin Franklin's son?"

"Yes, that's the one. He was leaving the Bishop's chambers just as I arrived on Monday afternoon."

"You saw the Bishop this past Monday?"

"I did," said the dandy, swinging his walking stick by the handle. "It was my hope to persuade the Bishop of the advisability of giving up his intention of delivering an impassioned attack on slavery before the Lords this Thursday."

"By appealing to his better nature?"

"Hardly. By threatening to have him blackballed from his clubs." Quillian sniffed. "You'll agree, I assume, that there is considerable difference between threatening to *blackball* a man and threatening to *blackmail* him? Hmmm?"

Actually, threatening to blackball a man struck Sebastian as a *form* of blackmail, but all he said was, "And Franklin?"

"As I said, the man was leaving as I arrived. Their exchange had obviously been heated, for as I entered the antechamber, I heard the Bishop say it would be a dark day in hell before he ever had dealings with a traitor's son. To which Franklin replied . . ." Here the exquisite hesitated, as if suddenly overcome by an eleventh-hour attack of scruples at the realization that he might be implicating a man in murder.

Sebastian dutifully prompted, "Yes?"

"To which Franklin replied, 'Hell is where men such as yourself belong.'" Quillian glanced over at Sebastian expectantly.

Sebastian said, "You're suggesting, I take it, that Franklin meant it as a threat?"

"Well, it could certainly be construed as such, could it not?"

"Perhaps. You wouldn't have any idea what their exchange was about?"

"I'm afraid not." Quillian brought the back of one hand to his forehead. "Merciful heavens. I do believe I am in danger of beginning to *perspire*. This is all your fault, you know. Expecting me to *walk* down the street like some milkmaid making deliveries." He raised his voice. "Chair! Chair, I say!"

A couple of chairmen lounging before a nearby public house jerked to attention and rushed toward him. "Carlton House," said Quillian, settling back against the sedan chair's quilted squabs.

"One more thing," said Sebastian, resting a hand on the chair frame to delay him. "Exactly where were you last night?"

Quillian's eyes widened in a show of indignation. "Why, with the Prince."

"All evening?"

"Of course," he snapped, and nodded to the chairmen to move on.

Sebastian took a step back, his eyes narrowing against the glare of the sun as he watched the chairmen trot away.

Chapter 11

One hand wrapped tightly around her kite's spar, the young girl raced down the grassy slope at the edge of Green Park, knees kicking against the muslin of her simple gown. She was a plain child, somewhere between twelve and fourteen years of age, with the nondescript brown hair and plump cheeks of her famous forebear, Benjamin Franklin. As Sebastian watched, the breeze filled the kite's red sails, flapping the silk. She held tight, shouting with delight to the small, rotund man who loped ahead of her.

William Franklin held a stout stick wound with the kite's line in one hand, the other hand playing out the twine as he ran. He was dressed in the frock coat and buckled breeches of an earlier age, his stocking-clad calves flashing in short, rapid steps as he hollered, "Now!"

The girl leapt up, releasing the kite. For a moment it dipped, threatening to crash to earth. Then the wind caught the sails and it soared high, a crimson splash against the clear blue sky.

"Take the line, quickly," shouted William Franklin, holding out the stick. She snatched it with a gay laugh, her skirts swirling around her as she raced across the park, the kite sailing above her.

Breathing heavily, Franklin bent to rest his hands on his knees. His plump cheeks were flushed and damp, but his small eyes danced with merriment as his gaze followed the plain, brown-haired girl with the kite.

"Your granddaughter?" said Sebastian, walking up to him.

The old man straightened. "Ellen. I've raised her myself from the time she was a wee babe." His eyes narrowed. "I know you, don't I?"

"Yes, although I'm surprised you remember me. The name's Devlin," said Sebastian, shaking the elderly gentleman's hand. "I came to one of your lectures on the Gulf Stream, many years ago."

William Franklin nodded to the girl with the kite. "It was Ellen's father—my son, Temple—who helped my father chart the stream, you know. On a voyage between London and America."

"I know."

"You've an interest in water currents?"

They turned to walk together across the grass. "I believe a man should strive to remain aware of the scientific advances of his day, yes."

"Hmm. Yet somehow, I don't think you've sought me out to talk about water temperatures, have you, Lord Devlin?"

At the use of his title, Sebastian shifted to face the small American.

Franklin smiled. "I knew your father many years ago—although I doubt he ever told you of our acquaintance."

"No. He didn't."

Franklin's head turned as he followed his grand-daughter's progress across the park. "We shared a ship's voyage together, once. Lord Hendon had been visiting the Colonies, while I . . . I was beginning my life of exile."

He was silent a moment. The humor that had briefly animated his features had gone, leaving his face bleak and sorrowful. "I'd just lost my first wife. She died while I was being held in a rebel prison." He let out a heavy sigh and shook his head. "I must beg your pardon for sounding maudlin. The older I get, the more the memory of those days lies heavily upon my heart."

They stood together, heads thrown back as they watched the kite dip and soar above them. After a moment, Franklin said, "You're here because of Bishop Prescott, I assume?"

Sebastian glanced over at him. "How did you know?"

Franklin tapped one snuff-stained finger against his temple. "I'm not in my dotage yet. You might have a passing interest in science, but your real passion is murder. It's not difficult to infer that someone told you I exchanged heated words with the Bishop of London recently."

"It's true then?"

"Oh, yes. Just because I'm not in my dotage doesn't mean I can't be foolish."

Sebastian shook his head. "I don't understand."

"I run an informal school for some local children— nothing fancy, just a small group of lads who gather in my parlor for an hour or so in the evening to learn the basics of reading, writing, and arithmetic. Ever since my Mary died, I've been finding it more and more difficult to keep the sessions going. I knew Prescott was an advocate of education for the poor, so I was hoping he might be able to find a place for a couple of the brighter boys in one of the city's charity schools." His lips tightened into a thin line. "I should have known better."

"He refused?"

"He wouldn't even hear me out. Became abusive, really—as I've no doubt you've heard."

They turned to walk together down the hill. "Ironic, isn't it?" said Franklin. "My own father disowned me as a traitor because I chose to remain loyal to the king he raised me to serve. But Prescott? As far as he was concerned, my father's loyalty to the land of his birth makes me a traitor."

Sebastian was silent, trying to reconcile two seemingly irreconcilable portraits of the Bishop: the dedicated philanthropist, and the narrow-minded bigot.

A faint smile rekindled in the depths of the American's eyes. "I see by your expression you don't believe me. You think, How could a man who fought for everyone from the poor slaves of the West Indies to the downtrodden Catholics of Ireland be so unreasonable in his dealings with an old man?"

"I suppose we all have our prejudices," said Sebastian.

"We do indeed. Prescott may have been a reformer, but he was no radical. As far as he was concerned, France and America were ungodly places, united by revolution and a dangerous philosophy he considered a threat to the future of civilization."

"But your own loyalty to England never wavered."

"It didn't matter. Prescott looked at me, and he saw my father. For him, that was enough."

"The war with America ended nearly thirty years ago."

Franklin shrugged. "For some, the passage of time

means little." He swung to face Sebastian again, his pale, watery eyes blinking in the bright sunlight. "If you want my advice, my lord, you'll look at more than the past few days if you want to find out who killed the Bishop of London. Some men keep their friends for a lifetime. But Francis Prescott, he preserved his enemies. Forever."

"Do you have any idea who some of those enemies might have been?"

"Me? No."

Franklin's granddaughter was beginning to reel in her kite, the crimson silk dancing against the clear blue sky. He watched it, eyes squinted against the light, his features set in troubled lines. After a moment, he said, "There is one rather curious aspect of my meeting with the Bishop."

"Yes?"

"When I arrived at London House, I found the Bishop paused on the footpath in conversation with a tradesman. A butcher. Prescott said the man was simply there over an account, but . . ."

"You didn't believe him?"

"When was the last time you dealt with your butcher over an account?"

Sebastian smiled. "I daresay I wouldn't recognize the man if I passed him on the street."

"Precisely."

"Had you ever seen the man before?"

"As a matter of fact, yes. I recognized him. He's a fellow by the name of Slade. Jack Slade. He has a shop near Smithfield."

"Smithfield?"

Franklin nodded. "Near the cathedral, although I'm afraid I couldn't tell you his exact direction. I remembered the incident because it was obvious the encounter troubled the Bishop. Deeply troubled him. I suspect it does much to explain why he reacted so angrily to my own request."

The wind gusted up, then suddenly died. Tipping back his head, Sebastian watched the kite falter, red wings vivid against the blue sky. Ellen Franklin let out a squeal as the kite plummeted downward, silk flapping, to land upside down in the branches of an elm tee, a torn scarlet splash against a sea of green.

"I want you to find someone for me," Sebastian told his tiger. "A Smithfield butcher by the name of Jack Slade."

Tom's eyes brightened. "Aye, gov'nor. Any idea what part o' the area 'e 'ails from?"

Sebastian gathered the gray's reins. "No."

Tom gave a cheery laugh and hopped down from his perch at the rear of the curricle. "I'll find 'im, gov'nor. Ne'er you fear!"

Chapter 12

*H*ero spent what was left of the day prowling the big Jarvis town house on Berkeley Square and awaiting the arrival of Bishop Prescott's appointment schedule from London House.

The discovery that the Archbishop of Canterbury had asked Viscount Devlin to investigate Prescott's death filled her with a driving sense of urgency. She knew Devlin, which meant she knew it was only a matter of time before he discovered the truth behind her recent visits to the Bishop. And once he knew that, she had no doubt he would be relentless in his determination to "do the honorable thing" and marry her. Wild and unorthodox Devlin might be, but he was still an officer and a gentleman. And in affairs of this nature, the gentleman's code was inflexible.

Of course, he could not *compel* her to marry him. Normally, Hero would have laughed at the suggestion that she might find it difficult to resist him. But she was discovering that pregnancy had the disconcerting effect of making even the strongest of females weak and—God help her—weepy. There were times, particularly in the dark, sleepless hours just before dawn, when she found herself actually considering such a solution. Which made it vitally important that the Bishop's murder be solved. Quickly. Before it was too late.

That evening, when the papers from London House had still not arrived, she pleaded a headache (which was real enough) and stayed home from a dinner at the Austrian ambassador's. She was convinced the schedule from the Bishop's chaplain would arrive at any moment.

But it never did.

That night, Sebastian dressed in a white silk waistcoat, black tails and knee breeches, and silk stockings, and directed his carriage toward Covent Garden.

He arrived late, after the fashionable crush of chattering society members had settled in their private boxes, and after the less-than-fashionable stampede of those taking advantage of the theater's practice of selling off all empty gallery seats at half price after the second interval.

For the better part of a year, Sebastian had carefully avoided the theater. Now, as he walked through the dim corridors and up the candlelit staircase, he breathed in the familiar scent of oranges and imagined for one painful moment that he caught the distant echo of a woman's sweet laughter, like a ghost from the past.

There'd been a time when Kat Boleyn, the most famous actress of the London stage, had been Sebastian's mistress and the love of his life. Then came the devastating revelations of the previous autumn, when Hendon rediscovered a previously unknown illegitimate daughter, and Sebastian . . . Sebastian lost forever the woman he'd hoped to make his wife.

He knew that painful truth should change the way he

felt about Kat, and in many respects, it had. But over the last months he'd been forced to acknowledge that a part of his heart would forever be hers, no matter how damned that might make him in the eyes of God and man.

The boxes, although private, were as brilliantly lit as the stage, for one attended the theater to see and be seen as much as to actually watch the production below. He was aware of heads turning, of whispers behind raised fans as he slipped, alone, into his box. His many months' absence from the theater had naturally been marked and speculated upon—coinciding as it did with the precipitous marriage of his longtime mistress to a gentleman of dubious reputation and questionable sexuality.

Sebastian kept his gaze on the stage below.

Resplendent in the red velvet robes of Portia in *The Merchant of Venice*, Kat was as beautiful as ever, her cheekbones exquisitely high and flaring, her dark hair touched with fire by the gleam of candlelight, her blue St. Cyr eyes flashing. He watched, his heart aching with need and want, late into the final act. Then he quietly left his seat and headed for the private dressing room he knew so well.

He was waiting for her when she swept in after the final curtain call, her eyes sparkling, her cheeks flushed with triumph. Then she saw him and froze.

"I'm sorry for coming here," he said, his shoulders braced against the far wall, his arms crossed at his chest. "But I couldn't see presenting myself at your new husband's house, and I need to talk to you."

She had full, sensuous lips, a child's nose, and slanting cat's eyes she'd inherited from the woman who'd once stolen Hendon's heart. Eyes she half hid with a downward sweep of her lashes as she closed the door quietly behind her. "You are always welcome there."

Nine months before, she had married an ex-privateer named Russell Yates, a dashing nobleman's son with long dark hair, a pirate's gold hoop earring, and a flair for making himself the darling of the ton. But theirs was a marriage of convenience only, for Kat had made herself Jarvis's enemy, and Yates had in his possession proof of a dirty little secret from the powerful man's past. In exchange for protecting Kat from Jarvis, Yates received the cachet of being married to the most beautiful, desirable woman on the London stage. Which was important, given that Yardley's sexual interests did not run to women.

When Sebastian returned no answer, Kat went to settle before her dressing table and began removing pins from her hair. "It must be important. You've been avoiding me for months now."

"You know why."

"Yes. I know why."

He drew a deep breath, but it did nothing to ease the ache in his chest. He shouldn't have come. He pushed away from the wall. "Last night, someone bashed in the head of the Bishop of London."

Her hands stilled at their task. "And you've been drawn into the investigation of his murder?" Sebastian's involvement in cases of murder had always troubled Kat. Of all the people in his life, she knew better than any—better even than Gibson—how much it cost him. "Oh, Sebastian."

He gave a negligent shrug. "My aunt asked it of me."

Her gaze met his in the mirror, her head tipping sideways. "You don't seriously think I was in any way acquainted with the good Bishop, of all people?"

"No. But there is some suggestion he was vulnerable to blackmail. I thought you might know why."

Once, she had labored to aid the country of her mother's birth—Ireland—by passing sensitive information to the agents of England's enemy, France. Ferreting out the secrets of the powerful and influential was an established technique in espionage. Which meant that if Bishop Prescott had indeed guarded a dangerous secret, then the representatives of Napoléon in London would have made it their business to know about it. Blackmail could be a powerful tool.

She understood at once the implication of his question. "I ended those associations months ago. You know that, Sebastian."

"Still?"

Her gaze held his in the mirror. "Still."

"But you would know whom to ask."

She took the last pin from her hair, letting it cascade in glorious waves around her shoulders. He had to tighten his fists to keep from reaching out and touching it. She said, "I could find out, yes."

He turned toward the door. "Thank you."

He had his hand on the knob when she said, "Sebastian—"

He glanced back at her. The flames of the candles at each end of her dressing table fluttered in the draft, dancing poignant shadows across the planes of her face. She said, "Sebastian, how are you? Really?"

He found he had to swallow before answering. "I'm well, thank you."

Her brows drew together in a frown. "You look thinner . . . wilder."

He gave a sudden laugh. "At least I've given up trying to drink myself to death."

No answering smile touched her lips. "That is an improvement."

"And you?" he said, his voice gruff. "How is your marriage?"

"As I would wish it," she said. Which could mean anything, or nothing.

He closed the door quietly behind him. He stood for a moment in the narrow corridor, breathed in the achingly familiar scents of oranges and greasepaint and dust.

Then he walked away, his footsteps echoing in the stillness.

He arrived back at Brook Street some hours later to find Tom awaiting him in the library.

"You shouldn't have stayed up for me," said Sebastian, holding himself painfully still.

Tom's eyes widened, taking in the slightly disordered cravat, the dangerous glitter that told of too many brandies downed too quickly. But all he said was, "I found yer Jack Slade. 'E 'as a shop in Monkwell Street, jist off Falcon Square, near St. Paul's."

Sebastian turned toward the stairs. "Good. We'll pay him a visit first thing in the morning. Best get some sleep."

"I asked around the neighborhood a bit, to see what manner o' man 'e is. From what I can tell, 'e's what ye might call an *unsavory character*. 'Im and 'is son, Obadiah, both."

Sebastian paused with one foot on the bottom step. "He has a son named Obadiah Slade?"

"That's right. Giant o' a man, with a lantern jaw and yellow 'air 'e wears cut short enough to show an ugly scar running across the side o' 'is 'ead." Tom tipped his own head sideways, studying Sebastian's face. "Why? Ye know 'im?"

"He was a corporal in my regiment, in Portugal. If it had been up to me, he'd have been hanged. As it was, he earned a hundred lashes and was cashiered from the Army."

Tom's face went suddenly solemn.

"What?" prompted Sebastian.

"They say 'e ain't been back in town long. But 'e's been talking big ever since 'e got back. About some officer 'e knew in the Army, some lord's son. Says if 'e ever sees 'im again, 'e's gonna kill 'im."

Chapter 13

*E*arly the next morning, Sebastian donned a rough brown corduroy coat and greasy breeches gleaned from the secondhand clothing stalls of Rosemary Lane. Wrapping a coarse black cravat around his neck, he rubbed ashes into his uncombed hair and unshaven cheeks. Under Jules Calhoun's amused eye, he settled an unfashionable round hat low on his head. Then he set out in search of Mr. Jack Slade.

Lying to the northeast of St. Paul's Cathedral, Monkwell Street proved to be a narrow lane of small shops that wound uphill toward the noisome churchyard of St. Giles Cripplegate and the vast burial ground beyond it. "There," said Tom, as Sebastian reined in the curricle at the base of the hill. "That's Jack Slade's place. Next to the knackery."

"Convenient."

"Maybe. If yer customers ain't bothered by bein' reminded o' where their vitals come from."

Sebastian eyed his young tiger with astonishment. "I'd no notion you harbored such exquisite sensibilities."

Tom grunted and took the reins.

Jumping down, Sebastian continued up the lane on foot. With each step he sank deeper into the role he intended to play. The grace of the horseman and the swordsman faded away, along with the easy assurance that came unthinkingly to an earl's son. His movements grew heavier, his demeanor pugnacious, argumentative. It was an acting trick Kat Boleyn had taught him years ago, when they'd been young and in love and blissfully, dangerously ignorant of the shared blood that flowed through their veins.

The footpath here was narrow, and crowded with a variety of goods spilling from the surrounding shops. Transformed now into Mr. Taylor, constable, Sebastian dodged stacks of tinware, trestle-mounted trays displaying colorful ribbons, a canvas piled with salted cod whose fishy odor mingled unpleasantly with the stench of freshly spilled blood and raw meat coming from the butcher shop and the knackery beyond.

A side of beef, a row of sheep's heads, and what looked like half a hog hung in the open shopfront. Ducking beneath the sheep's heads, Sebastian stepped onto a sawdust-covered floor where flies buzzed over trays of sausages and piles of tripe and blood pudding displayed on a long scrubbed bench; more flies coated the glistening joints hung from hooks screwed into the wall. Behind the bench, a grizzle-headed man in a bloody apron was hacking at a half-dismembered carcass lying on a thick block. A channel cut into the perimeter of the block caught the blood and drained it into a tin bucket below. As Sebastian's shadow fell across his work, the man glanced up, grunted, and turned away again.

He looked to be in his fifties, his face lined and darkened as if by years spent beneath a powerful sun. Several days' growth of gray beard shadowed his lean cheeks and pronounced jaw; his eyes were small and dark and wary beneath beetled brows. He was essentially an older, darker version of the Corporal Obadiah Slade who'd once raped a twelve-year-old Portuguese girl, then smashed in her head for the sheer joy of watching her die.

"You're Jack Slade?" said Sebastian, every trace of the aristocratic West End carefully scrubbed from his diction.

"Aye." Slade worked his cleaver free from between two ribs, then let it fly again. *Splat.* Small bits of gore splattered over the nearby wall. "What's it to ye?"

"I'm told you paid a visit to Bishop Prescott Monday afternoon."

The cleaver hesitated for one betraying instant, then fell heavily. "What if I did?"

"Care to tell us why?"

The butcher kept his gaze on his work, but Sebastian saw an angry muscle tighten along his heavy jaw. "What do ye mean, 'why'?"

"It's not a particularly obtuse question."

"I'm a simple man." *Splat.* "Ye want I should understand ye, ye'll need t' be usin' simple words."

"Simpler than 'why'?"

Jack Slade sank his cleaver into the side of beef and left it there, quivering. He straightened slowly, uncoiling a big body laced with muscle. "The Bishop likes me pork chops, see? I brung him some. It's as simple as that."

It was the most improbable tale Sebastian had ever heard. He said, "You do that often?"

"On occasion. It ain't somethin' I'd do fer jist anybody, ye understand. But the Bishop, he was a special customer."

"He must have been." Sebastian studied the sheep's heads hanging in the doorway. "Lamb chops, did you say?"

"That's right."

"So you're saying—what? That the Bishop didn't like the looks of your lamb chops?"

"What's that supposed to mean? Ask anybody on the street, they'll tell ye. Ye want fresh meat, ye go to Jack Slade."

"So maybe you brought him lamb chops when what he really wanted was your pork chops."

The butcher's nostrils flared. "Ye're tryin' t' be funny. Is that it?"

"What I'm trying to do is understand why a visit from a simple butcher would trouble someone like the Bishop of London."

Slade's eyes narrowed. "Who told you my visit troubled the Bishop?"

"Does it matter?"

"I s'pose not." Slade turned to pull his cleaver from the half-dismembered carcass. "Except that whoever said it, he's wrong." Slade kept his gaze fixed on the meat before him; Sebastian kept his gaze on that cleaver.

Sebastian said, "So you're suggesting the Bishop wasn't distressed?"

"No. I ain't sayin' that. Fact is, Prescott was already in a high dander when I seen him. What I'm sayin' is, it had nothin' to do with me." The man's fist tightened around the cleaver, his jaw clenching belligerently as he spat the words out. "Ye bulls just won't let a man alone, will ye? I done me fourteen years in Botany Bay. Lost me poor wife whilst I was there, then earned another seven for a spot o' trouble I got into in Sydney Town. It took me three years on top o' all that t' earn the wherewithal t' buy me passage back home. But I'm a free man now, ye hear? And there's nothin' the lot o' ye can do about it. So why don't ye get out o' here and go bother some other poor sod?"

The man's sun-darkened skin suddenly made sense. Sebastian said, "What were you transported for?"

"Like ye don't know." With a flick of the wrist, the butcher sent the cleaver flying to bite into the wooden board between them. It twanged a moment, then stilled.

"It was murder, wasn't it?"

"I'm closin' me shop now," said Slade. Ripping off his bloody apron, he pushed through the ragged curtain that screened an alcove in the back, leaving Sebastian alone with the flies and the stench of raw meat and blood.

Sebastian was heading back down the street when he saw Obadiah Slade.

The man came charging up the hill, his heavy fists clenched at his sides, his powerful jaw set hard. For one intense moment, he stared straight at Sebastian. But the rough clothes and grayed hair and unmilitary-like bearing confused him. Sebastian saw the man frown, as if trying to capture a fleeting memory.

Sebastian brushed past him and kept walking.

Obadiah Slade hadn't made the connection yet between this unfashionably garbed, subtly older Londoner and the young officer in the Peninsula who'd once tried to have him hanged.

But eventually, it would come.

Chapter 14

"Never tell me Obadiah Slade is involved in this?" said Paul Gibson, glancing up from the naked, eviscerated corpse stretched out on the stone slab before him.

Sebastian had driven here, to Gibson's surgery on Tower Hill, from Monkwell Street. Now he took one look at what Gibson was doing in the eighteenth-century cadaver's bowels, and shifted his gaze to the unkempt yard outside. "Maybe. Maybe not. But his father is definitely hiding something."

"Is the father anything like the son?"

"Yes."

"Then I suggest you be careful, my friend."

"I intend to."

With effort, Sebastian brought his gaze back to the grinning fright on the slab. "What can you tell us about this one?"

"Well . . . judging by his teeth and certain other features, I'd say our friend here was about forty years old when someone stuck that dagger in his back. He was an unusually large man, well over six feet tall, and probably twenty-five or more stone."

"A very large man," said Sebastian.

"From the condition of his internal organs, it's obvious he ate too much and drank too much."

"Not exactly unusual."

"Unfortunately, no. He still had most of his teeth, but at some point he must have broken his left forearm. It didn't heal well. See?"

Sebastian studied the discernible kink in the man's left arm, just below the elbow. "Anything of interest amongst his clothes?"

"Nothing to give us the man's name. He had a fine gold watch in his pocket, although unfortunately it wasn't engraved. His fob was in the shape of a rampant lion, rather than a family crest. And his purse contained only a few banknotes dated from 1778 and 1781. I've sent the lot over to Bow Street."

"From 1781? At least that narrows the date of death some." Sebastian studied the cadaver's dark, leathery face. "Any wounds besides the knife in his back?"

"Take a look for yourself." Heaving the corpse onto its side, Gibson pointed to a slit just below the left shoulder blade. "This is where I found the blade. But he was also stabbed here." He indicated another tear, toward the left. "And here."

"Three times. All in the back."

"The first two wounds were not particularly deep." Gibson eased the shriveled corpse onto its back again. "There may be more that I missed, given the condition of the body."

"No clue as to who might have killed him, or why?"

"Sorry."

Sebastian cast a quick look around the small, dank room. "Where's the Bishop?"

"Lying in state at London House."

"Ah. When's the funeral?"

"Next week sometime."

"Next week?"

Gibson shrugged. "The church needs to allow time for everyone to assemble the proper mourning clothes."

"At least the grave robbers won't have much interest in him by then."

An amused crease appeared in the Irish doctor's cheek. "Not in this weather."

Sebastian brought his attention back to the time-blackened corpse before them. "Anything that might connect the two murders?"

"I'm afraid not." Gibson rested his hips against the bench, his arms crossed at his chest. "It could simply be a coincidence, you know—the two bodies being found in the same place. The Bishop hurries out to Tanfield Hill to investigate the discovery of the original murder victim, and either surprises someone in the act of robbing the crypt, or is followed by some enemy who decides to take advantage of the darkness and bash our good bishop over the head."

Sebastian rubbed one bent knuckle against the side of his nose. "I don't like coincidences."

"Yet they happen."

"They do." Hunkering down, he studied the cadaver's distorted, sunken face, with its gaping mouth and shriveled nostrils and empty eye sockets. After a moment, he said, "Think anyone who knew this man thirty years ago would recognize him if they saw him today?"

"In a word? No."

"That's what I was thinking." Sebastian pushed to his feet. "You say you sent his clothes over to Bow Street?"

"Yes. Why?"

"It occurs to me that even if someone couldn't recognize our friend's face, they might remember his clothes. Or at least his watch and fob."

"After all this time?"

"If someone you loved disappeared into thin air, you don't think you'd remember what he was wearing—even after thirty or forty years?"

Gibson thought about it a moment. "You might have a point."

Sebastian walked around the slab, studying the withered cadaver from every angle. But from any angle, none of it made any sense.

Gibson said, "It seems to me that when you come right down to it, there are basically two possibilities. Either our eighteenth-century gentleman was killed by someone who had nothing to do with the Bishop's death, or they were both killed by the same man."

Sebastian looked up. "Why would a murderer wait thirty years or more to go after his second victim?"

"I don't know; you're the expert on murderers. I just read their victims' bodies."

"There is one other alternative," said Sebastian slowly.

Gibson frowned. "What?"

"That the Bishop killed our eighteenth-century gentleman. And then someone else killed the Bishop. In revenge."

When the information from London House failed to arrive by one o'clock on Thursday afternoon, Hero set forth for St. James's Square in her carriage, accompanied by her long-suffering maid.

"My dear Miss Jarvis," exclaimed the Bishop's chaplain, all obsequious goodwill as he received her in his chambers. "I was just now preparing to send the details you requested around to Berkeley Square. I am most dreadfully sorry for the delay, but the diary secretary only this instant completed making the necessary copies."

"Thank you," she said, slipping the packet he handed her into her reticule.

"You have heard, of course, that Archbishop Moore has requested the help of *Viscount Devlin* in investigating the Bishop's death?" He said the Viscount's name in the tone churchmen typically reserved for words like "Jezebel," and "heathen," and "Satan." Devlin had obviously not ingratiated himself with the Chaplain. Or perhaps his reputation for hard living had simply preceded him.

"I had heard," she said with a great show of sympathy. "How distressing for you."

He gave a soulful *tut-tut*. "It is, it is. But it is what the Archbishop wants, so we must, of course, do what we can to facilitate the arrangement."

"I suppose Devlin wanted to know all about the events of Tuesday night."

"Indeed he did. I told him everything, from the Reverend Earnshaw's arrival to the Bishop's own departure in his chaise."

"Everything?" said Miss Jarvis with a smile.

The Chaplain gnawed thoughtfully on the inside of one cheek. Then he seemed to come to a decision. "Well," he said, leaning forward as he dropped his voice to a whisper. "I did leave out one or two little details about *Monday*."

Hero listened to the Chaplain's words with an outward show of calm interest. But inside, she was anything but calm.

When he had finished, she said, "I'm convinced you were quite right to keep these, er, details to yourself. I can see no need for Devlin to know of them."

The Chaplain sat back and heaved a relieved sigh, although he still looked vaguely troubled. "I'm so glad to hear you agree."

Sebastian was eating a light nuncheon in his own dining room when he heard a distant, timid *tap-tap* at the front door. A moment later, his dour-faced majordomo, Morey, appeared to clear his throat apologetically and say, "A gentleman to see you, my lord. A clerical gentleman, in a high state of nervous agitation. He says his name is Mr. Earnshaw, from St. Margaret's in Tanfield Hill."

Sebastian pushed back his chair. "Show him into the drawing room. I'll be with him in a moment."

He found the reverend of St. Margaret's hovering before the empty hearth. A small, softly fleshy man with slightly protruding eyes and a receding chin, he held his black hat gripped in both hands before him like a shield.

"Mr. Earnshaw. An unexpected pleasure. May I offer you a glass of sherry? Or do you prefer port?"

A quiver of want passed over the man's features, but he said primly, "Nothing, thank you."

Sebastian indicated the cane chairs near the room's front bow window. "Please have a seat."

The Reverend shook his head back and forth in short, sharp jerks. "No, thank you. I've come to apologize for not being in a fit state to receive you yesterday."

"It's understandable," said Sebastian, pouring himself a glass of port. "You're certain you won't have something?"

Again, that quick, jerking shake of the head. "I'm told

the Archbishop has requested your assistance in dealing with this . . . unpleasantness. I am therefore here to answer any questions you might have."

The Archbishop had obviously expressed his displeasure at his underling's thoughtlessness in drugging himself into a twenty-four-hour stupor. One did not displease the Archbishop of Canterbury, even if that archbishop was old and dying.

"I think I've been able to piece together most of what happened that night," said Sebastian. "I gather that after the discovery of the body in the crypt, you traveled up to London to acquaint the Bishop with the situation?"

"That's right. Unfortunately, the Bishop had an important appointment scheduled for six that evening. Rather than return with me immediately to St. Margaret's, he arranged to drive out to Tanfield Hill afterward. It was my intention to meet him at the church, but . . ." The Reverend's voice faded away.

"But?" prompted Sebastian.

"One of my parishioners. Mrs. Cummings. She was ill. By the time I returned, the Bishop had already arrived. And it was too late."

The small, protuberant eyes blinked rapidly several times in succession. "I just keep thinking that if only Bishop Prescott could have returned with me to St. Margaret's right away, none of this would have happened!"

Sebastian took a slow sip of his wine. "Did the Bishop happen to mention the nature of the appointment he had that evening?"

"No. Only that he didn't feel he could cancel it. Something about an old friend in need of counseling."

Sebastian's fist tightened around his glass. "Really?" What had Miss Jarvis said? *The Bishop asked for my as-*

sistance in preparing the speech he was to give before the
House of Lords this Thursday.

The Reverend nodded again, his head moving up and
down in a way that reminded Sebastian of a pigeon
pecking at seed.

Sebastian took another sip of his wine. "It seems a
strange thing to have done—rushing off to the Bishop
simply because some workmen had stumbled upon an
old crypt. I mean, why the Bishop?"

"Because of the body, of course."

"You were concerned about . . . what? A scandal?
Over a decades-old murder victim?"

Mr. Earnshaw's eyes bulged alarmingly. "Good heavens. Can it be that you do not know?"

"Don't know what?"

"About the ring!"

"What ring?"

"Sir Nigel's ring! I recognized it."

Sebastian set aside his drink with a *click*. "You're saying you recognized a ring on the body in the crypt?"

"Yes, yes. An ancient Roman profile, carved in black
onyx and mounted in a setting of filigreed silver. Sir
Nigel wore it always on his right little finger."

"Who is Sir Nigel?"

The Reverend stared at him. "Why, Sir Nigel Prescott.
Bishop Prescott's eldest brother!"

Chapter 15

"*The* imbecile never mentioned the ring to anyone," said Sir Henry Lovejoy.

They were in Hyde Park, walking along the banks of the Serpentine. The magistrate had brought a loaf of stale bread and was crumbling it up to feed the ducks. Sebastian said, "But you have heard of Sir Nigel?"

"Oh, yes. We've had constables fanning out across the entire area, asking about men who disappeared thirty to forty years ago. His name came up right away."

Sebastian watched as a plump drake, its feathers iridescent in the sunlight, waddled out of the reeds toward them. "Sir Nigel was the Bishop's eldest brother?"

Lovejoy nodded. "By some thirteen years. He went missing in July of 1782. His horse was found wandering on Hounslow Heath, so it was generally believed he must have fallen victim to highwaymen. But his body was never found."

"How long was this before the crypt of St. Margaret's was bricked up?"

"Unfortunately, there was a fire in the sacristy some years ago that destroyed many of the church's records. We're still trying to ascertain the exact date of the closure."

Lovejoy threw a chunk of bread to the drake, who caught the morsel out of the air. "Sir Nigel's widow, Lady Prescott, still lives at Prescott Grange. A son inherited the estate."

"Sir Peter Prescott," said Sebastian.

Lovejoy kept his gaze on the task at hand. "You know him?"

"We were at Eton together."

The magistrate tossed the drake another handful of crumbs. "I understand he was a posthumous child, born some months after his father's disappearance."

Sebastian nodded. "He suffered a fair amount of grief over it at school—you know what boys can be like. But he always took it well." Sebastian watched the drake waddle away, tail feathers flashing in the sun. "I'm told there were originally five Prescott brothers. The middle three were all killed in the wars of the last century."

"Good heavens. I hadn't heard that. A most unfortunate family, indeed." Lovejoy emptied the rest of his bread on the grass. "If Bishop Prescott learned that his brother's body had been discovered, it would certainly explain why those who saw him after Earnshaw's visit described him as agitated."

"True. Except that William Franklin also described the Bishop as troubled. And he saw Prescott on Monday."

"It's my intention to take the victim's clothing, watch, and fob out to Lady Prescott this afternoon. Hopefully she'll be able to make some sort of identification without actually viewing the remains."

"What I want to know is, what happened to the ring?"

Lovejoy glanced over at him. "It wasn't on the body?"

Sebastian shook his head. "Earnshaw says he brought the ring up to London, to show the Bishop."

Lovejoy's lips flattened into a disapproving line. "Seems a ghoulish thing to have done—tugging a ring off a corpse's finger."

"Given the state of the body, I imagine it came off easily enough."

Lovejoy cleared his throat uncomfortably. "Yes, well . . ."

"According to the Reverend, he gave the ring to Bishop Prescott. But I checked with London House, and no such ring has been found in the Bishop's chambers. Gibson says it wasn't in the Bishop's pockets, or in his hand, when the bodies were delivered to him."

"I suppose the Bishop may have dropped it in the crypt," said Sir Henry, dusting the last crumbs of bread from his hands. "I'll send some of the lads to give the place another going-over."

"There is one other possibility."

Lovejoy raised an eyebrow in inquiry.

Sebastian said, "The killer could have taken it."

Later that afternoon, after she'd coaxed her mother out on a visit to one of Lady Jarvis's oldest friends, Hero settled on the window seat in her bedchamber and withdrew the Bishop's schedule from her reticule.

She ran through it quickly, relieved to see that there was nothing in the Bishop's calendar—except, of course, for his frequent meetings with Hero herself—that might betray her to Devlin. Satisfied of that, she went back to the beginning.

There, indeed, was the visit from Lord Quillian, just as she had suspected, on the afternoon of the Monday before the Bishop's death. "Ha. You see?" she said aloud, as if Devlin himself were actually in the room with her.

Then she frowned as she studied several other curious names on the schedule.

She might be nine-tenths convinced of Quillian's guilt in the Bishop's murder, but Hero liked to consider herself an open-minded person, which meant she had to remain receptive to other possibilities.

Pushing up from her window seat, she went in search of paper and pen. At the top of the page, she wrote, *Lord Quillian*, and below that, *William Franklin*. For a moment, she reconsidered and started to cross out his name, for the man was aged and infirm. But she reasoned that it did not require excessive strength or agility to hit someone over the head with an iron bar, so she left the American's name in place.

She glanced through the Bishop's schedule again, but came up with only one other interesting item: Sir Peter Prescott. Why, she wondered, would Sir Peter make an appointment to see his own uncle? She wrote his name on the list, then circled it in frustration.

One of the more tedious aspects of being an unmarried female was the extent to which it circumscribed her movements and activities. Having recently suffered a bereavement, Sir Peter was unlikely to attend any social functions. And try as she would, Hero could not come up with a sufficiently plausible excuse to visit him.

Decorum could, at times, be exceedingly aggravating.

That night, Sebastian made a rare appearance at his aunt Henrietta's rout.

One of London's most sought-after hostesses, the Duchess of Claiborne never failed to send her nephew an invitation to each of her many functions. Recognizing the summonses for what they were—thinly veiled attempts to introduce him to an endless line of suitable young debutantes—Sebastian invariably but politely refused.

As a result, the sight of her disreputable but still highly eligible nephew actually appearing in her drawing rooms that evening was such a shock that Henrietta staggered slightly, one hand groping for the quizzing glass that hung from a riband around her neck. "Good heavens," she said. "It is you, Devlin. Don't tell me you've finally decided to live up to the expectations of your house and look about you for a wife?"

"No," he said baldly, cupping her elbow to steer her toward a small withdrawing room. "I want to hear what you can tell me about the Prescotts."

"Ssshh," she whispered, shutting the door behind them with a snap. "I don't want Lady Christine to overhear."

"Who?"

"The Earl of Lumley's daughter. She really is lovely, Sebastian. But while I can assure you she is quite one of your admirers, it might be better if she didn't hear that you've once again involved yourself in murder—"

"I didn't involve myself in this murder; you did."

"Nevertheless, I'm afraid her sensibilities are such that—"

"Aunt," he said sternly. "I am not here to be enchanted by your latest ingenue, however lovely she may be. I'm here because I want to know what you can tell me about Sir Nigel Prescott."

"Sir Nigel Prescott? Why on earth would you want to know—" She broke off, her eyes widening. "Good heavens. Is *he* the decades-old body in the crypt?"

"In all likelihood, yes."

She sat down on a nearby swan-shaped pink silk settee with an inelegant thump. "Good heavens," she said again.

"You knew him, I presume?"

"Of course I knew him." The Duchess of Claiborne not only knew everyone—she knew all their dirty little secrets, too. And she remembered them forever. "A most disagreeable man," she said with a *tut-tut*. "Very bad ton. Nothing at all like his brother."

"Sir Nigel was the eldest?"

She nodded. "Yes. Of five brothers. He inherited the title while still up at Oxford. He was always a big man—tall, like the Bishop, but much bigger boned, and fleshy. He married a lovely woman by the name of Mary Mayfield, and made the poor dear miserable. She hadn't been dead of consumption a year when he married again—to Lady Rosamond, the second daughter of the Marquess of Ripon."

"When was this?" said Sebastian.

She frowned. " 'Seventy-six? 'Seventy-seven? Something like that."

"Sir Peter was his only son?"

She nodded. "There were no children at all from the first marriage. He was wed to Lady Rosamond for some five or six years before Sir Peter was born—and he was a posthumous child, born after his father disappeared."

Sebastian pulled forward a chair with gilded crocodile-shaped legs and sat down opposite her. "You say Sir Nigel was a disagreeable man. In what way?"

"He had a vicious temper. And a nasty reputation." She dropped her voice, even though they were alone and no one could hear. "Hellfire Club, you know."

Interesting, thought Sebastian; Squire Pyle had also mentioned the Hellfire Club. A notorious secret society of the previous century, the Hellfire Club had been dedicated to black magic, orgies, and political conspiracies. Meeting in the ruins of an ancient abbey, the "monks" specialized in defiling virgins, exhibitionism, voyeurism, and incest. At one time, its powerful members included the Prime Minister of England, the Lord Mayor of London, the Prince of Wales . . . and a certain homespun American named Benjamin Franklin.

The Duchess kept her voice low. "When he disappeared the way he did, it was assumed the club was somehow involved—an ungodly ritual gone awry, perhaps, or some poor young girl's family seeking their own revenge. There'd been other mysterious deaths and disappearances linked to that crowd—although mostly of young girls from the nearby villages." She paused to give him a significant look. "And a few young boys."

"What did you think happened to him at the time?"

"Me?" Henrietta sat back, her fierce blue St. Cyr eyes narrowing. She was a shrewd woman, able to see clearly through all the pretenses and flummery of her society. "Personally, I thought it more than likely that someone quietly slit his throat and dumped the body down an old well or some such thing. I told you: He was a disagreeable man. I don't think anyone was sorry to see him gone—least of all his wife."

"Tell me about her."

"Lady Prescott? There's not much to tell, really. She married Prescott at the end of her first season. There was talk of another suitor, but he was said to be a second son with no prospects. Her father, Ripon, was always badly dipped in those days. Gambling, you know. Most of the members of the Hellfire Club drifted pretty far into dun territory."

"Ripon and Prescott were both in the Hellfire Club?"

"So I'm told. All I know is that when Prescott offered for Lady Rosamond's hand, Ripon accepted."

"Sold to the highest bidder, was she?"

"Essentially. Ripon had half a dozen sons to see established in careers; he couldn't afford to let Lady Rosamond be picky. Particularly as there were rumors that Ripon had dragged her back from the border when she and her unsuitable suitor made a bolt for Gretna Green."

"Really? Who was this unsuitable suitor?"

"I'm not quite sure. It was all kept very hush-hush."

"It must have been, if you didn't hear about it," said Sebastian with a smile. "What can you tell me about Lady Rosamond's marriage to Sir Nigel?"

"I don't think she was ever very happy, poor dear. She went from being a rather vivacious, carefree woman to something quite *squashed*. That's the only word I can think of to describe it. After Sir Nigel disappeared, she essentially withdrew from society. He was eventually declared dead after the requisite number of years so that his son could inherit the title and estate, but she never remarried. If there's been any scandal attached to her name since that time, I've never heard of it."

Sebastian nodded. If the Duchess of Claiborne hadn't heard of any scandal, then there hadn't been any scandal. He said, "What about the Bishop? How well did you know him?"

Henrietta let out her breath in a long, troubled sigh. "He was a great favorite of the Archbishop's."

"But not yours?"

She pulled a face. "You know me; I've little patience for earnest clerics."

Sebastian smiled. "The Archbishop of Canterbury himself being the notable exception."

A rare bloom of color touched his aunt's cheeks. "John is different," she said, and looked away.

Sebastian studied his aunt's plump, carefully rouged and powdered face. She had been married at the age of eighteen to the heir to the Duke of Claiborne, who assumed the title on the death of his father not long after the wedding. For fifty years she had reigned as one of the acknowledged queens of society, imperious, assured, and seemingly more than content with her lot in life. Odd that it had never occurred to Sebastian, until now, that the onetime Lady Henrietta St. Cyr might have nourished a *tendre* all these years for the poor but ambitious cleric who had eventually risen to become the most powerful churchman in all of England.

She said, "I know the Archbishop had hopes that Prescott would be named his successor. But it never would have happened."

"Why's that?"

"In theory, the selection of the new Archbishop of Canterbury will fall to the Prince Regent. But you know as well as I do that when it comes to affairs of state, Prinny doesn't sneeze without consulting Jarvis first. And Prescott was far too reform-minded to ever find favor with Jarvis. You mark my words: When the time comes, Charles Manners-Sutton will be named Archbishop. Mark my words."

"Jarvis's dislike of Prescott was well-known?"

"To anyone who gave it much thought. The two men tangled on everything from slavery in the West Indies to child labor here in England."

Interesting, thought Sebastian, that Miss Hero Jarvis hadn't bothered to mention it.

"Not that I'm suggesting," the Duchess continued, "that Jarvis had anything to do with the Bishop's death—however convenient that death may be for him."

"'Will no one rid me of this troublesome priest?'" quoted Sebastian softly.

The Duchess heaved to her feet with a soft grunt. "I assume your involvement in this affair is the reason you were seen walking with Miss Jarvis at the Chelsea Royal Hospital yesterday afternoon?"

"Good God," said Sebastian. "Do you have spies everywhere?"

"Not spies. Observant connections. And while I know I have been pressing you of late to set about the business of selecting a wife, I wouldn't want you to take that as in any way suggesting that you—"

Sebastian gave a sharp bark of laughter. "Never fear, Aunt; I have it on the best of authority that Miss Jarvis considers matrimony under England's current laws a barbaric institution that gives husbands the same rights over their poor wives as an American master might exercise over his slave."

"Good heavens; she said that?"

"Yes."

"Well." His aunt's worried frown cleared. "Seeing as how you are here, why not take a moment to meet Lady Christine? She's—"

"No, Aunt."

"But she's—"

"No." Sebastian opened the door for her, then stopped her by saying, "Was there any connection that you know of between Jarvis and Sir Nigel Prescott?"

She hesitated, her brows drawing together in thought. "I believe there was something. . . ." She let out her breath in a harsh sigh, and shook her head. "I must be getting old. But don't worry; it will come to me. Eventually."

Chapter 16

Sebastian returned home that night to be met by his majordomo.

"A packet arrived in your absence, my lord. From London House."

"Thank you," said Sebastian.

Carrying a branch of candles into the library, he slit the seal on the sheaf of papers and spread them open on his desk. The top sheet proved to be a curt note from the Bishop's supercilious chaplain, Simon Ashley. Sebastian could imagine the cleric's nose twitching with disapproval as he wrote it.

> *My lord Devlin,*
> *As per the Archbishop's instructions, herewith find enclosed a list of the Bishop's most recent appointments. At His Grace's suggestion, I have annotated the list for your edification.*

It was signed with a single initial: "A."

The next two pages had obviously been copied from the Bishop's appointment diary by someone with a painfully neat hand, most likely the diary secretary. The

Chaplain's own annotations were, in contrast, hurried scrawls, although thorough.

Settling back in his chair, Sebastian ran through the list of names, dates, and times. Most of the Bishop's appointments over the past week appeared to be routine meetings with church functionaries or parishioners. Sebastian found the appointment with William Franklin on Monday. Although late in the afternoon, it appeared to have been the Bishop's first scheduled appointment of the day, and it was followed immediately by the meeting with Lord Quillian. Interestingly, the Bishop had also met with his nephew, Sir Peter Prescott, at four o'clock on Tuesday afternoon, the day of his death. For what purpose was not made clear.

Rising thoughtfully to his feet, Sebastian glanced through the previous week's schedule again, but only one other name caught his attention: Miss Hero Jarvis.

In addition to her six-o'clock appointment on Tuesday, she had met with the Bishop of London no fewer than three times in the previous week.

Sebastian's dreams took him many places.

Sometimes he dreamt of cannonballs that whistled through the air to explode in bloody geysers of mud and horseflesh and torn men. Sometimes he dreamt of the sharp stench of burned timbers and a child's pale cheeks, brown eyes wide and sightless. And then there were those dreaded nights when he dreamt of a woman with blue St. Cyr eyes, who touched her fingertips to his and then slipped away, lost to him forever.

She came to him again that night, as a storm blew in off the North Sea, bringing with it the bite of an unseasonably cool wind. He felt her soft lips tremble against his. Felt her tear-slicked cheek, warm and wet against his neck. Beneath his touch, her body shivered. . . .

And he knew a start of horror that brought him instantly, heart-poundingly awake.

He lay for a moment, his breath coming harsh and ragged. Then he swung his legs over the side of the bed and went to fill a glass with brandy.

He drank it down, shuddering. Setting aside the empty glass, he jerked open the drapes and threw up the sash. The growing wind scuttled heavy clouds across the dark sky and bathed his hot skin with the cool air of the night. In the street below, the oil lamp at the corner flickered, went out.

But Sebastian had the keen eyesight of a creature of the night. Resting his palms on the sill, he leaned forward, his attention caught by the figure of a man crouched in the pool of shadow cast by the front steps of the house opposite.

As Sebastian watched, the man raised a cheroot to his lips and drew deeply, the glowing embers illuminating his bony features and narrowed eyes.

"Bloody hell," swore Sebastian. Shoving away from the window, he snatched up his breeches and the small pistol with an ivory handle and double barrels he kept primed and ready, and turned toward the door.

Obadiah Slade had the lit cheroot halfway to his mouth when Sebastian pressed the muzzle of his flintlock against the man's broad temple and drew back both hammers.

"Do the world a favor," said Sebastian, "and give me an excuse to blow your brains out."

For the briefest instant, the other man froze. Then he

rested the cheroot against his lower lip and inhaled sharply. "What? A fine, moral gentleman like yerself, committing murder on the streets of London?" The former corporal exhaled a blue stream of smoke, his lips pursing insolently. "I don't think so."

Sebastian kept his arm extended, the muzzle biting into the flesh of the other man's forehead. "Why are you watching my house?"

"Ain't no law sayin' an Englishman can't stand on the street smoking a cheroot, now, is there?"

"Depends on the Englishman, and the street."

Obadiah took another drag on his cheroot. "Took me a while, after I seen ye in Aldersgate today. But I finally figured it out. Me da told me ye were at 'im over the Bishop. He thought ye was a constable. He don't know what ye did in the Army. How ye could pass yerself off as everythin' from a Spanish peasant to a French general."

"Is that why you're here? Because of Jack Slade?"

"Nah." Obadiah took a final drag on his cheroot and let it fall to the footpath. "Ye know why I'm here."

Sebastian stepped back, the pistol still held at full cock. "Come around here again and I'll call the watch on you."

Moving deliberately, Obadiah brought the heel of one massive boot down on the glowing tip of the cheroot. "Know what a hundred lashes do to a man's back?"

"If it had been up to me, you would have hanged."

Obadiah's teeth glowed white in the darkness. "Takes a long time to lay a hundred lashes on a man's back. Ye know how I survived it?"

When Sebastian remained silent, the other man ground his boot back and forth, pulverizing the cheroot beneath the heel. "There's lots o' different ways to kill a man. The one I picked for ye, ye're gonna wish ye'd pulled them triggers."

Sebastian felt his finger tighten against the cold metal in his hand, then willed himself to relax. "You're not worth it."

Obadiah smiled and turned away, his gait a languid, contemptuous threat. "Ye say that now."

Chapter 17

*A*rising early the next morning, Hero Jarvis took one look at the platters of eggs and sausages, tomatoes and mushrooms set out on the buffet in the breakfast parlor, and turned away to order her horse brought around.

The previous night's wind had brought a heavy cover of angry clouds to hang low over the city. As she trotted her big bay up and down the Row in Hyde Park, her groom following at a tactful distance, the first drops of rain began to fall. She ignored them.

It had occurred to her at some point in the middle of a long, sleepless night that by focusing all her thoughts and energy on the murder of Bishop Prescott she had been avoiding dealing with the disastrous effect of his death on her own future. Yet every time she tried to think about it, she found her mind shying away.

The thunder of approaching hooves drew her attention to the gate. Looking up, she saw the lean figure of Viscount Devlin cantering toward her. She checked for the briefest instant, then trotted on.

"It's raining," he said, bringing his Arab in beside her bay. "Or didn't you notice?"

"If one doesn't ride in the rain in England, one seldom rides."

His eyes narrowed with amusement. "True."

"I assume you've sought me out for a reason," she said bluntly, anxious to have him gone. "What is it?"

"Several things, actually. First of all, I'm wondering why you failed to mention your father's opposition to Prescott's translation to Canterbury during our discussion yesterday."

She let out a huff of breath that fell somewhere between a laugh and a genteel expression of derision. "What, exactly, are you imagining? That my father played the role of Henry the Second to Bishop Prescott's Thomas Becket?"

"The thought had occurred to me."

"Don't be an ass."

He was startled into a sharp burst of laughter. A silence fell, filled with the creak of saddle leather, the squishing thunder of their horses' hooves. Once again, she was the one to break it.

"You said 'several things.' What else?"

He kept his gaze on the distant treetops. "I fear, Miss Jarvis, that you have been less than honest with me about the purpose of your recent visit to Bishop Prescott. Or should I say *visits*?"

She kept her hands and seat relaxed. But some inner agitation must have communicated itself to the bay, for it began to sidle. She corrected it immediately.

After a moment, he said, "No comment?"

She turned her head to study his fine-boned, handsome face, but she could detect no sign that he had discovered her secret. "The Bishop is dead. How, pray, do you presume to know what passed between us?"

The rain began to fall harder, slapping the leaves of the chestnuts along the Row, drumming on the turf. The Viscount readjusted his hat. "A remark the Bishop made about an old friend in need of counseling."

Inside, her stomach did an unpleasant flip-flop. But she had herself well in hand now. "There is obviously some sort of confusion," she said evenly.

"Perhaps. Although I can't help but wonder: three visits? Over one speech?"

The rain was coming down now in buckets. Water ran down the Viscount's cheeks, found its way down the back of Hero's collar. She said, "Perhaps we should continue this conversation at some future date in a less damp environment." Signaling her groom, she turned the bay's head toward home. "Good day, my lord."

She was aware of his gaze upon her, of him watching her, as she left the park.

She did not look back.

Returning home to Berkeley Square, Hero dismissed her maid, stripped off her riding habit, and went to stand in front of her dressing room mirror.

She stared at her reflection dispassionately, her hands splayed across her lower abdomen. Her body was still slim, her stomach flat. But for how much longer? One month? Two? For how long could she continue to move amongst the *haut ton* of London? The high-waisted, fashionable dresses of the day would disguise her changing shape for a while, but the time was coming when she would need to go away.

It had been her intention to spend the coming autumn and winter in the Welsh mountains, at the home of a dear cousin. Hero knew the name of the couple who was to receive her child, but they had been carefully kept in ignorance of her identity. And without Prescott, her ability to transfer the child to its adoptive parents without betraying her own identity was seriously compromised.

She thought about contacting the couple directly, then rejected the idea out of hand. To do so would mean condemning herself to a lifetime of looking over her shoulder, worrying always about exposure and blackmail. She needed to find some other alternative. Quickly.

She was running out of time.

Chapter 18

*B*y the time Sebastian made it back to Brook Street, his riding jacket and breeches were soaked.

"Murder investigations can definitely take a toll on a gentleman's wardrobe," said Jules Calhoun, collecting the discarded garments.

Sebastian smoothed the folds of his fresh cravat. "Tempted to quit, Jules?" Until he had discovered the unflappable Calhoun, Sebastian had endured everything from vapors to temper tantrums from valets unused to serving a gentleman who regularly found himself involved in all the down-and-dirty particulars of murder investigations.

Calhoun looked around, affronted. "Who, me? Of course not, my lord!"

Changed into dry clothes, Sebastian ordered his curricle brought round and set forth in search of the Bishop of London's nephew, Sir Peter Prescott.

He found the Baronet sprawled in one corner of a high-backed, old-fashioned bench in a tavern known as the Jerusalem Gate, near Hans Place. It was just past ten in the morning, and from the looks of things, Prescott had yet to make it to his bed. A half-empty bottle of brandy rested on the small octagonal table before him; his cravat was disordered and stained with sweat. A day's growth of blond beard shadowed his cheeks, and his well-tailored coat of olive drab was creased and muddied near the cuffs. When Sebastian pulled a chair opposite him, Sir Peter looked up without shifting his posture and announced unnecessarily, "I'm foxed."

"My condolences on the death of your uncle, the Bishop," said Sebastian, ordering two tankards of ale.

Sir Peter let his head fall back against the bench's high wooden slats. He was a slim man of medium height, with fine fair hair that curled against his forehead. Combined with his soft blue eyes, that halo of golden curls had given him a deceptively angelic appearance as a boy. Now, the curls were plastered against his forehead with sweat, the eyes bloodshot. "Dear Uncle Francis," he said. "Leave it to the Bishop to get himself murdered in a church."

Sebastian studied the Baronet's flushed, strained features. The two men had known each other for some twenty years, first as schoolboys, then as young men on the town. But after that, their lives had diverged. While Sir Peter settled down to the management of the ancestral estate that had been his since birth, Sebastian's days had filled with the tramp of red-coated soldiers and the howl of artillery shells he sometimes still heard exploding in his dreams.

Sebastian took a sip of ale, his gaze on his old friend's familiar face. "I was always under the impression you and your uncle were quite close."

"Close." Sir Peter gave a peculiar shudder. "I suppose. I mean, it worked out well, didn't it? He didn't have a son, and I didn't have a father. A match made in heaven, you might say. Or in hell."

"I take it you quarreled recently?"

"I didn't know he was going to die," said Sir Peter, scrubbing a shaky hand across his lower face. "You try having the bloody Bishop of London as your bloody uncle. If I had aspirations toward sainthood I'd have become a bloody priest, like him."

"No, I never thought you had any aspirations for sainthood."

A ghost of a schoolboy's grin lifted the edges of the other man's lips. "Me? I may be the one who loosed that goat in the old headmaster's bedchamber, but you're the one who dreamt up the prank in the first place."

Sebastian gave a soft laugh. The truth was, Bishop Prescott should have had little to complain of in his nephew. The ebullient schoolboy had matured into a good-natured but responsible landowner far more interested in his herds and the latest strain of oats than in the turf or the dice box. Sebastian could think of only one way in which the Baronet strayed from the path of respectability: Like Sebastian, Sir Peter had never taken a wife, preferring to allow his mother to continue as chatelaine of his estate's ancient, rambling house while he himself divided his time between the Grange and a certain dark-haired, dark-eyed opera dancer he kept in rooms in town.

Sebastian leaned back in his seat and stretched out his boots to cross them at the ankles. "Heard about your opera dancer, did he?"

Sir Peter hunched forward to wrap one fist around his tankard, and sniffed. "To listen to him, you'd have thought I was a bloody Turkish pasha with a harem. Didn't look good, I suppose, for the nephew of the bloody Bishop of London to be consorting with a *low woman*—especially when the Bishop of London has a shot at becoming the next Archbishop of Canterbury."

"Is that what he wanted to talk to you about on Tuesday?"

Sir Peter looked up in surprise. "How'd you know about that?"

"The Bishop's diary secretary."

He took a deep draught of ale. "Says something, don't it, when a man needs to make an appointment to see his own bloody uncle?"

"How was he when you saw him?"

Sir Peter's eyes narrowed. "What's that supposed to mean?"

"Did he seem . . . unusually distressed by anything?"

"No. Why would he be?"

Sebastian raised his tankard and took a slow sip. Both Miss Jarvis, who saw the Bishop at six that evening, and William Franklin, who met with Prescott the previous afternoon, had described the Bishop of London as unusually agitated about something. Either Sir Peter was a particularly insensitive nephew, or he was being less than truthful. "So tell me," said Sebastian, "who do you think killed him?"

"Me? What would I know of it?"

"You must have some thoughts on who might be responsible."

Sir Peter cast a quick glance sideways, then leaned forward, one forearm pressing into the tabletop between them as he dropped his voice. "Seems to me, what the authorities ought to be asking is, Who would have the most to gain from the Bishop of London's death?"

"Good question," said Sebastian. "What would you say is the answer?"

Sir Peter flopped back in his seat. "That's where it gets tricky. Uncle Francis wasn't afraid of making enemies of the kind of men who can be dangerous."

"Did he ever mention anyone in particular?"

Sir Peter gave a sharp laugh. "What, you mean besides everyone from Jarvis and Quillian to Liverpool and Canning?"

"He sounds like a quarrelsome man."

"Quarrelsome?" Sir Peter frowned, then shook his head, some of the anger and resentment seeming to leech out of him. "No. He wasn't particularly quarrelsome. He simply believed passionately in the ideals of his faith. Justice. Charity. Peace."

"In other words, an admirable man."

"Yes." Sir Peter drew in a deep breath. Suddenly, he didn't look so drunk. "Yes, he was."

Sebastian glanced across the taproom, to where he could see raindrops chasing one another down the old leaded glass panes of the windows. "Where were you Tuesday evening?"

Sir Peter's eyes darkened. "In Camden Place. Why?"

"Camden Place?"

"I keep rooms there."

"Ah." Sebastian studied his former schoolmate's trembling hand, the day's growth of beard shadowing his normally ruddy cheeks. From the looks of things, Prescott had been drinking steadily since hearing the news of his uncle's death. Sebastian said, "When was the last time you saw Lady Prescott?"

"M' mother?" Sir Peter frowned. "Yesterday. Why do you ask?"

By now, Sir Henry Lovejoy would have made the awkward journey out to Prescott Grange bearing a tattered coat of blue velvet, a stained satin waistcoat, and an old-fashioned gold pocket watch and fob. If their supposition was correct, if the decades-old corpse in blue velvet was indeed Sir Nigel, then Lady Prescott had just learned she was a widow.

Sebastian said, "You do know they found another body in the crypt with your uncle—the body of a man who was apparently murdered there thirty years ago?"

The Baronet went suddenly still. "You say *thirty* years ago?"

"That's right."

Whatever color Sir Peter had left drained from his face. "What are you saying?"

Sebastian pushed to his feet and dropped a hand on his friend's shoulder. "I'm saying you might consider returning to the Grange. I suspect you'll find Lady Prescott in need of your support."

Chapter 19

*S*ebastian was driving up Whitehall, headed toward Bow Street, when he spotted Charles, Lord Jarvis, coming out of the Foreign Office. The rain had eased up for the time being, leaving the gutters running and the pavement glistening with wet beneath heavy gray skies.

Sebastian drew in close to the curb. "I wonder if I might have a word with you, my lord?"

"Only if you're willing to walk with me," said Jarvis without breaking his stride.

"Follow along behind us," Sebastian told his tiger, and jumped down from the curricle's high seat.

Jarvis continued walking as Sebastian fell into step beside him. The two men shared a tangled history of animosity stretching back nearly two years. Sebastian never made the mistake of underestimating either Lord Jarvis's intellect and power, or his malevolence.

"I hear you're making inquiries into the death of Bishop Prescott," said the big man. "It's rather undignified, don't you think? The son of a peer of the realm, continually involving himself in murder investigations like some common Bow Street Runner?"

"As long as I don't do anything truly sordid, such as

accept payment for my activities, the reputation of the house of St. Cyr should survive."

Jarvis grunted and kept walking.

Sebastian said, "I understand you and the Bishop of London had differences."

"Differences?" Jarvis threw him a sideways glance. "I should rather think so. You'd be hard-pressed to find a member of the House of Lords who didn't have 'differences' with the Bishop of London—and that includes his fellow ecclesiastics on the Bishops' Bench. The man was a bloody radical."

"You mean because of his stand on slavery?"

"I mean because of his stand on everything. He even wrote a poem about *peace.*" Jarvis spat the word out as if it were an abomination.

"He was a man of God, after all."

"And this country does God's work." Jarvis paused at the curb to let a two-wheeled cart piled high with casks and pulled by a gray mule rattle past. "Although not, of course, in Prescott's reckoning. 'Princes are privileged to kill, as if numbers sanctify the crime,'" he quoted derisively.

"Prescott was in favor of pursuing peace with the French?"

"With the French, *and* with the bloody Americans."

"Despite the fact that he held both nations in considerable contempt?"

Jarvis made a rude sound. "Don't ask me to make sense of the man's twisted reasoning."

Sebastian studied Jarvis's arrogant, aquiline profile. "I understand you opposed Prescott's translation to Canterbury."

"I should rather think so."

"Because of his opposition to the war, or because of his stand on abolition?"

"What do you think?"

"I think the Bishop of London seems to have accumulated a number of enemies."

The big man drew up on the footpath outside Carlton House. "That tells you something about a man, does it not?"

His words echoed something Jarvis's own daughter had said. "I suppose," said Sebastian. "A lot depends on the nature of that man's enemies."

A gleam of amusement touched the other man's hard gray eyes. "So it does. Good day to you, my lord."

Sebastian waited until Jarvis was passing through the gate in the screen separating the Mall from the palace courtyard before raising his voice to say, "What about the Bishop's brother? What manner of man was he?"

Jarvis swung slowly to face him again. "Francis Prescott had four brothers. To which are you referring?"

"The eldest."

"Sir Nigel?" A quiver of distaste passed over the Baron's aristocratic features. "Bishop Prescott was a tiresome, meddlesome fool. But Sir Nigel was something far worse. He was, pure and simply, bad ton. I wasn't the least surprised when someone finally murdered him."

Sebastian blinked. He himself had good reason to believe Sir Nigel had spent the last thirty years lying face-down in the crypt of St. Margaret's with a dagger in his back. But that fact was as yet not well-known. He said, "*Was* Sir Nigel murdered? I was under the impression the man simply . . . disappeared."

"Of course he was murdered. Do you think men of his ilk simply disappear?"

"Who do you think killed him?"

"I honestly don't know. But if I did, I'd be inclined to buy the man a drink." Jarvis paused as the bell towers of the city began to toll the hour, a harmonious jumble of high and low *dong*s ringing over the rooftops. "Now, good day to you, my lord."

Sebastian watched the Baron cross the courtyard toward the palace steps.

"Gov'nor?" said Tom, reining in the chestnuts beside him.

Sebastian stood for a moment, frowning after the King's powerful cousin. Then he leapt into the curricle and turned his horses toward Bow Street.

"I don't think there's much doubt about it," said Sir Henry Lovejoy, his features set in serious lines. "Our mysterious eighteenth-century victim is in all likelihood the Bishop's long-missing brother, Sir Nigel. Lady Prescott identified the blue velvet coat and satin waistcoat as identical to what her husband was wearing when he disappeared. The watch and fob were his, as well."

The two men had left the Public Office in Bow Street and were pushing through the crowds that thronged the nearby arcades fronting Covent Garden Square. By now the tumult that characterized the early-morning market had died down, the heavy wagons of the merchants and traders giving way to the handcarts of the costers and strolling hawkers selling buns and oysters, knives and pocketbooks.

"And the crooked left arm?" asked Sebastian.

"She says he broke it as a boy. At Eton," added the magistrate, watching a stout, thick-necked woman with a basket balanced on her head stagger past. The air was heavy with the scents of coffee and fresh flowers and drying horse droppings.

"How did Lady Prescott receive the news his body had been found?"

"She wept."

"What did she tell you of the circumstances surrounding Sir Nigel's disappearance?"

"As I understand it, the Baronet was last seen on the twenty-fifth of July. He left the estate after an early dinner, intending to pass the evening at one of his clubs. Only he never arrived."

"His horse was found wandering on Hounslow Heath that night?"

"The next day."

"Any blood on the saddle or horse?"

"Not that anyone remembers."

They paused beside a medicinal stall selling everything from leeches and dried herbs to snails for a healing broth. "Yet they attributed the man's disappearance to highwaymen?" said Sebastian. "Seems a bit of a stretch, does it not? When was the last time you heard of thieves leaving a purebred horse and saddle, and stealing their victim's dead body?"

"The authorities assumed the horse bolted when Sir Nigel was set upon. Hounslow Heath was particularly notorious in those days."

"Was there no suspicion at the time that the Baronet might have met with foul play at the hands of some enemy?"

"Oh, yes, there was considerable speculation. I gather Sir Nigel had a rather unsavory reputation."

"I've heard he was a member of the Hellfire Club."

"That, too." The magistrate peered thoughtfully at a

mound of dried mint on the table before them. "He seems to have had a talent for arousing the passions of his enemies."

"Somewhat like his brother," observed Sebastian. "Although not, obviously, for the same reasons."

"How true." Lovejoy paid for a measure of the mint, and slipped the packet into his pocket. "I understand that, at first, suspicion focused on the son of a former tenant who was nursing a powerful grudge against the Baronet. But the lad possessed a solid alibi for the evening in question."

"What sort of alibi?"

They turned back toward Bow Street. "He was locked up in a roundhouse here in London."

Sebastian thought about the Renaissance dagger that had been found in Sir Nigel's corpse. He could see a disgruntled farmer taking a sickle to the Baronet's back. But an antique Italian dagger? Aloud, he said, "What was the nature of the lad's grudge?"

"Seems his father had quarreled with Sir Nigel over some trifle. Sir Nigel retaliated by having the family evicted from their cottage. It was in the midst of a dreadful snowstorm and the entire family froze to death on the heath trying to make it into London. Mother, father, two young girls. The only reason the lad survived was because some uncle had arranged for him to be apprenticed to a butcher in London, so he wasn't with them."

Sebastian drew up short, the tumult of the busy square swirling around him. "You say the lad was a *butcher's* apprentice?"

Lovejoy looked over at him in surprise. "That's right. Why?"

"Do you know his name?"

"Slade. Jack Slade."

Something of Sebastian's reaction must have shown in his face, because Lovejoy said, "You know him?"

"I know him," said Sebastian.

Chapter 20

Finding the butcher shop on Monkwell Street closed, Sebastian tracked Jack Slade to the nearby vast livestock market of Smithfield.

Once, these death-haunted acres had echoed with the crackle of burning faggots, the jeers of angry mobs, the shrieks of dying martyrs as Protestant monarchs burned Papists, and Catholic monarchs burned heretics. Now the open ground was crowded with pens of bleating sheep separated by foul lanes where long lines of cattle stood, their heads tied to the rails.

Working his way down a narrow pathway, Sebastian found Jack Slade with his foot propped up on the nearest low rail, a drover's boy beside him as they inspected a long-horned Spanish cow tied up outside the sprawling bulk of St. Bartholomew's Hospital. The air was heavy with the smell of manure and wet hides and unwashed men.

At a nod from Sebastian, the drover's boy drew back, his jaw slack with wonder. This time, Sebastian had made no effort to disguise who or what he was.

"You didn't tell me you grew up on Prescott Grange," said Sebastian.

His foot sliding off the rail, Slade straightened slowly, his eyes narrowing as he took in Sebastian's blue coat of superfine, the exquisitely tailored doeskin breeches, and gleaming Hessians. But all he said was, "Ye dinna ask."

Sebastian hooked one elbow over the top rail of the fence beside him, his gaze drifting over the sheep milling in the pen. "You still maintain you went to see Bishop Prescott on Monday afternoon to take him some pork chops?"

Slade sucked on the plug of tobacco distending his lower lip. "Why else would I go see him?"

"I'm told you threatened to kill his brother thirty years ago."

Slade pursed his lips and spat a thick stream of tobacco juice that hit the cobbles in a yellowish brown splat. "That were no threat. That were a promise. And I'd o' done it, too, if somebody hadna beat me to it."

Beside them, the cattle shifted restlessly, steam rising from their hides. A roar of voices from a nearby public house mingled with the barking of dogs and the whistling of the drovers and the frightened chorus of bellowing and bleats coming from the doomed animals.

Slade spat again. "What ye thinkin'? That I done for Sir Nigel thirty years ago, then went after the Bishop on Tuesday night? I had no quarrel with the Bishop. He was a good, God-fearin' man. Unlike his hell's spawn o' a brother."

"Where were you Tuesday night?"

"With me mates at the local. Why?"

"What time did you get there?"

Slade smiled, revealing two rows of rotten, tobacco-stained teeth. "What time did the good Bishop get hisself killed? Because whene'er it was, I've a dozen mates who'll swear I was at the public house the whole night."

Sebastian watched a hawker working the crowd, his tray piled high with sausages. "I hear you were locked up in a watch house the night Sir Nigel disappeared."

"Yeah. On the Strand. What of it?"

"Convenient."

"Weren't it just?"

Sebastian studied the butcher's creased, sun-darkened face. "Who do you think killed him?"

"You mean Sir Nigel?" Slade sniffed. "I don't know. But if I did, I'd buy the bastard a bloody drink."

"That seems to be a common sentiment."

"Yeah? Well, that tells ye somethin', don't it?"

"I assume you've heard by now that Sir Nigel's body has been found?"

A muscle bunched along the butcher's prominent jaw. "No. Where?"

"In the crypt of St. Margaret's. It seems he was murdered down there, not long before the crypt was sealed."

To Sebastian's surprise, Jack Slade threw back his head and laughed.

Sebastian said, "That's amusing?"

"Course it's amusin'." He glanced sideways at Sebastian. "Ye don't find it amusin'?"

"I'm obviously missing something."

Slade laid a forefinger beside his nose and winked. "Seems our good Bishop had more'n his fair share o' secrets, hmm?"

"Did he?"

"Kinda makes ye wonder, don't it, why he ordered that crypt bricked up all them years ago?"

"The Bishop?" Sebastian frowned. "What did the Bishop of London have to do with the decision to seal the crypt of St. Margaret's?"

Amusement danced in the other man's small, dark eyes. "Ye don't know, do ye?"

"Evidently not," said Sebastian drily.

Slade used his tongue to shift his plug of tobacco to his cheek. "Who ye think was the priest in residence at St. Margaret's thirty years ago?"

Sebastian said, "The Bishop began his ecclesiastical career as a doctor of classics at Oxford."

"Maybe." Slade leaned toward him, his breath heavy with the odors of rotten teeth and half-masticated tobacco. "But I knows what I knows. Ye look into it. Ye'll see." He paused, his small eyes practically disappearing into the folds of flesh as he smiled. "*Captain* Lord Devlin."

"You've been talking to your son," said Sebastian, his gaze drifting over the lowing cows, the pens of milling, bleating, terrified sheep. "I don't see him around today."

"Nope. But that don't mean he ain't here, watching ye." Slade ran his hand down the Spanish cow's flank. The cow shied away, bellowing, its hooves churning the mud and muck of the passage. "Ye think about that," he said, and walked off into the noisy, pushing throng of men and beasts.

It seemed at first improbable to Sebastian that the Bishop of London might be the shadowy reverend who ordered the crypt of St. Margaret's bricked up all those years ago. Yet the more he thought about it, the less certain he became. The exact year of the closing of the crypt had been forgotten, and no one had bothered to inquire too closely into the Bishop's own past.

Leaving the market at Smithfield, Sebastian turned his horses toward the West End, to London House in St. James's Square.

He found the Bishop's chaplain seated on the floor of the Bishop's official chambers, surrounded by piles of paper and looking harried. "I beg your pardon, my lord," he said, shifting a large stack of folders, "but now is not a good time."

"Just one question," said Sebastian, pausing in the doorway of the disheveled chambers. "Was Bishop Prescott ever the priest in residence at St. Margaret's in Tanfield Hill?"

Frown lines appeared in the Chaplain's forehead. "Why, yes, of course. Back in—" He broke off suddenly, his eyes widening as comprehension dawned. "Good heavens."

"Exactly."

They went for a walk in the Square, skirting the perimeter of the octagonal-shaped iron fence that railed off the vast circular pond in the center.

"I was under the impression," said Sebastian, "that the Bishop began his career at Oxford."

"He did." The Chaplain clasped his hands together behind his back, the black skirts of his cassock swirling around his ankles as he walked. "He believed, initially, that his vocation lay in scholarship. But then he discovered he possessed an affinity for ministry. When the benefice at Tanfield Hill fell vacant, it was given to him."

"St. Margaret's is in the Prescott family's gift?" More than half the livings in England were under the control of private landowners, who either gave them to a younger son or cousin, or sold them like an investment.

"Yes. Before Francis Prescott took it up, I believe it was in the possession of a distant cousin."

"When exactly was this?"

"That Dr. Prescott was in residence at St. Margaret's?" The Chaplain thought about it a moment. "From sometime in the late 1770s until the end of 1782, I believe."

"So it would have been Prescott's decision to seal the crypt at St. Margaret's?"

The Chaplain blew out his breath in a long sigh. "I suppose it must have been, although I couldn't say for certain without looking at the records." He glanced over at Sebastian. "I know what you're thinking, but you're wrong. The Bishop was a man of God. A good, gentle soul, repulsed by violence. He could never have killed his own brother and then bricked up the crypt to hide the deed."

Sebastian studied the Chaplain's pale, troubled features. In his experience, most people were capable of murder, if pushed hard enough. And Sir Nigel certainly sounded like the kind of man who had pushed many men hard enough to goad one of them into murder.

"I was acquainted with him, you know," said the Chaplain.

Sebastian glanced over at him in surprise. "You mean Sir Nigel?"

The Chaplain nodded. "I was only a child when he disappeared, but he was . . . most memorable. A huge man, loud and rather frightening, actually."

"How did the two brothers get along?"

"Sir Nigel was . . ." The Chaplain hesitated, searching for the right words. He eventually settled on," . . . a difficult man."

"In what way?"

The Chaplain's lips tightened into a thin line. "I see no point in speaking ill of the dead."

"Even when one is dealing with murder?"

They walked along in silence for a moment, the Chaplain's features set in troubled lines. After a time, he said, "Sir Nigel could be charming, even gracious. Yet he could also be quick-tempered, vicious, and vindictive. He was cruel to everyone, from his wife and servants to his dogs. The only creatures I ever saw him treat with any restraint and affection were his horses. As a child, I soon learned to avoid him whenever possible."

"How did he get along with his brother Francis?" Sebastian asked again.

"Bishop Prescott was the youngest of five brothers and two sisters, with Sir Nigel the eldest. Given the large difference in the two men's ages, I doubt there was much interaction between them."

"But that would have changed, surely, when Francis Prescott took up the living at St. Margaret's?"

"I suppose." They had completed their circumambulation of the pond. The Chaplain glanced up at the crepe-hung facade of London House. "I wish I could help you more. But it was all so long ago."

Sebastian nodded. "Thank you. You've been a tremendous help." He turned toward where Tom was waiting with the horses, then paused to look back and say, "Did the Bishop ever talk much about his time at St. Margaret's?"

"No. To be honest, I can't recall ever having heard him mention it. I suppose that's why I didn't make the connection sooner."

"You don't find that unusual?"

The Chaplain frowned. "That he didn't talk about it, you mean? At the time, I didn't. But now that I think about it?" He let out a long sigh that left him looking suddenly older than his years, and considerably more likable. "It's worrisome, yes. Very worrisome."

Chapter 21

"*S*ounds pretty simple to me," said Gibson, his head bowed as he worked to carve a slice of meat from the serving of pork ribs on the table before him. "The Bishop obviously murdered his brother, then bricked up the crypt to hide the body."

"I suppose it's possible," agreed Sebastian, leaning back in his seat. They'd come here, to an old inn near the Irishman's surgery on Tower Hill, so that Gibson could grab something to eat. Sebastian wasn't hungry. "By all accounts, Sir Nigel was unpleasant enough to provoke even a saint to murder. And while the Bishop might have been a far more pleasant individual than his brother, he doesn't exactly sound even-tempered himself."

Gibson glanced up. "Yet you're not convinced. Why?"

"There are other possibilities."

"Such as?"

"That Sir Nigel met with foul play on Hounslow Heath after all, and his killer shifted the body to the crypt to hide it, knowing the crypt was about to be sealed."

Gibson's brows drew together in a thoughtful frown. "Sounds like a risky thing to have done, if you ask me.

There are nasty penalties for those caught lugging bodies around churchyards in the dark."

"True. But those types are generally taking bodies *out*, not bringing them in."

The surgeon gave a soft laugh. "Still. What if the workmen had decided to take one last look around the crypt before bricking it up? The body would have been found thirty years ago."

"At which point suspicion would have fallen on the priest in residence—namely Sir Nigel's brother. Actually, when you think about it, it would have been a clever way for someone with a grudge against the Prescotts to get back at *both* brothers: kill Sir Nigel, and then set up Francis Prescott to take the blame."

"Except that the body wasn't found."

"No. It wasn't."

"The problem with that scenario," said Gibson, working on his pork with a surgeon's thoroughness, "is that Sir Nigel was a big man—not an easy burden to shift when you're dealing with a deadweight. If you ask me, he was killed in that crypt."

Sebastian watched his friend's flawless dissection of his pork ribs with something approaching awe. "Two men could have lifted the body. Two strong men."

"They could have," Gibson acknowledged.

"The problem with having Sir Nigel killed in the crypt is that it then begs the question, What the devil was a forty-year-old baronet doing down in the crypt of the village church in the middle of the night?"

Gibson took a drink of ale. "What if someone he loved had recently died? Someone who was buried in the crypt? He could have been grief-stricken enough to want to be near them."

"From what I've heard of Sir Nigel's character, it seems unlikely. Although I suppose it could be possible." Sebastian thought about those moldering stacks of coffins, the dark-stained bones and grinning skulls. "Ghoulish, but possible."

"You did say he was a member of the Hellfire Club, did you not? Black magic rituals and all that."

"Yes. Except . . ."

"Except what?"

"It occurs to me that the gate at the top of the stairs would have been kept padlocked. If he broke the lock, it would have been remarked upon. So he must have had a key."

"The living was in his patronage, right?" said Gibson. "He may well have had a key. If he left the gate to the crypt open behind him, his killer could have followed him down, killed him, then taken the key from his body and secured the padlock again when he left, with none being the wiser."

Sebastian sat for a time, drinking his ale in thoughtful silence. "There is one other aspect to all this we've yet to consider."

Gibson looked up questioningly.

"There were originally five Prescott brothers, with Sir Nigel the eldest and the Bishop the youngest. The three middle brothers all chose to make the Army their career. By 1782, all three were dead, leaving Francis Prescott as his brother's heir presumptive."

"What are you suggesting? That the Bishop killed his older brother for the *inheritance*?"

"It does happen. Although I must admit, it sounds decidedly out of character in this case."

Gibson finished picking the ribs clean and shoved his

plate away. "If it is true, it must have been something of a shock to the Bishop when Lady Prescott gave birth to a posthumous heir some months later."

Sebastian drained his tankard. "And none of it explains who killed the Bishop himself, or why."

"Could have been the son, Sir Peter. He discovered his uncle killed his father for the inheritance, so he killed his uncle in revenge."

"I don't think so. I *know* Sir Peter."

"You knew him as a boy. People change." Gibson watched Sebastian push to his feet. "What do you plan to do next?"

"Drive out to the Grange in the morning and talk to Lady Prescott."

"What do you think she can tell you?"

"I'm not sure. What her husband was doing down in that crypt would be a nice place to start."

That evening, Sebastian took a copy of Aeschylus's *The Libation Bearers* from his shelves and settled down to read with a brace of candles and a glass of port at his elbow.

The second in the famous Athenian playwright's bloody trilogy on the curse of the House of Atreus, *The Libation Bearers* told an agonizing tale of murder and vengeance and hints of madness. But Sebastian could find nothing in that ancient Greek myth that seemed of any relevance to the death of the Bishop of London. He was halfway through the third act when Kat came to him.

Ushered into the drawing room by Morey, she brought with her the scent of beeswax and oranges and the cool air of the night. She paused just inside the door, one hand pushing back the hood of her cherry velvet cloak while she waited for the majordomo to discreetly bow himself from the room. The light from the candles gleamed over her pale cheeks and the shiny dark fall of her hair, and she was so beautiful she took his breath.

"I have an answer to your question," she said.

The book slid to the floor as he rose to his feet. He did not step toward her. "And?"

"There has been speculation for some time that the Bishop of London hid a secret of some sort from his past. But none of the attempts by various agents to discover the nature of that secret were successful."

Sebastian met the brilliant blue intensity of her gaze. "You're certain?"

"Yes." She turned to go.

He stopped her. "May I offer you something? A cup of tea? A glass of wine?" What he was really saying was, *Stay*.

She hesitated, a sad smile playing about her lips. "No, thank you." *You know that would not be wise*.

He stared at her from across the room. *Yes, you're right*. But he still couldn't stop himself from saying, "How are you, Kat? In truth? Does Yates treat you well?"

She gave a faint shrug. "He is never anything but a gentleman. We go our own ways."

As hard as it was for Sebastian to imagine her with another man, it was even harder for him to think of her trapped in a loveless marriage. He said, "It doesn't sound like much of a marriage."

"It's the kind of marriage I want. We are friends."

"I would like to see you happy, and in love."

She gave a sad smile. "And you, Sebastian? Hendon is desperate for an heir."

"I will take no woman to wife unless I can give her a whole heart." *Or unless I must*, he thought, *to preserve her honor*.

She nodded, and drew her hood back up over her hair.

"Thank you," he said with a painful formality that hurt him almost as much as anything else.

"I spoke to Gibson," she said, her hand on the door, as if she knew she should leave but could not quite bring herself to go. Through all that had happened in the past ten months, she and the Irish surgeon had remained friends. "He told me about Obadiah Slade." She hesitated. "Please be careful, Sebastian."

Somehow, he managed to give her a jaunty smile. "I'm always careful."

"No. You're not. You're never careful. That's what worries me."

After she had gone, he retrieved his book from the floor. But the words swam before his eyes and he imagined the scent of her lingered still in the room, like a sweet memory just beyond his grasp.

The Reverend Malcolm Earnshaw sank before the high altar of St. Margaret's, his hands clasped in supplication before him as he let out a low moan.

Beneath his aching knees, the worn stone paving of the aisle felt cold and cruelly hard, but he welcomed the pain as a kind of penance. The jewel-toned stained glass of the soaring windows of the apse before him showed only black against black, while the distant recesses of the church were lost in the gloom of the night. He let his head fall back, his throat working to swallow as he stared up at the intricately carved groins of the ancient vaults above him, alive now with strange, ghostly shadows cast by the flickering flames of the two heavy candles flanking the altar.

He squeezed his eyes shut, his lips moving in a soundless prayer. *Oh, Lord, thou hast searched me and known*

*me. Thou knowest my lying down and my rising up; thou
understandest my thoughts afar off....*

It was so difficult to know what to do in such a situation. One shrank from accidentally implicating the innocent, but what if ... What if the innocent were not
truly innocent? How was one to know? Never had Earnshaw felt more in need of guidance and wisdom.

"'Thou compassest my path and my lying down,'" he
whispered, finding solace in speaking the words aloud.
"'Whither shall I go from thy spirit? Whither shall I flee
from thy presence?'"

At some point, the rain had started up again. He
could hear it beating on the slate roof above him, and he
shivered with the cold and the damp and a quick leap of
unaccountable fear.

"'Surely thou wilt slay the wicked, O God,'" he said,
his voice rising shrilly. "'Depart from me therefore, ye
bloody men.'"

From somewhere startlingly near came a soft thump.

The Reverend pushed to his feet, his knees creaking,
his breath bunching hot in his throat as he whirled about
to peer helplessly into the gloom. "Who's there?"

His own voice echoed back at him. He swallowed
hard, feeling an odd mixture of foolishness and terror.
"Is anybody there?"

The urge to bolt toward the west door was strong. But
the fat beeswax candles flanking the altar were atro-
ciously dear; he never should have lit them. It had been
a foolish extravagance, however spooked he might be.

Bent on extinguishing the flames quickly, he lurched
up the step toward the altar, stumbling in his haste. Then
he threw another frightened glance toward the nave and
whispered, "*Oh, my God.*"

Chapter 22

*T*he next morning, Sebastian drove out toward Prescott Grange, intending to speak to the widow of Sir Nigel Prescott. But when he passed through Tanfield Hill, he found the village green crowded with men fanning out under the direction of the Squire, Douglas Pyle.

"What's all this?" asked Sebastian, reining in beside him.

"That fool priest," said the Squire. "He's gone missing. According to Mrs. Earnshaw, he went out last night, saying he couldn't remember if he'd locked the sacristy door. Nobody's seen him since."

Sebastian glanced over at the ancient church, its heavy sandstone walls looking dark and brooding beneath the cloudy sky. "Did you check the crypt?"

The Squire drew in a deep breath that lifted his broad chest, and blew it out slowly. "Aye, we did. He's not there, thank God. Although we did find *this*." He slipped something from his waistcoat and held it out.

Sebastian found himself staring at a black carved classical profile mounted on a heavy silver setting. "Sir Nigel's ring?"

The Squire nodded. "One of the lads found it in the rubble near those old collapsed coffins. Musta got kicked back there somehow, which is why we didn't see it before."

Sebastian handed the ring back. "Does Earnshaw do this often? Visit the church at night, I mean?"

"His wife says sometimes. When he's troubled."

"He was troubled?"

"She says he seemed to be."

"Does she know about what?"

The Squire shook his head. "He's been acting queer ever since he found the bodies in the crypt. But then, who wouldn't?"

"True," said Sebastian. He studied the Squire's pleasant, fleshy face. "How well did you know Sir Nigel Prescott?"

"Sir Nigel? Not all that well. He was a good bit older'n me." The Squire rubbed the back of his neck with one hand. "I hear they're saying the fright in blue velvet was him."

"So it would seem."

The Squire shook his head. "It's unsettling to think about it, him lying there with a knife stuck in his back right beneath our feet, every Sunday, for close onto thirty years. And no one knew it."

Sebastian watched the men moving off in all directions. "I understand he was an unpleasant man."

"Unpleasant?" The Squire grunted. "You'd be hard-pressed to find anyone around here with something nice to say about him."

"It's not often you see brothers so unlike each other."

The Squire rubbed a hand over his jaw and looked away, as if choosing his words carefully. "I've heard tales about old Lady Prescott—Sir Nigel's mother—if you know what I mean? There wasn't a strong family resemblance between Francis Prescott and the rest of his brothers and sisters."

"Yet Prescott Grange would have passed to the Bishop, would it not, if Sir Peter hadn't been born?"

"Aye, that it would," said the Squire, shaking his head. "Who'd have thought, with five sons?" He shook his head again, as if to underscore the point. "Five sons. And if not for that wee posthumous babe, the youngest would have inherited it all."

The estate Sir Peter Prescott had inherited at birth from his dead father lay just to the north of the village, on the edge of Hounslow Heath. Sebastian drove through well-tended, ripening fields of barley and wheat and oats waving gently in the July breeze. Fat brown cows grazed pastures edged by sturdy stone walls and thick hedgerows. Children played outside thatched cottages with dogs that loped, barking, behind the curricle as he bowled up the lane to the ancient manor house.

The house itself was a picturesque, rambling conglomerate, some parts half-timbered, some of red Tudor brick, others of medieval stone, all grouped around a broad paved quadrangle and centered on a great hall with an arch-braced roof that must have dated back to the thirteenth or fourteenth century.

Lady Prescott, mother to the current baronet and widow of Sir Nigel, was in the gardens that stretched to the east of the ancient hall. She had a basket looped over one arm and secateurs in hand as she worked snipping blooms from the wide, riotous border of peonies and roses, hollyhocks and lavender that that ran along the grassy embankment of what had once been a moat. She was a small, slim woman, her guinea-gold hair fading slowly to gray, her soft blue eyes sad beneath the wide brim of her hat as she turned at Sebastian's approach. Now somewhere in her fifties, she wore a plain black gown made high at the neck, as befitted a woman in deepest mourning for both her husband and her husband's brother.

"I'm sorry my son isn't here to receive you," she said, extending her hand to Sebastian. "But he should return presently. I believe he's conferring with workmen making repairs on some of the cottages." She passed the flower basket and secateurs to the footman who'd escorted Sebastian and said to the man with a smile, "Ask Mrs. Norwood to put these in water for me, will you, Frederick?"

"Actually, I saw Sir Peter yesterday," said Sebastian as the footman withdrew with a bow. "I was hoping I might be able to speak with you."

She nodded. "Sir Henry told me the Archbishop had asked for your assistance in this dreadful business. I'm willing to help in any way I can."

They turned to walk together along the border. The day was warm despite the clouds, the pinks and scarlets of the rambling roses bright in the flat light. She said, "You'd think that after thirty years, I wouldn't find the discovery of Sir Nigel's body such a shock. But somehow, thinking someone is dead and knowing it for certain are two entirely different things."

Sebastian studied her fine-boned face, the gentle fan of lines that bracketed her eyes. She was still a remarkably attractive woman; in her prime, she must have been stunning. He said, "What did you think had happened to Sir Nigel when he disappeared?"

"At first? When his horse was discovered wandering the heath, I thought he must have suffered some sort of accident. That he'd be found under a bush, injured."

"And when he wasn't found?"

"In all honesty? I assumed someone had killed him."

"Any idea who?"

She glanced over at him, the faintest hint of an odd smile touching the edges of her lips. "Tell me something, Lord Devlin: You've obviously spoken to people who knew my husband. Have you found anyone who knew him well and still had anything good to say about him?"

Sebastian returned her smile. "I believe someone said he could be charming."

"Oh, yes, he could indeed be charming. When he wished to be." She reached out to pluck a pink hollyhock from the riot of blooms in the border beside them. "Do I shock you?"

"I admire your candor."

She twirled the hollyhock back and forth between gloved fingers. "Thirty years ago I would not have been so honest. But three decades of living as neither wife nor widow have had their effect."

She glanced back toward the terrace, to where a gardener in a smock was working manure into an empty flower bed. After a moment, she said, "I'll be even more frank with you, Lord Devlin. I didn't care what had happened to him, as long as he was indeed dead so that I would never have to see him again." She raised her chin, her jaw hardening. "There; I've said it. Think of me what you will."

He studied her pale, strained face. What manner of man, he wondered, could have inspired such passionate, enduring animosity in his gently bred young wife? And yet . . .

And yet, according to Lovejoy, she had wept when shown the evidence that Sir Nigel was, indeed, dead.

Aloud, Sebastian said, "I'm told Sir Nigel's brother, Francis Prescott, was the priest in residence at St. Margaret's at the time your husband disappeared."

"Yes. He was a tremendous comfort to me at the time." Turning away from the ancient moat, they followed a track that wound toward a distant copse of elms and chestnuts. "Why do you ask?"

"Do you remember the circumstances surrounding his decision to brick up the church's crypt?"

"Very clearly. Francis had wanted to seal it off for some time. The smell was truly appalling, particularly in the heat of summer. And there were concerns that the air wafting up from the decomposing bodies might expose the congregation to disease. Unfortunately, the Dowager Lady Prescott—my late mother-in-law—was adamantly against the idea. She was determined to be buried in the crypt, beside two daughters who had died as children. She begged him to wait until after she was gone, and he did."

"When did she die?"

"That June, not long before Sir Nigel disappeared. After her funeral, Francis moved quickly to have the crypt closed."

"You never connected the sealing of the crypt with the disappearance of your husband?"

She turned to face him, her soft blue eyes wide in a pale face. "No. Why ever would I?"

Why, indeed? thought Sebastian. Aloud, he said, "I understand it was Sir Nigel's intention to visit his clubs the evening he disappeared."

"Yes."

"Any idea as to why he might have changed his mind and gone to St. Margaret's instead?"

She looked at him blankly. "No."

"You can't think of any reason he might have decided to visit the crypt?"

She shook her head. "I can't imagine. It was such a frightful place."

"What can you tell me of his activities in the days immediately preceding his disappearance?"

"His activities?" She made a vague gesture with one gloved hand. "How much do you remember about a particular point in time thirty years ago?"

"I wasn't born thirty years ago."

She gave a soft laugh. "No, I suppose you weren't. Neither was my son." She walked on for a moment, lost in memories of the past. Then she said, "As I recall, he was very busy in those last weeks, riding back and forth to London nearly every day for meetings at the Palace and at Whitehall. He was something of a leader in the Commons, you know—allied with Pitt. If he hadn't died, he would probably have been named foreign secretary when the government was reorganized. I know he wanted the position. It's one of the reasons he went on the mission to the Colonies."

Sebastian drew up short. "Sir Nigel was in America?"

"Why, yes; didn't you know? He'd only just returned."

Sebastian watched the gardener load his tools in the now empty wheelbarrow and push it back toward the stables. The rattle of his rake and shovel carried clearly on the breeze as he bumped over heavy ground. It seemed oddly inevitable that Sir Nigel had only just returned from the American Colonies. Somehow, everything kept circling back to the Americas.

Sebastian said, "In 1782, we were still at war with the rebels."

"Yes, but there was growing opposition in Parliament to the King's determination to continue the war effort. In the end, Lord North and the King agreed to send a mission to evaluate the true state of affairs in the Colonies."

"Who were the other members of the mission?" Sebastian asked, although somehow, he already knew the answer.

She tipped her head to one side and hesitated, as if wondering how he would receive what she was about to say. "There were three of them: Sir Nigel; Charles, Lord Jarvis; and your own father, the Earl of Hendon."

Chapter 23

Sebastian found his father at the Horse Guards.

"Walk with me," said Sebastian, coming upon the Earl in the small circular hall overlooking Whitehall.

Hendon glanced at the ormolu clock on the mantel of the vestibule's empty fireplace. "I've a meeting with Channing at—"

"This won't take long."

Hendon raised his eyebrows, his jaw working thoughtfully in that way he had as he studied his son's face in silence. "Very well," he said, and turned toward the door.

Sebastian waited until they'd reached the gravel path that ran along the canal in St. James's Park before saying, "Thirty years ago, you were one of three men sent by the King to evaluate the situation in the American Colonies."

Hendon's forehead furrowed in a frown. "That's right. Why do you ask?"

"The other two men were Charles, Lord Jarvis, and Sir Nigel Prescott?"

"Ah. I see. Yes, Sir Nigel was with us. I heard his body had finally been found. Who'd have thought, after all these years?"

"How long after the three of you returned from America did Sir Nigel disappear?"

Hendon's lips pursed with the effort of memory. "A week. Perhaps less."

Sebastian frowned. Lady Prescott had spoken of "weeks." Yet after thirty years, one's memory might be expected to grow distorted. "Did you think at the time his disappearance might have something to do with your recent mission to America?"

Hendon glanced at him sharply. "No. Why would I?"

Sebastian studied his father's unexpectedly closed, angry face. "I don't know. I'm not entirely certain I understand why the three of you were sent to the Colonies in the first place."

Hendon was silent for a moment, the fingers of his right hand running absently up and down his watch chain. He said, "The King took the Americans' rebellion against his authority personally. Very personally. He was determined they be punished for it. The problem was, once the French and Spanish entered the war against us, our ability to actually subdue the colonists was seriously compromised. We simply didn't have the troops to fight the French and Spanish in every corner of the world, and occupy the rebellious colonies, too. We'd send the Army into an area and occupy it, but as soon as the Army left, the rebels would take control of it again."

"There was opposition in Parliament to continuing the war?"

"That's right. But the King remained adamant that it could be won. His idea was to concentrate on fighting the French in India and the West Indies while crushing the Americans financially—basically by destroying their maritime trade, burning their coastal towns, and supporting the natives on the frontiers, until the rebels came begging to be taken back under the King's protection."

"Even after Yorktown?"

Hendon sighed. "Yorktown was undeniably a turning point. The King remained resolute, but the surrender of Cornwallis emboldened the peace party in Parliament to move against His Majesty's Prime Minister, Lord North. In the end, it was actually North who convinced the King to send a delegation to America, to evaluate the situation at first hand—and, if possible, to open channels to the members of the Confederation Congress, urging them to accept some form of dominion status, with a separate parliament loyal to a common king."

"Why the three of you—you, Sir Nigel, and Jarvis?"

Hendon shrugged. "We were young, and willing and able to undertake what was potentially a dangerous voyage. I was in the Lords, Prescott was a powerful voice in the Commons, and Jarvis . . . Jarvis has always been the King's man."

"How long were you there?"

"Not long. In the end, our mission was overtaken by events here in London. Shortly after our departure, the House of Commons voted against continuing to fund the war, North's government fell, and Parliament empowered the King to negotiate for peace."

"So what did you do?"

"When word reached us in the Colonies in May, we wound up our affairs and sailed for home the following month. As I remember it, Sir Nigel was particularly furious about the vote in the Commons. He was convinced the rebellion could still be put down if the King could only prevail upon Parliament to devote the necessary funding to the cause."

"And you?"

Hendon sighed. "You know my opinion of Republican principles and radical philosophies. Before we left for America, I would have told you the rebellion *had* to be put down at any cost, that the very future of civilization depended on it. But . . ." His voice trailed off.

"But?" prompted Sebastian.

Hendon worked his jaw back and forth. "I wasn't in the Colonies a fortnight before I came to the conclusion that any continued attempt to subdue the Americans by military force was futile. It's my opinion that we could have kept troops in America for a hundred years, and we still wouldn't have defeated the insurgency."

The sun had come out, throwing splotches of light and shade across the path and surrounding grass as they turned to walk beneath a row of elms. Sebastian studied his father's aged, troubled face. "And Jarvis? What was his opinion of the situation?"

Hendon shrugged. "Whatever his conclusions, Lord Jarvis kept his views to himself."

They walked along in silence, each lost in his own thoughts. Then Sebastian said, "The three of you arrived back in England in June?"

"July. We sailed from New York at the beginning of June. The passage took six weeks."

"You're certain it was July?"

Hendon snorted. "It's not a voyage I'm likely to forget. The ship was dreadfully crowded with dozens of Loyalists fleeing the persecution of their countrymen, poor devils. There was one woman on board who'd watched her husband and fifteen-year-old son stripped, tarred and feathered, and then scalped, right before her very eyes. As for what the rebels did to the woman herself . . . Well, let's just say it was enough to make me reconsider the wisdom and righteousness of abandoning so many of the King's faithful subjects to the brutal rule of the mob."

"The Loyalists on board were from New York?"

"Some. Others were from Massachusetts and Vermont. We even had the King's former Governor of New Jersey aboard. I remember him particularly because he quarreled so violently with Sir Nigel."

I once shared a voyage with your father, William Franklin had said. Sebastian's step faltered. "Are you telling me William Franklin was on the ship with you and Sir Nigel?"

"That's right. Benjamin Franklin's son."

Chapter 24

*H*ero Jarvis learned of the identification of Sir Nigel Prescott's mummified remains in the same way as the rest of London: She read about it in the *Morning Post*. When she and her mother set off after nuncheon on a round of morning visits (amongst those of a certain class, morning visits, like breakfasts, were always held in the afternoon), they discovered that conversation in the drawing rooms of Mayfair revolved around little else.

"Sir Nigel?" said Lady Jarvis to their hostess. "Why, I remember when he disappeared."

Hero looked at her mother in surprise. "You do?"

"Oh, yes," said Lady Jarvis as her friend turned away to greet a new arrival. "It was right after he returned from that dreadful mission to the Colonies with your father and Lord Hendon."

Hero set her teacup down with enough force to rattle it dangerously. *"What?"*

"Mmm, yes." Lady Jarvis lowered her voice. "There was quite a stir at the time in government circles. Seems Sir Nigel had discovered evidence of treason, in the form of letters written by someone styling himself 'Alcibiades.' The letters disappeared with Sir Nigel. It was all *most* mysterious. Not that your father told me about any of it, of course. But I overheard him talking to Lord North."

Having chafed impatiently through the remainder of their social visits, Hero hurried home to find her father preparing to set forth for his clubs. "Your mission with Sir Nigel to the American Colonies," she said, coming upon him in the library. "Tell me about it."

Jarvis looked up from organizing some papers. "Wherever did you hear about that?"

"The whole town is talking about the discovery of Sir Nigel's body," she said vaguely.

Jarvis locked his papers in a desk drawer and straightened. "There's not much to tell, really," he said, and proceeded to give her a succinct rundown.

Listening to him, she found herself wondering, inevitably, what he was leaving out. She asked, "You never discovered the identity of this 'Alcibiades'?"

"No." He went to splash brandy in a glass. "What are you thinking? That Sir Nigel was killed by the traitor?"

"It's possible, isn't it?"

"I suspect it's more than possible." He set aside the crystal brandy decanter.

"Or you could have killed him."

"Really, Hero, I am not responsible for every dead body that turns up in London."

She gave an inelegant harrumph.

Her father said, "Why are you now interesting yourself in Sir Nigel's death?"

"Perhaps I like puzzles."

He took a slow sip of his brandy, his gaze on her face. "No. That's not it." When she remained silent, he said, "Do you plan to make a habit of this?"

She turned toward the door. "A habit of what?"

"Involving yourself in murder."

She looked back at him. "Would you find that more or less objectionable than my more radical projects?"

He pulled a face. "I'm really not certain."

The aged American rested on a weathered bench in a slice of sunshine that cut down through the ancient yews and elms of the vast churchyard of St. Pancras. He sat hunched forward, both hands wrapped around the handle of the walking stick he held upright between his knees, his eyes closed as if in sleep.

Sebastian had followed him here, to the sprawling burial ground on the outskirts of the city, after a conversation with the old man's granddaughter. When Sebastian settled on the other end of the bench, Mr. William Franklin grunted and said, without appearing to open his eyes, "I figured you'd be back."

Sebastian let his gaze wander over the jumble of moss-covered, ancient tombstones and sunken earth. The burial ground was actually the intersection of two churchyards, that of St. Giles adjoining that of St. Pancras, said by antiquarians to be one of the oldest churches in England.

"You told me you'd sailed from America with my father," said Sebastian. "What you didn't tell me was that the Bishop of London's brother was on that ship, as well."

Franklin opened his eyes. "Didn't seem important at the time. How was I to know Sir Nigel's body had been found in that crypt, along with the Bishop's?"

"You wouldn't have any idea what Sir Nigel was doing down in that crypt, would you?"

"Me? No. Why would I?"

Sebastian studied the old man's florid, sagging face, creased with lines left by eighty-odd years of laughter and heartache. "I think you know far more than you're letting on."

Franklin chuckled at that, his protuberant belly in its snuff-stained, old-fashioned waistcoat shaking up and down. Fumbling in his pocket, he came up with a battered snuffbox he flipped open with the practiced grace of a Macaroni.

Sebastian said, "I understand you and Sir Nigel quarreled during the course of the voyage."

"Of course we quarreled. Sir Nigel was an abrasive, arrogant man. He quarreled with everyone—including your father."

"Over what?"

"The war, mainly. Sir Nigel was adamant that the only reason the King hadn't managed to put down the rebellion was a lack of firm resolve on the part of Parliament. He was convinced that a sustained surge in the number of troops on the ground would be sufficient to subdue the rebels once and for all."

"You didn't think so?"

Franklin lifted a pinch of snuff to one nostril. His hands shook with age, dusting the fine grains over his knees as he leaned forward. "As punishment for my decision to remain loyal to my king, the Revolutionary government seized everything I owned. My home. My estates. Even my liberty for two years. You think I didn't want to see the King prevail in reestablishing control over the Colonies? But what a man wants and what he recognizes as within the realm of possibility aren't necessarily the same thing."

A whirl of pigeons, their wings beating the air as they

rose up from beside the church walls, drew Sebastian's gaze to the massive old west tower of St. Pancras, with its crumbling thirteenth-century arches and broken weather vane. He said, "Lord Jarvis sailed with you, as well?"

"Yes. Why?"

"Did he ever quarrel with Sir Nigel?"

"Jarvis? Not within my hearing, no."

Sebastian had to keep reminding himself that thirty years ago, Lord Jarvis would have been a young man in his twenties, while Hendon wouldn't have been much older than Sebastian himself. Would they have been any different, then? he wondered. Somehow, Sebastian doubted it.

He said, "Your ship docked . . . where? Portsmouth?"

"London. Thirty years ago this month." Franklin dropped the snuffbox back into the pocket of his frock coat. He was silent for a moment, gnawing thoughtfully on the flesh of his inner cheek. At last, he glanced over at Sebastian and said, "You do know about the papers Sir Nigel was bringing back with him?"

Sebastian shook his head. "What kind of papers are we talking about?"

"Letters, actually. Letters from London, written to a member of the Confederation Congress. They were passed to Sir Nigel by a Loyalist from Philadelphia. A woman."

"What woman?"

"Her name isn't important. She's long dead. It was my understanding she stole the letters from their original recipient."

"Who wrote the letters?"

"I never knew. They were simply signed 'Alcibiades.' But from their contents, it was obvious they were written by someone either in the Foreign Office, or else very close to the King."

"Someone passing on sensitive information to the rebels?"

"Yes."

The pigeons on the roof of the dilapidated church began to coo. Sebastian squinted up at them, his eyes narrowing against the glare of the late-afternoon sun. "Why did Sir Nigel tell you about the letters?"

Franklin gave a wry smile. "To my knowledge, he didn't tell anyone. I only knew of the letters' existence due to my acquaintance with the woman who gave them to him."

"But someone else could have known about them?"

"I suppose so. Sir Nigel and I were hardly intimates, now, were we?"

Sebastian studied the old man's aged, paper-thin skin, the watery, nearly lashless eyes. "When Sir Nigel disappeared, it didn't occur to you that it might have something to do with the letters he brought back from America?"

"Of course it occurred to me. Which is why I'm telling you about it now. Did I mention it to anyone at the time? No. Sir Nigel called me a traitor's spawn and spat in my face. As far as I'm concerned, whoever killed him did the world a favor."

"That seems to have been a common sentiment."

Franklin grunted. "So why waste a perfectly fine July day sitting in a churchyard talking to an old man about long-ago events now best forgotten?"

"Because four nights ago, someone killed the Bishop of London in the exact same spot where his brother died thirty years ago. Unlike his brother, the Bishop was a man who accomplished much that was good in his life and would doubtless have accomplished more, had he lived. I don't think the man who killed him did the world a favor."

Franklin tightened his grip on the knobbed handle of his walking stick and pushed to his feet. "Yes, well . . . You know my opinion of the good Bishop."

"We all have our faults."

The aged, watery eyes blinked. "So we do. Perhaps when you know all the good Bishop's faults, you'll know who killed him."

Sebastian watched the American walk away through the tumble of gray, moldering tombstones, his back still surprisingly straight, his gait solid and steady, despite his age. Then Sebastian's gaze fell to the tombstone nearest the bench. Newer than all the others, its inscription was still crisp and easy to read:

HERE LYETH Y^E BODY OF
MARY FRANKLIN
BELOVED WIFE OF WILLIAM
DEPARTED THIS LIFE
SEPTEMBER 1811

Sebastian looked up. But the old man had gone.

Hendon sat with his chin propped on one fist, the scowl on his face deepening as he studied the chessboard before him.

"There is a way," said Sebastian.

Hendon raised his brilliant blue eyes to his son's face. "Don't tell me that."

Sebastian settled deeper into his seat and crossed his

outstretched boots at the ankles. "It's what you used to tell me."

They were in the library of the vast St. Cyr town house on Grosvenor Square. It had become their habit of late to meet in the afternoons when both were free for a game of chess, as they had done so often when Sebastian was a boy. A warm breeze billowed the curtain at the open window, bringing them the *clip-clop* of horses' hooves and the laughter of children at play in the square.

"I used to tell you that when you were four. By the time you were five, you were wiping the board with what was left of my pride."

Sebastian smiled, but said nothing.

Hendon leaned forward to nudge his queen. "Take that."

"There was a way," said Sebastian, carefully relocating his knight. "But that wasn't it. Checkmate."

"Hell and the devil confound it," said Hendon, but softly, as a man acknowledging the inevitable.

A knock sounded at the front door. A moment later, a footman appeared with a note on a tray.

"Message for Viscount Devlin, my lord. From Bow Street."

Hendon let out a disapproving huff. Like Kat, he disliked his son's involvement in cases of murder, only for a different reason. He simply found such activities sordid and unseemly. But since Sebastian's involvement in this particular case had come about on the intervention of Hendon's own sister, he really couldn't say anything.

"Good God," said Hendon, watching Sebastian's face as he broke the seal and glanced through the magistrate's hurried scrawl. "Not another murder?"

Sebastian pushed to his feet. "I'm afraid so."

Chapter 25

"The Squire discovered the corpse himself," said Lovejoy as they drove in Sebastian's curricle toward the village, with Tom clinging to his perch at the rear. "Seems someone stuffed the Reverend's remains in a cupboard in the vestry. One wonders how the searchers failed to find him sooner."

"Not a likely place to look for a missing priest, I suppose," observed Sebastian.

"There is that."

The setting sun had sent the temperature dropping, and Lovejoy had wrapped himself in a greatcoat for the drive. As they crested a ridge, a brisk wind buffeted the carriage, and the magistrate settled deeper into his coat. "It makes one wonder if perhaps our investigation into the Bishop's death has veered off in a faulty direction. Perhaps Bishop Prescott's murder has less to do with events in the Bishop's own life than with the ecclesiastical affairs of St. Margaret's."

"Perhaps," said Sebastian, steadying his horses for the curve ahead.

Lovejoy glanced over at him. "What other explanation is there?"

Rounding the bend, Sebastian dropped his hands, giving the chestnuts their heads as they raced across the heath. Thick bands of clouds obscured the moon and cast the road into deep shadow. But Sebastian had the night vision of a cat or a wolf; even without the moon he could see quite clearly for miles.

He said, "Perhaps Reverend Earnshaw knew something he failed to disclose to us. Something that could have led us to Prescott's killer."

Lovejoy frowned. "But why would the man keep such information back?"

"He may not have realized the significance of what he knew. At least, not until it was too late."

Sebastian stood just inside the door to the vestry, his arms crossed at his chest, and watched Sir Henry peer into the gloom, eyes narrowed to a squint, his candlestick held high.

The light flickered over a bloated, pale face and wide, sightless eyes. "*Good God*," exclaimed the magistrate, jerking back so violently that the candle splashed hot wax over his hand.

"It's a ghoulish sight, no doubt about it," agreed Squire Pyle, raising his own horn lantern high to better illuminate the scene before them.

The air in the vestry was chill and close, the stale scent of old incense overlaid by the pungent odors of dried blood and death. A small chamber built to one side of St. Margaret's main altar, it was lined with cupboard doors and chests with wide, shallow drawers in which were stored the church's vestments. At the narrow end of the room, a tall locker had been thrown open to expose its grisly contents.

Some five and a half feet high and perhaps four feet wide, the cupboard had a row of hooks that ran across the top. One of these hooks had been thrust through the back of the Reverend's collar so that his body hung there, head squashed to one side. Sebastian found the effect disconcertingly similar to a side of beef hung up for display in a butcher shop.

"I thought it best to leave him like that till you got here," said the Squire, wiping one hand across his lower face. "So's you could see it yourself."

"Yes ... well ... we've seen it." Lovejoy took another step back, holding his candlestick more carefully. "Pray, take him down now."

Pyle nodded to his constable, a big, burly man in a leather waistcoat, who hefted the Reverend's body off its hook. Rigid with rigor mortis, the corpse thumped awkwardly against a nearby bench before crashing to the floor.

"Sorry," mumbled the constable.

Lovejoy dabbed at his lips with a wadded-up handkerchief and swallowed.

Sebastian said, "Any indication as to how he was killed?"

Pyle jerked his chin toward the Reverend's bloodstained waistcoat. "There's a neat slice in his waistcoat and shirt, just above his heart. I'd say he was stabbed. But then, I'm no doctor."

Lovejoy tucked away his handkerchief. "We'll have the corpse conveyed to Paul Gibson, at Tower Hill, for a full postmortem."

Pyle nodded to his constable. "Aye. I'll get the lads on it right away."

Sebastian glanced around the vestry. "A wound like

that would have bled significantly. Any traces of blood elsewhere in the church?"

"The cleaning lady found a bit near the altar. Looks as if somebody took the trouble to try to clean it up, which is why we didn't notice it sooner. You can see something of a trail from there to the vestry, although it was pretty much wiped up, too."

"Show us," said Lovejoy.

Lovejoy studied the smeared stains near the altar, his head bent, his hands clasped behind his back as he followed the smudges back to the vestry. Then he walked outside to stand beneath the aged porch and draw the cool air of the night deep into his lungs.

"Why hang up the Reverend's corpse in his own vestry cupboard?" he asked when Sebastian walked up behind him.

Sebastian stared out over the shadowy churchyard, with its pale, tumbled tombstones glowing faintly beneath the darkened canopy of oaks that shifted in the growing wind. "To delay discovery, one presumes."

"Yes, I suppose." Lovejoy was silent a moment, huddled deep in his coat, lost in his own thoughts. The wind gusted up even stronger, banging a shutter someplace in the night. He shivered, and turned toward where Tom walked the chestnuts. "And people claim London is a dangerous place."

By the time they dropped the magistrate at his house on Russell Square, the wind had grown increasingly violent, churning the heavy clouds overhead and bringing with it the smell of coming rain.

"Out with it," Sebastian said to his tiger as the tired chestnuts turned toward Brook Street.

Tom made his eyes go round with innocence. "Gov'nor?"

"You've been looking smug ever since we left Tanfield Hill. What have you discovered?"

Tom grinned. "While you and Sir 'Enry was in the church, I got to talkin' to one of the ostlers at the Dog 'n' Duck."

"The what?"

"The Dog 'n' Duck. It's the inn down by the mill-stream."

"Ah. Go on."

"This ostler—'is name is Jeb, by the way: Jeb Cooper. Anyway, it seems 'e was a groom in the stables at the Grange thirty years ago."

Sebastian swung onto Bond Street. The footpaths and pavement were eerily dark and empty, the unpleasant wind having driven most of the city's inhabitants indoors. "You mean when Sir Nigel was still alive?"

"Aye." A gust snatched at Tom's hat, and he smashed it down on his head with his free hand. "'E remembers the night Sir Peter's da disappeared weery well. Weery well, indeed. Says there were strange goings-on at the Grange that night. Weery strange."

"How's that?"

"'E says Sir Nigel didn't jist ride into town that night. Says 'e took off in a 'igh dudgeon. That's why nobody thought much about it when 'e dinna come back. Not till the next day, when 'is 'orse was found wanderin' on the 'eath."

Sebastian blew out a long breath. "Why is it," he said, drawing up in front of his house on Brook Street, "that every time I begin to think I'm getting a handle on the events surrounding this murder, I suddenly discover I really don't know what's going on at all?"

The street was unnaturally dark, the wind having blown out a good half of the tall oil lamps that marched in a line up the block. But thanks to Morey's vigilance, the two lamps bracketing Sebastian's front door still burned brightly, casting a pool of light over the short flight of steps and the pavement before it.

"Give 'em a good rubdown," said Sebastian, handing the tiger the reins. "I'll drive the grays tomorrow."

Tom scrambled into the seat. "Ye'll be goin' back out to Tanfield 'Ill?"

"Sounds as if I need to have a conversation with this ost—" Sebastian broke off, his head turning as the booming discharge of a long gun crackled through the night.

Chapter 26

With a startled cry, Tom started up, half spinning around in the seat.

"*Bloody hell.*" Grabbing the boy, Sebastian dragged him off the exposed high perch and into the inadequate shadows cast by the delicate carriage.

The rifle crackled again. Heads tossing, the chestnuts whinnied in terror, their hooves clattering on the cobbles as they sidled nervously. Sebastian was hideously conscious of the boy's head lolling against his shoulder, could feel the slick wetness of blood on his hands. "Tom," he whispered. "*Tom!*"

The boy let out a low moan, just as the gun boomed once more. Sebastian caught his breath. A *third* shot?

He scanned the dark, empty street before them, his eyes narrowing as he spotted the shadow of a man crouched in the area steps of a house some three doors down.

"Morey!" Sebastian bellowed.

Sebastian's front door crashed open, spilling a flood of golden light down the steps. The majordomo charged out, blunderbuss in hand. "Where are they?" demanded the former gunnery sergeant. "I'll get 'em, Captain."

Sebastian yanked the majordomo down into the shadows and snatched the blunderbuss. "Here. Take care of the boy."

Already, Sebastian could hear the sound of running feet, disappearing fast. "Bloody hell."

Pushing up, he sprinted down the darkened street, blunderbuss in hand. A good three-quarters of a block ahead of him, a cloaked figure with a hat pulled low darted toward the corner.

"*Watch!*" bellowed Sebastian. "Watch, I say!" As the figure reached the corner, Sebastian paused to raise Morey's blunderbuss and fire.

But the short-barreled, stocky muzzle loader was designed to do maximum damage at minimum range. The heavy shot blew a chunk out of one of the corner stones of the end house. The running figure veered out of sight.

"Bloody hell," swore Sebastian, and ran on.

He heard the creak of saddle leather, the clatter of hooves on cobbles. Bursting around the corner onto Davies Street, he saw the flick of a horse's tail disappearing into the night.

He expelled a long, frustrated breath. "Son of a bitch."

Fist tightening around the stock of the empty blunderbuss, he swung back toward Brook Street. He was passing a house halfway down the block when he saw the gleam of a metal gun barrel lying near the service door at the base of the house's area steps. Running lightly down to the darkened service area, he picked up the long, elegant rifle abandoned by his would-be assassin.

Sebastian stood in the doorway of his best guest bedchamber, his gaze on the small, dark-haired boy sleeping beneath the covers. "How bad is it?"

Paul Gibson collected his instruments in his bag and straightened. "Barring any serious infection, he should be fine. I was able to extract the bullet from his shoulder without doing serious damage to either bone or sinew. I suspect he fainted from shock as much as anything. He was certainly hollering lustily enough while I was trying to sew him up. I've dressed the wound with some basilicum powder, and given him a couple drops of laudanum to help him sleep."

Sebastian kept his gaze on the boy's pale face. "That bullet was meant for me."

Gibson clapped Sebastian on the shoulder. "Come. I could use a drink and so could you. The boy'll be fine."

"So who do you think it was?" said Gibson, lounging in one of the leather chairs in Sebastian's library. "Obadiah?"

"Perhaps." Sebastian splashed generous measures of brandy into two glasses and handed one to his friend. "Perhaps not. I keep thinking of Reverend Earnshaw, hanging in his own vestment locker like a side of beef."

"What's to say that wasn't Obadiah's work, as well?"

"It's certainly possible." Picking up the rifle, Sebastian held it out. "Ever see a butcher carry a weapon like this?"

"What the devil is it?" asked Gibson, studying the rifle's strange screw mechanism.

"It's a Ferguson breech-loading rifle."

"A *breech-loading* rifle?"

Sebastian nodded. "The problem with rifles has always been that they're so damn slow to load. That, plus they can't be fitted with bayonets." He turned the screw handle to open the breech. "This mechanism got around both those problems. I've heard it said that a man who knows what he's doing can fire six rounds a minute and hit a target up to two hundred yards away with this gun."

"Six rounds a minute? You're lucky you weren't killed."

Sebastian pointed to the clogged screw mechanism. "The problem is, the breech threads have a nasty habit of clogging up around the third shot. It's one of the reasons the Army never adopted the Ferguson. They're quite rare."

Gibson ran a hand over the weapon's well-oiled stock. "I suppose Obadiah could have lifted it from some dead officer in the field and brought it back from the Peninsula with him."

"He could have," said Sebastian, going to stand beside the window overlooking the darkened street.

Gibson cleared his throat. "Is it wise, do you think, to expose yourself at the window in that way?"

Sebastian swung to face him. "What would you have me do? Hide in the house?"

"No. But . . . just draw the drapes, would you?"

Sebastian drained his glass with a laugh and stepped away from the window. "Did you get a chance to look at Earnshaw's body?"

Gibson shook his head. "The constable from Tanfield Hill was still drinking a tankard of ale in my kitchen when your footman arrived with news that Tom had been shot. I'll start on your Reverend first thing in the morning."

Sebastian went to pour himself another drink. "I'll be surprised if his body has much to tell us."

"The Constable said something about a stab wound?"

"That's what it looked like."

Gibson finished his own brandy in one long pull. "Just like Sir Nigel Prescott."

"Yes. Only this one wasn't stabbed in the back." Sebastian raised the carafe of brandy in a silent inquiry.

"No more for me, thanks," said the surgeon, pushing to his feet. "You'll be riding out to Tanfield Hill again in the morning?"

"Yes."

Gibson nodded. He turned toward the door, then paused to look back and say, "Just be careful, Devlin."

Chapter 27

Sunday, 12 July 1812

*T*he next morning dawned heavily overcast and blustery, with an unseasonably chill north wind that whistled in the chimneys and sent trash scuttling down the city streets.

Before leaving the house, Sebastian checked on Tom and found the boy sitting up in bed, pink-cheeked and cranky.

" 'Tain't nothin' but a scratch," he said. "If'n Morey'll let me 'ave me breeches—"

Sebastian touched the boy's forehead and found him hot. "You're not going anywhere, and that's an order."

"But the grays don't *like* Giles—"

"I'm not taking the curricle. I'll be riding out to Tanfield Hill on Leila. Alone." Sebastian had no intention of getting another groom shot. "And you are staying in bed until Gibson says otherwise."

"But—"

"No buts." It was said in the officer's voice that had once quelled the rebellious murmurings of a battle-hardened regiment.

Tom flushed scarlet and hung his head. "Aye, my lord."

Beneath the sullen, wind-tossed sky, the village of Tanfield Hill lay unnaturally quiet and somber. As Sebastian trotted his Arab up the high street, a woman with a dark shawl drawn over her head threw him a quick, anxious glance, her hand tightening its grip on the child beside her. Sebastian supposed having two clerics murdered in your church in less than a week might tend to make the locals nervous.

He found the Dog and Duck nestled in a curve of the millstream, just beyond the churchyard. A plain-fronted, two-story brick building dating back to the early eighteenth century, it had a cobbled rear courtyard sheltered on two sides by the attached livery and carriage house.

"Aye," said Jeb Cooper, happy to talk while he worked rubbing down the Arab just inside the livery's wide doors. "Time was, I was groom to Sir Nigel Prescott himself." A slim, wiry man somewhere in his late forties or fifties, just below average height, the ostler had a head of thick, short gray curls and a bony face shadowed by several days' growth of beard.

"I ain't surprised to hear he was lyin' dead all these years," said the ostler. "I figured somethin' bad musta happened to him, when they found Lady Jane."

Sebastian frowned, not understanding. "Lady Jane?"

"Sir Nigel's mare. Dapple gray, with four white stockings. The sweetest-goin' thing you ever did see. Trained her hisself, he did."

Sebastian propped his shoulders against the whitewashed wall, his arms crossed at his chest. "The mare was found running loose on the heath the next day?"

"That's right. The next mornin'."

"Did you think at the time Sir Nigel might have been set upon by highwaymen?"

The ostler looked at Sebastian over the mare's back. "Me? Nah. I never believed it for a minute."

"Why not?"

"Couldn't see Lady Jane boltin' and leavin' Sir Nigel. That horse was his baby. If he were hurt, she would'nta left him."

Sebastian studied the groom's rawboned, grizzled features and wondered if the man would have said the same thing a week ago, before the Baronet's mummified corpse had been discovered in the crypt of St. Margaret's. He said, "How long were you at Prescott Grange?"

"Near ten years."

"Why'd you leave?"

Jeb rubbed the side of his nose with one finger and winked. "I run into a spot o' trouble with one o' the housemaids, if ye know what I mean? Lady Prescott herself asked me t' leave. But then, she'd had it in for me, ever since that night."

Sebastian frowned, not understanding. "You mean the night Sir Nigel disappeared?"

"That's right." The ostler sniffed. "Big row they had, up at the house. Jist afore dinner."

"An argument? Between whom?"

"Why, Sir Nigel and Lady Prescott, of course."

"Did they quarrel often?"

Jeb paused to consider it. "Well, Sir Nigel had the devil of a temper. He was always shoutin' at somebody or t'other. But her ladyship didn't often stand up to him."

"Yet she did that night?"

"Aye. I could hear her pleadin' with him when he slammed out o' the house callin' for his horse." Jeb raised his voice into a falsetto and opened his eyes ridiculously wide. "'Please don't do this!'"

Sebastian frowned. "Please don't do what?"

The ostler's voice returned to its normal pitch. "Leave, I suppose."

"But Sir Nigel left anyway? Despite her ladyship's pleadings?"

"Aye. I saddled Lady Jane for him, and he rode off toward London."

Sebastian stared out the open stable door, at the millstream flowing sluggishly past. The village of Tanfield Hill lay on the lane between the Grange and the main road to London. He said, "Did Sir Nigel actually tell you he was bound for London?"

Jeb Cooper screwed up his mouth with the effort of thought. "Can't rightly say, now, after all these years."

"You don't have any idea what Sir Nigel's quarrel with her ladyship was about?"

Jeb shook his head. "That I couldna say. But Bessie could maybe tell ye."

"Bessie?"

"Bessie Dunlop. Her ladyship's old nurse—and Sir Peter's, when he come along. Most folks'll tell ye she's a witch." He paused, a strange, faraway look coming into his eyes. "I'm not telling ye she ain't a witch, mind ye. I'm jist sayin', there ain't much Bessie misses. Course, whether she'll be willin' t'tell ye everythin' she knows, now, that's somethin' else agin."

"Where might I find this Bessie Dunlop?"

"She lives on up the millstream. Maybe half a mile. A place called Briar Cottage."

Sebastian straightened. "Thank you," he said, pressing a guinea into the ostler's hand. "You've been most helpful."

He was in the yard, tightening the girth on the Arab's saddle, when Jeb Cooper came up to him. "There's one other thing was queer about that night I was thinkin' ye might want to know about."

Sebastian lowered the stirrup and turned to face him. "Yes?"

"Weren't more'n five minutes after Sir Nigel left that Lady Prescott called for *her* horse to be brought 'round. Rode off without even a groom."

"Lady Prescott? Are you saying she rode after Sir Nigel?"

"I don't know about that. But she rode toward London, too; that I do know."

"When did she come back?"

Jeb Cooper pressed his lips together and shook his head. "That I couldn't say. When I awoke the next mornin', her ladyship's mare was back in her stall, still wearin' her saddle."

"Did it look as if it had been ridden hard?"

"Well, she didn't show signs of having worked up any kind of a sweat, that's fer sure. So I'd say, no, that horse hadn't been ridden far at all."

The witches' cottages of Sebastian's childhood imaginings had been dark, decrepit places, with mold-slimed walls and grimy, cobwebbed windows and broken shutters that creaked ominously in the wind. The witches themselves, of course, were all hideous creatures—bent, skeletal crones with wild hair and hooked noses and drooling, toothless grins.

But when he followed the dark, overgrown path that wound through the mingling willows and oaks that grew along the banks of the millstream, he came upon a tidy, recently whitewashed cottage with a newly thatched roof and a profusion of rambling roses in a riot of pink and scarlet. Chickens scratched in the well-swept yard. A snowy-white gander preened himself in the reeds beside the stream, and finches chirped cheerfully from the branches of a nearby willow. On a low stool beside the cottage's open door, a white-haired woman sat with a butter churn gripped between her knees. When Sebastian rode into the yard, she set aside her churn and rose gracefully to her feet.

"I was wondering when you'd get here," she said, then added with a smile, "My lord."

Chapter 28

Sebastian swung out of the saddle, his gaze taking in the doe that grazed unconcernedly at the edge of the clearing, the rabbit foraging in the nearby undergrowth. "You knew I was coming, did you?"

Bessie Dunlop gave a soft chuckle. "They told you I'm a witch, didn't they?"

The woman's hair might be white, but her face was surprisingly unlined. If she'd served as nurse to both Sir Peter and Lady Prescott before him, Sebastian knew that Bessie Dunlop had to be at least in her seventies. Yet her cheeks still bloomed with good health and vigor. Small and plump, with a fan of laugh lines radiating out from merry black eyes, she looked far more like a jovial baker's wife than a witch.

She nodded to a little girl whose dark head peeked around the edge of the doorway. "Missy, take his lordship's mare and put her in the lean-to so she'll be out of this wind."

Sebastian handed the child his reins. "Thank you."

"My granddaughter," said Bessie Dunlop, studying Sebastian through suddenly narrowed eyes. And it oc-

curred to him that while she might look like a jolly baker's wife, appearances could be deceiving.

"Do you know who I am?" he said.

She gave a soft cackle that sounded decidedly unjo-
vial. "Oh, I know who you are, Lord Devlin." She
dropped her voice and leaned forward to whisper, "The
question is, do you know? And, more important, do you
want to know?"

"What's that supposed to mean?"

She straightened. "When you're ready to understand,
you will."

He cast a more searching gaze about the clearing. "I
assume Jeb Cooper told you to expect me?" It occurred
to him that a child like Missy, running along a more direct path, could conceivably have reached the cottage
ahead of a horseman following the winding millstream.

"In a manner of speaking." She turned to pick up a
bulky meal sack resting on a shelf built against the cottage wall.

"He says you were at Prescott Grange thirty years
ago, the night Sir Nigel disappeared."

"That's right." Opening the meal sack, she thrust her
hand inside and came up with a fistful of grain she tossed
to the chickens in the yard. The wind caught the seed,
scattering it unexpectedly far.

Clucking and jostling for position, a dozen chickens
descended upon them, feathers ruffled by the brisk wind.
Sebastian felt his initial spirit of goodwill toward this
maddeningly smiling woman begin to wane. "He says Sir
Nigel and Lady Prescott quarreled that night, and that
you would know the subject of their quarrel."

She shrugged one shawl-draped shoulder. "I know

what I heard. It's no different from what the others in the house that night heard."

Sebastian waited patiently. It was a moment before she continued. "Afterward, there was all sorts of wild talk, of course. Sir Nigel disappearing like that. Especially when it became known that her ladyship was with child."

Sebastian studied the woman's half-averted profile. "When was Sir Peter born?"

"Late February. He came early. He was expected in April."

Late February would have been seven months after Sir Nigel disappeared, Sebastian thought. And just over seven months after the Baronet had returned from America. No wonder Lady Prescott had been vague about the dates of her husband's return.

A scratching sound drew Sebastian's attention to a ratty brown hen pecking and clawing at the shiny surface of his Hessians. He shifted his feet, but the hen persisted. *Careful*, he thought, *or you'll end up in a stew pot, my fine feathered friend.*

"I keep the hens for their eggs," she said, as if he had spoken the thought aloud. "Not for the pot."

She laughed when he looked up at her, startled. "I eat no flesh of my fellow beings. It's why the creatures of the forest know they need have no fear in approaching me."

Sebastian glanced over to where he'd seen the doe, but the deer was gone. He said, "You still haven't told me the reason Sir Nigel quarreled with Lady Prescott that night."

"Nor will I." Tossing the last of the grain, she turned back toward the cottage. The loyal family retainer, loyal to the end.

Sebastian followed her. "Three men are dead."

"And you think it's because of that quarrel?"

"I don't know."

For the first time, she looked vaguely troubled. Seating herself on her stool again, she reached for the churn. "I haven't seen Lady Rosamond in some time," she said in an apparent non sequitur. "It was Sir Peter gave me this cottage."

"Lady Rosamond being Lady Prescott?"

The old nurse worked her churn. "She'll always be Lady Rosamond to me, just like she was when she was a little girl." She paused. "Now, Sir Peter, he comes to visit me regularly. Why, he was here just last week."

Sebastian watched her work her butter. He said, "You haven't actually told me anything. You know that, don't you?"

She stopped churning long enough to look up at him. "Oh, but I have." Lifting her head, she called to her granddaughter, "Missy, fetch his lordship's horse. He'll be wanting to make it to Prescott Grange before the rain starts."

The first raindrops began to fall just as Sebastian clattered into the centuries-old courtyard. It hadn't been his intention to call again at Prescott Grange. But too many questions about Sir Nigel's last, fatal night remained unanswered.

He found Lady Prescott even paler and more wan than he remembered her, her soft blue eyes huge with what looked very much like fear. She received him in the Grange's ancient hall, a graceful medieval chamber with tapestry-draped stone walls and a massive fireplace and a decorated wooden ceiling supported by stone corbels carved into fanciful shapes.

"We've heard the dreadful news about Reverend Earnshaw," she said, gripping his hand tightly for a moment before turning away to order tea. "I do hope you're here to tell us there's been some progress in identifying this killer?"

"I'm afraid not." Adjusting the tails of his riding coat, Sebastian settled on a hard, stiff-backed settee covered in a faded tapestry worked in the style of the previous century. "But I had an interesting encounter this morning with your old nurse."

The widow sank into a low chair beside a work basket and a stand supporting an embroidery frame. "Bessie Dunlop?" she asked, drawing the frame to her.

"I understand she has something of a reputation as a witch."

Lady Prescott took up her needle. "Old women living alone in the wood often give rise to such speculation."

"She does seem uncannily prescient."

Lady Prescott bent her head to focus her attention on her stitches. "Bessie is unusually observant, and a good student of human nature. That is enough to make her a witch in the eyes of the villagers."

"She's fortunate not to have lived in a less enlightened century."

"As are we all."

Sebastian studied the widow's hollow cheeks and downswept lashes. "She is very loyal to you."

Lady Prescott looked up, her eyes twinkling with unexpected amusement. "In other words, she wouldn't tell you what you wanted to know."

Sebastian gave a soft laugh. "No, she wouldn't."

The widow tipped her head to one side. "And precisely what is it you wished her to tell you?"

Sebastian met her gaze squarely. "I understand you and Sir Nigel quarreled the night he disappeared."

"I wouldn't doubt it." She bent over her embroidery

again, her equanimity unruffled. "My husband had a violent temper. He quarreled with everyone, about anything and everything. It would have been unusual had we not disagreed that night."

Sebastian watched the woman's half-averted, faintly flushed face. He could hardly say to her, *Did your husband come home from America to discover you pregnant with another man's child? Was* that *the topic of that fatal night's confrontation?* Even if it were true, she would never admit it.

He said, "I understand you rode after him that night."

Her eyes narrowed. "Jeb Cooper told you that, did he?"

"Is it true?"

"I had Jeb saddle my mare, yes. Nigel was—" she paused as if choosing her words with care "—a very difficult man. I fell into the habit of going for a ride when I was . . . upset."

"Even at night?"

She touched her left eyelid with her fingertips. Then, as if becoming aware of what she was doing, she curled her hand into a fist and rested it on her lap. "At such times, one has little care for one's own safety."

It was a remark that told Sebastian volumes about her marriage. He said, "So you didn't follow Sir Nigel to London?"

"The last thing I wanted at that moment was to see him again."

"Do you recall the nature of your disagreement?"

She shook her head. "Sir Nigel had a vicious temper. He could fly into a rage over the simplest of things, from a badly swept chimney to a dinner of fish or veal when he was fancying lamb. One never knew what would set him off."

Sebastian said, "I'm told Sir Nigel returned from America with a set of papers. Letters written to the Confederation Congress by someone either at Whitehall or in close association with the King. Do you know anything about that?"

She jabbed her needle into her embroidery so violently that she pricked her finger. "Do you mean to say he had evidence of some treason?"

"So it would seem, yes."

She brought her pricked finger to her lips and sucked on it. It was a childlike gesture, and had the effect of suddenly making her look both younger and more vulnerable. She said, "I know Sir Nigel came home from America preoccupied and surly—unusually so, even for him. But if he had evidence of high treason within the government, this is the first I've heard of it. I'm afraid he never discussed his affairs with me. He never even explained completely the purpose of his mission to America."

"They left for America—when? Late January? Early February?"

Her forehead puckered with thought. "Oh, no, it was sometime in December. I don't remember the exact date, but I know it was before Christmas."

Sebastian stared at her. He knew a peculiar tingling sensation, as if every nerve in his body were suddenly, painfully heightened. He could hear the laughter of a housemaid in a distant room, smell the bitter tinge of stale ashes on the hearth. He felt his breath fill his lungs, and had to force himself to exhale.

He was aware of her looking at him strangely. It was an effort for him to speak, to keep his voice even, as if every facet of his life didn't depend on her answer.

He said, "You're certain?"

"Why, yes. I'm afraid I don't recall the exact date, but I do know it was before Christmas. We still follow the old tradition of St. Thomas's Day here at the Grange, when needy women are allowed to go begging from door to door for Christmas 'goodenings.' I remember it distinctly because that was the first year I distributed our charity to the women personally."

"Did the entire mission sail together?"

The question seemed to puzzle her. "Of course. Why wouldn't they?"

He pushed to his feet. "You'll have to excuse me."

She set aside her embroidery and stood with him. "But surely you'll stay for tea?"

"What? Oh. No, thank you."

Somehow, he managed to murmur the requisite polite phrases, to take possession of his hat and riding quip, and call for his horse.

He had only the vaguest memories of mounting the Arab at the worn old block in the corner of the court and setting her on the long road back to London. The wind blew in short, sharp bursts that stung his cheeks with a needlelike spray of rain. He blinked, wiped the water from his eyes, and rode on.

In three months' time, on the nineteenth of October, Sebastian would celebrate his thirtieth birthday. But if what Lady Prescott had told him were true ... If the Earl of Hendon had indeed left England for the American Colonies in December of 1781, then Hendon could not possibly be Sebastian's father.

And his name should not, in truth, be Sebastian St. Cyr.

Chapter 29

A thousand recollections rode with Sebastian through the howling wind and driving rain. Raw memories of a disapproving father whose harshest words had always been reserved for his youngest child, the son so unlike all the others, the son who grew tall and lean when his brothers were built solid and big-boned, and whose eyes were a strange amber in place of the vivid St. Cyr blue. The son with the preternatural hearing and vision, the quick reflexes and uncanny ability to see in the dark. The son who by some cruel twist of fate had lived to become Hendon's heir when both his brothers died.

He remembered snatches of hushed conversations the child he'd once been was never meant to overhear. Voices raised in anger and in pleading. Words that had made no sense, until now.

The white blur of a tollgate loomed out of the mist. Sebastian reined in hard, fists clenching with impatience, the mare's hooves churning the mud while he waited for the grumbling attendant to lumber from his cottage, head bent and shoulders hunched against the downpour. Reaching down to hand the toll to the attendant, Sebastian realized he was shaking. Shaking with pain and denial.

Yet as the gate swung open and he set his spurs to the Arab's flanks, Sebastian was aware of a small spark of hope fed by a burning rage. Because if Alistair St. Cyr were not, in truth, Sebastian's father, then the horror of incest that had driven him from Kat Boleyn was all a mistake. No, not a mistake: a lie.

One more lie in a long string of deceptions stretching back nearly thirty years.

Still booted and spurred from the ride back to town, Sebastian went straight to the great St. Cyr pile on Grosvenor Square. But he found Hendon out and the painfully proper butler unable to say where the Earl had gone or when he would be back. Drawing the same blank at Hendon's clubs, Sebastian was on Cockspur Street, striding toward Whitehall, when he heard a man calling his name.

"Lord Devlin."

Sebastian kept walking.

"I say, Lord Devlin!"

Turning, Sebastian was surprised to find Bishop Prescott's chaplain weaving his way through the traffic, the hem of his cassock lifted clear of the droppings scattered across the wet pavement by a passing mule team.

"I'd formed the intention of seeking you out later this afternoon," said the Chaplain, leaping nimbly onto the footpath, "so this meeting is quite fortuitous."

"You wished to see me?" said Sebastian, holding himself still with effort.

The Chaplain had been smiling faintly. But whatever he saw in Sebastian's face as he walked up to him caused the smile to slip, his forehead puckering. "Are you all right, my lord?"

Sebastian found he had to draw in a breath, then another, before he could speak. "Yes, of course. Did you have something for me?"

The Chaplain held out a folded square of paper. "You may have noticed there was a gap in the Bishop's itinerary on Monday afternoon."

"Yes. I'd assumed he had official duties scheduled at that time."

The Chaplain shook his head. "In fact Bishop Prescott paid a call upon a family in Chelsea. I was originally hesitant to pass the information on to you, but I've discussed the situation with the Archbishop, who assures me we can rely upon your discretion. It may not be relevant, of course, but I've written down the information for you."

"Thank you," said Sebastian, barely glancing at the scrawled name and address before tucking the paper into his waistcoat pocket.

The Chaplain cleared his throat. "Word reached London House last night about Reverend Earnshaw. A troublesome development. Deeply troublesome."

Sebastian studied the cleric's pale, pinched face and noticed for the first time the fear that widened the man's eyes and flattened his lips. So it was fear that had driven this normally persnickety, disapproving man to suddenly become more cooperative.

A new thought occurred to Sebastian. He said, "How much contact was there between Bishop Prescott and Malcolm Earnshaw? Before Tuesday night, I mean."

The Chaplain looked blank. "None that I am aware of."

"Yet the living is in the Prescotts' gift, is it not?"

"In Sir Peter's, yes."

"Was Earnshaw related in some way to the Bishop?"

"A distant cousin of some sort, I believe. Why do you ask?"

"He recognized Sir Nigel's ring, which means he must have known the man."

"I can make inquiries into the exact relationship, if you'd like."

"That would help," said Sebastian, already turning away. "Thank you."

Drawing a blank at the Admiralty, Sebastian extended his search for Hendon to the Horse Guards, and from there to Downing Street, all without success.

Leaving the Chancellor's chambers, he stood for a moment outside Number Ten, his gaze fixed unseeingly on the heavy gray clouds bunching overhead.

Then he turned and strode rapidly toward the Mall and Carlton House.

Charles, Lord Jarvis, was reading through a set of dispatches at the table in his chambers at Carlton House when Viscount Devlin thrust aside Jarvis's indignant, sputtering secretary and strode into the room.

"*My lord!*" protested the secretary. "You can't go in there!"

The Viscount paused just inside the entrance to the chambers, bringing with him the scent of fresh country air and warm horseflesh. He was dressed in a riding coat of blue superfine, with buff-colored buckskin breeches and high-topped riding boots splashed with mud. His strange amber eyes glittered dangerously.

Hopping ineffectually from one foot to the other, Jarvis's secretary wrung his hands in despair. "I do most humbly beg your pardon, my lord Jarvis. I did try to—"

"Leave us," snapped Jarvis.

"Yes, my lord." The secretary bowed and withdrew.

"I trust you have a good reason for this intrusion?" said Jarvis, leaning back in his seat.

Devlin prowled the room, the spurs on his boots clinking. "Thirty years ago, you formed part of a mission sent by the King to the American Colonies. The other two members of that mission were my father and Sir Nigel Prescott."

Jarvis set aside his dispatches and smiled. This promised to be an interesting conversation. An interesting conversation, indeed. "That's right."

"While the mission was in America, a woman provided Sir Nigel with evidence of treason at the highest levels of government—evidence in the form of a collection of letters written to a member of the Confederation Congress by someone styling himself 'Alcibiades.' Someone who was obviously in the Foreign Office or close to the King, given the sensitive nature of the information the letters contained."

Jarvis reached for the gold snuffbox he kept in his pocket.

The Viscount watched him, his jaw set hard. When Jarvis remained silent, Devlin said, "You know all this, I gather?"

"Of course."

"Sir Nigel told you?"

Jarvis flicked open the lid of his snuffbox with one artful finger. "I have my own sources of information."

"And was the identity of the traitor known to you, as well?"

Jarvis lifted a thumbnail full of snuff to one nostril and sniffed. "Unfortunately, no."

The Viscount came to press his palms flat on the surface of the table and lean into them. "You never discovered who this 'Alcibiades' was?"

"No."

Devlin shoved away from the table in disgust. "You seriously expect me to believe that?"

Jarvis raised one eyebrow. "Whether you believe it or not is of no consequence to me."

"What happened to the letters?"

"They disappeared. Along with Sir Nigel."

"And you found none of this cause for concern?"

Jarvis closed his snuffbox with a snap. "Of course it was cause for concern. Lord Grantham—the Foreign Secretary—and I contrived several clever stratagems to lure the individual involved into revealing himself. Unfortunately, none worked. A preliminary peace agreement with the Americans was negotiated later that year and signed not long thereafter. Alcibiades was never revealed."

"When Sir Nigel disappeared so soon after your return from America, did you not suspect that his death might in some way be connected to those letters?"

"Obviously," said Jarvis drily. "We saw no reason to advertise that fact, however."

"How many people knew of your mission to America?"

"In point of fact, the information was very tightly held."

"But surely your absence from London would have been remarked upon?"

Jarvis put his fingertips together, wondering how much the Viscount knew, and how much he merely suspected. "Not really. It's easy to lose track of the movements of one's acquaintances, is it not? What with house parties and weeks of seclusion in hunting lodges and the need to attend to one's estates."

A muscle bunched along the Viscount's jaw, but he said nothing.

"In Sir Nigel's case, of course, things were a bit more difficult," Jarvis continued, "owing to the proximity of his estate to London. I believe he gave it out he was traveling in Ireland."

There was a tense pause. Jarvis waited for the inevitable query to come. But either Devlin already knew the truth, or he couldn't bring himself to pose such a question to Jarvis, because all he said was, "Given your opposition to Francis Prescott's translation to Canterbury, I find your previous association with his dead brother . . ." Devlin hesitated, as if searching for the right word. "Shall we say, suggestive?"

Jarvis pushed to his feet. "I wouldn't refine too much on it, if I were you. I hardly see how what happened to Sir Nigel thirty years ago could have any bearing on the Bishop's more recent demise—even if the two men did meet their fate in the same somewhat bizarre locale."

The Viscount smiled sardonically. "Men whom you oppose do have an unfortunate tendency to turn up dead."

"True. But I had no quarrel with Sir Nigel."

"You considered him bad ton."

"Believe me, if I went around removing men simply because they happened to be bad ton, London would soon be very thin of company."

"Yet you did oppose Francis Prescott's translation to Canterbury."

"True again. However, the situation hardly called for

drastic measures. Do you seriously think the Prince would make such an important appointment without consulting me?"

"There's a difference between consultation and capitulation."

"You underestimate my powers of persuasion."

Devlin went to stand at the window overlooking the Mall, his eyes narrowing as he watched the traffic below.

Jarvis studied the younger man's strained profile. "I hear the priest in residence at St. Margaret's has been slain, as well," said Jarvis. "I don't suppose it has occurred to you that you are allowing a penchant for high drama to cause you to read too much into all this? That perhaps someone in the neighborhood of Tanfield Hill simply does not like priests?"

Devlin glanced over at him, a hint of amusement touching his lips. "And Sir Nigel's thirty-year-old corpse mummifying in the church's crypt?"

"Could well be irrelevant to the current murders. Curious, but irrelevant."

"It could be," agreed Devlin, pushing away from the window.

"But you don't believe it is?"

"No," said Devlin, turning toward the door. "No, I don't."

Chapter 30

*S*ebastian sat, alone, in a leather armchair beside the empty hearth in the library of the St. Cyr town house in Grosvenor Square. The dark shadows of evening had long since filled the room. But when one of Hendon's footmen came to light the candles in the wall sconces, Sebastian waved him away.

Outside, the rain had begun again. Sebastian could hear it drumming on the lime trees in the square, hear the splash of carriage wheels as members of the *haut ton* left their elegant town houses for their evening rounds of dinners and card parties, routs and balls. Sebastian raised his glass of brandy and took a slow swallow that burned all the way down.

He was on his third brandy when he caught the approach of familiar footsteps that shifted to climb the front steps. He heard a low exchange of voices in the hall. Then Hendon appeared in the doorway, a taper in one hand.

"I'm told you've been looking for me," said the Earl.

"Yes."

The golden light from the taper played over the broad, beloved features of the Earl's face. He stood for a moment, jaw working thoughtfully back and forth before he went to touch his flame to the nearest sconce. "You won't mind if I light the candles? We don't all have the night vision of a cat."

Sebastian settled deeper into his chair, his outthrust boots crossed at the ankles. "A trait I inherited, perhaps, from my real father? Do you even know who he was, I wonder? Or did my mother take that little secret with her when she sailed away the summer I was eleven?"

Hendon froze, his hand extended toward the next sconce. Hot wax dripped, splashing on the polished surface of the table below. He calmly resumed his task, although Sebastian noticed his hand was no longer steady. "I'm not certain I understand what you mean to imply by that statement."

"Don't you?" Sebastian thrust up from the chair. "I had an interesting conversation with Lady Prescott this morning. The widow of Sir Nigel Prescott. She tells me the three of you—you, her husband, and Lord Jarvis—sailed for the American Colonies in December of 1781."

Hendon had given up lighting the sconces and simply stood on the far side of the room, the taper clenched in his hand. "She is mistaken."

"Don't." Sebastian drew in a harsh breath that shuddered his chest. "Don't . . . lie to me anymore."

"It's not a lie. We sailed at the beginning of February. The fifth."

"From where?"

"Portsmouth.

"The name of the ship?"

"The *Albatross*," said the Earl without hesitation.

Sebastian knew a leap of hope at war with a whisper

of despair. His voice, when he spoke, was a ragged tear. "Why should I believe you?"

"What are you suggesting? That I deliberately raised a son I knew was not my own?" Hendon swiped his arm through the air before him, as if brushing aside an unwanted presence. "Don't be ridiculous."

"You would hardly be the first peer to do so. Look at the Harleian Miscellany." The Earl of Oxford's wife was famous for having taken so many lovers in her life that the resultant brood of bastards was known collectively as the "Harleian Miscellany."

"No one ever doubted the parentage of Harley's heir," said Hendon.

"True. Yet you had no way of knowing what lay ahead when you acknowledged me as your third son."

A heavy silence fell as the two men's gazes clashed from across the length of the room. It was Hendon who turned away.

"You have never been much like me," he said gruffly. "Either in temperament or interests. It made relations between us difficult at times. I won't deny that. But I never doubted for a moment that you are my son."

The pressure in Sebastian's chest was suddenly so great he found it impossible to speak.

Hendon said, "We sailed at the beginning of February, and we returned in the middle of July. If you know when Lady Prescott's son was born, then you'll understand that she has her own reasons for obfuscating the exact dates of her late husband's departure and return."

When Sebastian still remained silent, the Earl made another jerky, angry gesture and took a step forward. "For God's sake, Sebastian, *think*! Jarvis was on that mission. Do you seriously believe that if he had proof my son and heir was not the fruit of my own loins, he wouldn't have used that information against me years ago?"

Sebastian's hand tightened around his brandy, reminding him of its existence. He raised the glass to his lips and drained the contents in one long pull. "Perhaps he has his own reasons for leaving the mission cloaked in obscurity."

"Such as?"

Sebastian shook his head. "I don't know."

Hendon's jaw hardened. "We sailed in early February."

Sebastian set aside his empty glass with a click. "If you are not my father, then Kat is not my sister."

Something shifted in the depths of the Earl's intense blue eyes. "So that's what this is about, is it? My God. Do you love her so much that you would wish yourself not my son? *Simply so that you could have her?*"

"Yes."

Another long silence fell between them. This time when Hendon spoke, his voice was hushed, almost gentle. "I'm sorry, Sebastian. But you are my child. And so is Kat."

"You've lied to me before. Why should I believe you now?" Sebastian turned toward the door.

"I'm not lying about this."

Sebastian kept walking.

"You hear me, Sebastian?" Hendon called after him. "I'm not lying about this."

Sebastian returned to Brook Street to find a message from Paul Gibson awaiting him.

I've finished with your Reverend, wrote the surgeon. *I'll be attending at St. Bartholomew's this afternoon, but I should be at the surgery after four.*

Somehow, amidst all the revelations of that day, Gibson's planned postmortem on the Reverend of St. Margaret's had been forgotten. Sebastian glanced at the clock.

It was nearly eight.

He arrived at Gibson's ancient house near the Tower to find the Irishman eating ham and cooked cabbage in solitary state at one end of his dining room table. A brass candlestick heavily splashed with old dried wax sat at his elbow; the other end of the table lay buried beneath piles of books and gruesome-looking specimen jars.

"I didn't know you kept such a fashionably late dinner hour," said Sebastian, drawing out one of the empty chairs beside his friend.

"There was an accident in one of the breweries near the hospital," said Gibson, spearing a large slice of ham with his fork. Neither death nor its leavings ever seemed to dull the surgeon's appetite. He nodded to the half-carved joint resting on a nearby platter. "Like a plate?"

Sebastian suppressed a shudder. "No, thank you. You say you've finished with Earnshaw?"

"This morning." Gibson took one last mouthful of ham and pushed up from the table. "Come. I'll show you."

Lighting a horn lantern in the kitchen, the surgeon led the way across the tangled, rain-soaked garden to push open the door to his small stone outbuilding. The Reverend lay upon the central slab, his flesh pallid, his body neatly eviscerated. The small stab wound in his chest stood out like a puckered purple tear against the dead white skin.

"What kind of knife?" asked Sebastian, studying the wound.

"A dagger. About ten inches long, I'd say. Aimed well by someone who either knew what he was doing, or got very, very lucky." Gibson limped over to lift one of Earnshaw's plump, soft hands. By now, the rigor mortis had largely faded from the Reverend's limbs, leaving them limp. "You'll notice there are no signs of any defensive wounds."

"So he may have known his attacker."

"Either that, or he was taken by surprise and was simply too frightened to react."

Sebastian drew in a deep breath that filled his head with the stench of dank stone, decay, and death. "Anything else?"

"I'm afraid not."

He went to stand looking out over the dark, rain-soaked garden. The wind had come up again, thrashing the half-dead trees and scuttling the heavy clouds overhead. He kept trying to bring his mind back to the murder of the man lying on that slab behind him, but all he could think about was the gleam of pride he'd glimpsed in Hendon's eyes the day an eight-year-old Sebastian first brought his hunter smoothly over one of the worst ditches in Cornwall, or . . .

Or the way Kat's eyes glowed with love when Sebastian brushed his lips against her cheek.

Gibson came up beside him. "You look like hell," he said, his gaze on Sebastian's face.

Sebastian gave a sharp, humorless laugh and stepped out into the wind.

Gibson secured the door to the building behind him. "Come on, then. I'll buy you a drink."

The wind blew sharp bursts of rain against the leaded windows of the old Tudor inn at the base of Tower Hill as the two friends settled into a dark booth in the corner. Fortified with ale, Sebastian ran through his conversations from that morning, with the ostler Jeb Cooper and with the old nurse Bessie Dunlop. He told Gibson of the quarrel that was said to have taken place between Sir Nigel and Lady Prescott on the night of Sir Nigel's disappearance, and the child that arrived barely seven months after his father's return from the Colonies.

He did not tell Gibson about the controversy surrounding the departure dates of the mission to the Colonies, nor what a December sail date would imply about Sebastian's own legitimacy.

"Very few infants born at seven months survive," said Gibson.

"Yet it is possible?"

"Yes, it's possible. But I'd say it's far more likely Sir Nigel's lady was unfaithful."

Sebastian was remembering what his aunt Henrietta had told him about Lady Rosamond's unsuitable suitor and the desperate bolt to Gretna Green thwarted by her enraged father.

Gibson leaned forward. "It makes sense, does it not? Sir Nigel returns from America to find his wife pregnant by another man. Husband and wife quarrel. Sir Nigel slams out of the house, calling for his horse. He rides off into the night, determined to confront the man who cuckolded him, and—"

"And ends up dead in the crypt of the local church," finished Sebastian wryly.

Gibson sat back. "Ah. I was forgetting that part. You've no notion of the identity of this suitor?"

"No. There're also the Alcibiades letters to be taken into account. Sir Nigel may have ridden away from the

Grange that night in a passion over his wife's infidelity, but I think those letters are the key to his death."

Sebastian found himself gazing at the young barmaid laughing with the innkeeper as she scooped up fistfuls of tankards. She looked no more than sixteen, with a heavy fall of auburn hair and a wide, infectious smile, and she reminded him so much of Kat at that age that his chest ached with yearning for all that had been lost, and all that might have been.

"What is it, Sebastian?" asked Gibson softly. "There's something you're not telling me."

"What?" Sebastian brought his gaze back to his friend's face and shook his head. Rather than answer the surgeon's question, he said, "You do realize, of course, that none of this even begins to answer the question we actually started with."

"What question?"

"Who killed the bloody Bishop."

"And the Reverend Malcolm Earnshaw," Gibson reminded him.

"And the Reverend Earnshaw," said Sebastian.

It was when they were leaving the tavern that Sebastian reached into his pocket and pulled out a small folded square of paper. *Dr. and Mrs. Daniel McCain, Number 11 Cheyne Walk, Chelsea.*

"What's that?" said Gibson, watching him.

Sebastian frowned down at the scrawled direction and resurrected with difficulty the memory of the Bishop's chaplain accosting him in Whitehall that afternoon with some babble about a hiatus in the Bishop's appointments.

"It's an address," said Sebastian. "The name and address of a family in Chelsea the Bishop visited the Monday before he died." He could be wrong, but he had a disquieting suspicion that McCain was the name of the doctor he'd seen escorting Miss Hero Jarvis around the Royal Hospital.

"Chelsea?" said Gibson. "What the bloody hell was Prescott doing in Chelsea?"

"I don't know. But first thing tomorrow morning, I intend to find out."

Chapter 31

Monday, 13 July 1812

The next morning dawned cool and gray, with a heavy mist that blanketed the wet city and hung in dirty wisps about the chimney pots. Sir Henry Lovejoy was in his chambers at Bow Street's public office, a scarf wrapped around his neck and the *Hue and Cry* spread open on the desk before him, when Sebastian strolled into his office.

"My lord," said the little magistrate, leaping to his feet. "Please have a seat."

"No, thank you," said Sebastian, shaking his head. "I won't be but a moment." He drew a folded slip of paper from his pocket and laid it on the open pages of the weekly police gazette. "I have here the name and sailing date of a vessel that was said to have left Portsmouth in February of 1782. But it is also possible the ship sailed from London sometime in mid-December of 1781, headed for the American Colonies. I'd like you to verify when and where it sailed."

"'The *Albatross*,'" read Lovejoy, fingering the paper.

"The Board of Trade should have the information you require. I can go there this afternoon." He glanced up. "I take it this is related in some way to the deaths of Bishop Francis Prescott, the Reverend Earnshaw, and Sir Nigel?"

Sebastian felt a rare suggestion of heat touch his cheeks. "Yes. But I'd appreciate it if you could keep whatever information you discover confidential."

Sir Henry gave one of his jerky little bows. "You may, of course, rely upon my utmost discretion."

"I know," said Sebastian, turning toward the door. "Thank you."

"I'm not entirely certain I understand this continuing fascination of yours with America," said Sir Henry, stopping him.

Sebastian turned. "You don't find it curious, the way the events surrounding both Prescott men's deaths keep circling back to the Colonies?"

The magistrate shrugged. "Most men of affairs in London have ties to America. I would imagine your own father has had dealings with the Colonies."

Sebastian blinked, and kept his peace.

"Personally," continued Lovejoy, "I find the Bishop's recent encounter with Jack Slade far more telling."

"Jack Slade was locked up in a watch house here in London the night Sir Nigel disappeared."

"True. But he could easily have had an accomplice who committed the actual murder for him."

Sebastian shook his head. "If I were going to kill the man I held responsible for the death of my entire family, I'd want to watch him die. And I'd want to make certain he knew exactly *why* he was dying."

The magistrate looked oddly pinched, as if the flesh

had suddenly stretched taut across the features of his face. He cleared his throat and glanced away. "Yes . . . well . . . perhaps. But you must admit that the reappearance of Slade in the Bishop's life at just such a time is curious."

"I won't deny that," said Sebastian.

Half an hour later, Sebastian was rubbing gray ashes into his hair in his dressing room at Brook Street when Tom appeared in the doorway.

"I 'ear yer lordship is goin' to Chelsea this mornin'," said the tiger, his arm resting rakishly in a sling, his voice strained by the effort to appear nonchalant. "Ye want I should bring the curricle 'round?"

Sebastian glanced over at him and frowned. "What are you doing up?"

"Dr. Gibson said I could."

"Getting out of bed and going back to work are two different things."

"But I'm gonna be fit fer nothin' but Bedlam, sittin' around 'ere with nothin' to do! *Please*, gov'nor."

Sebastian wrapped a cheap black cravat around his neck. "I fear your sanity must be sacrificed to a higher cause—in this case, your health."

Tom's scowl deepened. "Never say you're taking *Giles*?" Tom had a long-standing rivalry with Sebastian's middle-aged groom.

"No, I'm not taking Giles. I have no intention of arriving in Chelsea in a gentleman's curricle. I'm taking a hackney."

"A hackney? Gov'nor, no!"

"A hackney," repeated Sebastian, slapping the false padding around his stomach. "I've no doubt Mr. Brum-

mell would sympathize with your revulsion. But then, the
Beau would also swoon at the sight of this neckcloth and
coat, so there's no hope for it, is there? If I'm recognized
by any of my acquaintances, my reputation is ruined."

Rather than smile, the tiger simply looked troubled.
"The thing is, ye see, there's this cove what's been 'ang-
ing round the 'ouse, like 'e's watching for ye. I seen 'im
last night, and agin this mornin'. Early."

Sebastian crossed to the window and carefully parted
the drapes. "Where?"

" 'E's not there now." Tom dug the toe of one boot into
the carpet. "Even if ye take a hackney, I could still come
with ye—"

"No."

"Ye need somebody t' watch yer back."

Sebastian gave a sharp laugh. "In Chelsea?"

"Ye never know—"

Sebastian slid his dagger into the hidden sheath of his
boot. "I'll be fine."

Much to her father's disgust, Hero Jarvis spent a good part
of that morning at London House, investigating church
records. What she discovered was curious. Very curious.

She devoted several hours during the afternoon to
accompanying her mother on a tour of cloth warehouses
and mantua makers. Lady Jarvis returned to Berkeley
Square tired, but happily laden down with bandboxes
and piles of brown paper–wrapped packages. At first she
protested she had no appetite, but Hero managed to
coax her into drinking tea and eating some cakes. Then,
when her mother went to lie down for a rest, Hero ordered her carriage brought 'round, and set off with her
maid for Tanfield Hill.

Chapter 32

*B*y the time Sebastian paid off his hackney outside the Old Bun House at the end of Jew's Row in Chelsea, the rain had started up again, a slow but steady drizzle that dripped off the nearest roofs and ran in the gutters. Ducking beneath the colonnade that projected out over the foot pavement, he stood for a moment, his gaze assessing the empty wet street before he entered the fragrant interior of the Old Bun House.

The girl behind the counter was young and pretty, with honey-colored hair and dimpled cheeks. Sebastian bought a couple of buns and lingered, talking to her of the endless rain and the mud and the high price of corn. He complimented her on the buns, which were justly famous throughout the metropolitan area. Then he said casually, "I've come to Chelsea to see a Dr. McCain. Dr. Daniel McCain, lives in Cheyne Walk. Do you know him?"

"Oh, yes," said the girl, slipping the tray of buns back onto its rack. "He and his missus come in here regular-like, in the evenings. Buy a pocketful of buns, they do, then go for a walk along the river."

"He's been in Chelsea long?"

"Long as I can remember," she said, which didn't ex-

actly mean much, given that she didn't look much above
fourteen or fifteen. "He's nice," she volunteered. "So's his
lady. They always buy extra buns to give to the cottagers'
children, down near the waterworks." For nearly a hundred years, the Chelsea Water Works had supplied water
to Westminster and much of the West End, two powerful
steam engines now doing the work of the old waterwheels
to lift water from a series of river-fed ponds into the pipes.

"The McCains have children of their own, do they?"
asked Sebastian, nibbling on one of the buns.

The girl's smile dimmed. "Oh, they've had four or five
babies, at least. But the poor wee things never seem to
live more than a day or two."

Sebastian stared out the paned window at the rain
dripping off the edge of the colonnade's roof, at the
muddy fetlocks of the team hauling a loaded wagon toward the river. A horrible possibility had begun to form
in his mind, a confluence of events and interests and circumstances that he found profoundly, personally disquieting. He said, "Have you ever seen the Bishop of
London around here?"

The girl gaped at the shift in topic. "You mean him as
got killed last Tuesday?" She cast a quick glance left and
right, as if verifying that no one could overhear. They
were alone in the shop, but she still leaned over the
counter, her voice dropping confidingly. "He was in here
just last Monday, you know."

"The Bishop of London?"

"That's right. The day before he was murdered."

"Was he ever in here before?"

Her eyes suddenly widened. "That's why you're here,
isn't it? Why you're asking me these questions. Are
you . . ." She cast another conspiratorial glance around

and gave a little shiver of excitement. "Are you a Bow Street Runner?"

"Shh," said Sebastian, putting a finger to his lips. "Don't tell anyone."

Cheyne Walk proved to be a cobbled lane faced by a single row of redbrick houses overlooking the river. Trimmed in white and varying in size from modest to prosperous, most looked to date back to the days of Queen Anne. Only a low stone embankment shadowed by an avenue of dripping limes and chestnuts separated the terrace and its narrow lane from the water.

Plying the knocker at Number Eleven, Sebastian expected to find only Mrs. McCain at home at this hour. But when he introduced himself to the young housemaid as Mr. Simon Taylor, he was quickly escorted to the parlor, where both Mrs. McCain and her stout, mustachioed physician husband awaited him—the same stout, mustachioed physician Sebastian had seen not a week before escorting Miss Jarvis around the Royal Hospital.

He'd discovered long ago that he didn't need to actually say he was from Bow Street; all he had to do was look the part and say he was investigating a murder, and most people assumed the connection. "Mr. Taylor," said the physician's wife, a smile trembling on her lips as she extended her small white hand. "How may we be of assistance to you?"

She was a tiny woman, well under five feet and small-boned, with soft brown hair and large gray eyes fringed with thick dark lashes. She looked to be about thirty, with an air of quiet sadness underlined by the half mourning of her gray, high-necked gown.

"Thank you for agreeing to see me," said Sebastian,

his voice and manner carefully wiped clean of any trace of the West End and the Earl's son.

Dr. McCain's eyes narrowed with puzzlement. "Have we met before, Mr. Taylor?"

"I don't believe so," said Sebastian, adjusting the modest tails of his brown coat as he took the seat indicated by his hostess. "I beg your pardon for the intrusion, but this shouldn't take long."

"You are investigating the death of Bishop Prescott?" said McCain, taking a seat opposite him.

"Yes. I understand the Bishop visited you and Mrs. McCain last Monday?"

"In the afternoon," said McCain.

"Do you mind if I ask why?"

There was a moment's uncomfortable silence, while husband and wife exchanged glances. It was Mrs. McCain who answered, saying quietly to her husband, "I don't mind, Daniel." To Sebastian, she said, "In the past eight years, we have buried seven babies. None lived longer than a month."

"I am sorry," said Sebastian. "Please believe me when I say that anything you choose to tell me from here on out will be treated with the strictest confidence."

She nodded, her slender throat working as she swallowed. "Thank you. You see, I have always wanted—" She glanced at her husband and corrected herself, "Dr. McCain and I always wanted very much to have a family, to have children. But God in his infinite wisdom has not seen fit to allow our own children to live. So we thought . . . It seemed perhaps that He was telling us He wanted us to . . ." Her voice trailed away.

Sebastian said, "I take it Bishop Prescott spoke to you of adopting a child?"

"That's right," said McCain. "The usual scenario. A young gentlewoman not in a position to keep her child . . ." He cleared his throat in obvious embarrassment at discussing so delicate a topic. "You know how these things are."

A gust of wind pattered the rain against the windowpanes as thunder rumbled in the distance. Somehow, Sebastian managed to keep his voice casual, disinterested. "And has the child been born already?"

"Oh, no," said Mrs. McCain. "The child is not expected until sometime late this coming winter. But the mother is particularly anxious to have the necessary arrangements in place well ahead of time. As are we."

Sebastian had no need to silently count off the months to know that if he and Miss Jarvis had indeed conceived a child during those moments of despair in the subterranean vaults of Somerset House, such a child would be born late in the coming winter.

As if from a long distance, he heard McCain clear his throat. "The idea was for Mrs. McCain to go away for a few months to visit a sister in Bath when the appropriate time came, and return with the child."

Sebastian thrust to his feet and reached for his hat and gloves. "I understand. Please accept my apologies for intruding on your privacy."

Mrs. McCain rose quickly beside him. "Won't you stay for tea, Mr. Taylor?"

"What? Oh, no, thank you." Sebastian's fingers tightened on the brim of his hat. Then, because he knew the occasion required it, he added stiffly, "My congratulations on the coming adoption of the child."

"But that's just it," said Mrs. McCain, looking stricken. "We don't actually know the gentlewoman involved. We were never meant to know her. Bishop Prescott was the only link between us. Now that he is dead . . ." She lifted one hand, only to let it flutter helplessly back to her side.

"That is unfortunate," said Sebastian. Although in truth, he found the thought of a child of his being raised by this stout, stuffy physician revolting. He knew an overwhelming urge to storm back to London, hunt down Miss Jarvis, and shake the truth out of her. "I've no doubt another such opportunity will arise in the future. Thank you for your help."

"I was just on my way back to the hospital," said Dr. McCain, following Sebastian out into the hall. "Walk with me for a ways, Mr. Taylor?"

"Of course," said Sebastian, chafing at the delay while he waited for the physician to outfit himself with great-coat, hat, gloves, and umbrella. "Please accept my apologies for any distress I may have caused Mrs. McCain."

"It's been a severe disappointment to her. I'll not deny it."

"I would imagine that as a physician you must come into contact with many such cases."

McCain sighed. "No doubt that's true of most physicians. Unfortunately, I work with old men." The housemaid opened the door to a solid rain, and McCain paused to put up his umbrella. "Charlotte—Mrs. McCain—is so desperate for a child she'd be more than happy to pick up a foundling from the gutter, but . . ."

"But?" prompted Sebastian as they stepped off the shallow porch into the downpour.

McCain turned their steps toward the hospital. "Well, let's just say I've bred enough horses and dogs in my day to know that characteristics such as temperament and intelligence are as likely as blue eyes and brown hair to be passed down from sire and dam. If I'm to adopt a child, I want to know something about the stable. The Bishop was able to vouch for the character of this babe's mother and father. Reassured me both were young and healthy, and of good moral fiber. Superior in every way."

Sebastian stared off through the rain, to where a wherryman in an oil slicker and a slouch hat was unloading his fare at the base of a set of wooden steps leading down to the wind-whipped river. "Prescott never said anything to give you some clue as to the identity of the child's mother—or its father?"

McCain glanced at him in surprise. "Surely you don't think the unborn child could have something to do with the Bishop's death?"

"I don't see how. But I honestly don't know."

The physician shook his head. "I'm sorry, but he was very careful not to give us any particulars."

"I understand." They had reached the edge of the hospital's courtyard by now, the redbrick walls and white columns of the facade half obscured by the driving rain. Sebastian drew up. "Thank you again for your help."

The physician frowned, stopping beside him. "You know, I'd swear I've met you before. It's something about the eyes . . ."

Sebastian swiped the forearm of his rough coat across his wet face. "You don't see many men with yellow eyes, I'll admit."

"True, true," said McCain. "Although I met a highwayman with yellow eyes, once. Held me up and robbed me on Hounslow Heath, not three years ago."

"I trust you're not suggesting I might be a highwayman?"

The physician laughed. "Hardly. The man who robbed me was younger than you. Dark-haired, and lean."

"I was dark haired and young once myself. And lean."

McCain laughed again. "Weren't we all? It's odd, though, because I was thinking about that highwayman just the other day. Someone else must have recently reminded me of him . . ." His voice trailed off, and he shrugged. "It will come to me."

"Perhaps it will." Sebastian took a step back, boots splashing in the puddling water. "Thank you again for your time."

"I wish I could have been of more assistance. He was a good man, Bishop Prescott."

"Yes, he was."

Head bent against the downpour, Sebastian turned to walk rapidly toward the road. But when he reached the footpath and glanced back, he saw McCain still standing beneath the portico of the east pensioner's ward, his umbrella held aloft as he stared thoughtfully into the rain.

A hackney loomed out of the mist, harness jingling, the rawboned bay between the poles snorting as the jarvey pulled up in response to Sebastian's raised hand.

"Where to, gov'nor?" shouted the jarvey, a big, broad-shouldered Cockney with a slouch hat pulled low over a beard-grizzled face.

"London. Brook Street."

"Aye, gov'nor." The hackney rolled forward as Sebastian leapt up and slammed the door behind him.

The inside of the carriage was damp, the straw on the floor old and foul, the ancient leather seats cracked. Sebastian settled gingerly into a corner, his arms crossed, his chin sinking to his chest as he listened to the rain drumming on the roof of the old carriage, the splash of the horse's hooves as the hackney swung away from the curb.

Lost in a swirl of troubled thoughts, he was only dimly aware of the hackney lurching and bumping over the rutted road, of the air growing heavy with the stench of burning coal. He heard the hiss of steam, the roar of engines, and looked up suddenly.

Two tall, narrow towers loomed out of the rain, some four or five stories high and linked by a heavy timber scaffolding. Built of brick, the engine houses crowned a nearby small rise. He could see the sullen gleam of a series of ponds, the rain-pocked expanse of a channel that stretched back toward the river. And suddenly, he knew where he was: the Chelsea Water Works.

He was reaching up to signal the jarvey when the hackney came to a plunging halt and a heavy hand jerked open the door.

"Welcome, *Captain* Viscount," said Obadiah Slade, his fist tightening around a stout cudgel.

Chapter 33

Surging forward, Sebastian gripped the scarred wood framing the ancient carriage door and levered up off the tattered seat to swing both feet through the open doorway.

Driven hard by the momentum of the swing and packing Sebastian's full weight, his boots caught Obadiah square in the chest. He staggered back with a grunt, his scarred, shaven head jerking, his powerful arms flailing as he fought to keep his balance in the mud.

Rain pounded on the old wooden roof of the hackney carriage, slapped into the dull, muddy surface of the ponds that stretched out into the mist. Sebastian jerked the knife from his boot and leapt from the carriage.

He landed in the wet, grassy verge, knife held low, body crouched in a street fighter's stance. He could hear the roar of the engines from the nearby waterworks, the hiss of steam, and the splat of a pair of rough boots landing in the muddy lane as the hackney driver dropped off the box behind him.

Sebastian tightened his grip on his knife, his breath coming hard and fast. He now had one man before him, one man at his back. He heard the whistle of a whip cutting through the air and threw himself sideways, the tip of the driver's horsewhip flicking across his temple.

"You bloody bastard," swore Sebastian, swiping the sleeve of his rough coat at the warm wetness spilling into his eyes.

The jarvey lashed at him again. But Sebastian was already moving in on him. Throwing up his left arm, Sebastian caught the blow on his forearm, the lash wrapping around his wrist like a hot wire as he pivoted to drive the blade of his dagger deep into the jarvey's chest.

Eyes wide with bewilderment, blood spilling from his mouth as his jaw sagged, the driver dropped heavily to his knees, then pitched forward onto his face in the mud before Sebastian had time to yank his dagger free.

"Lost yer knife, have ye?" Obadiah gave a harsh, ringing laugh. "What ye gonna do now? Hmm, Captain Viscount?" He slapped the cudgel against his palm, lips peeling back from his teeth in a grin.

Sebastian still had the lash of the driver's whip wrapped around his left arm. Now, his gaze on the other man's rawboned, scarred face, he closed his right fist on the thong some three feet closer to the handle and took two quick loops of the leather around his wrist.

Obadiah hawked up a mouthful of spittle and spat it into the mud at Sebastian's feet. "By the time I'm done wit' ye, yer own da ain't gonna recognize ye."

Stepping forward, he swung the cudgel at Sebastian's face, the heavy wood whistling through the air. Sebastian jerked the whip up, the leather thong held taut between both fists. The blow bounced off the whiplash, sending shock waves down Sebastian's arms and throwing Obadiah off balance.

Kicking out, Sebastian knocked the big man's lead

foot out from beneath him. Obadiah went down hard, his right hand reflexively letting go of the cudgel to break his fall. Sebastian kicked again and the club went spinning through the rain to land with a plop in the muddy water of the pond lapping at the grassy verge beside the lane.

"*Ye bastard*," spat Obadiah. Wrapping his arms around Sebastian's legs, he brought him down like a roped calf.

Sebastian hit the muddy ground with a painful grunt. Scrabbling around, he kicked out to free himself from the other man's hold. Obadiah grabbed fistfuls of Sebastian's coat, and the two men rolled together across the grassy verge and down a gentle incline to hit the murky surface of the pond with a splash. Sebastian felt the cold water closing over him and barely had time to suck in one last breath before his head went under.

He fought his way to the surface, feet scrabbling for purchase on the silty, shifting bottom. He swung around, breath coming in quick gasps, eyes filmed with water and mud and blood as he scanned the churning, rain-pocked surface of the pond, its far banks obscured by a haze of mist mingling with steam from the pounding engines of the waterworks.

He swiped his wet sleeve across his face and heard Obadiah rise up behind him with an angry roar. Before he could spin around, a massive arm clamped around Sebastian's neck to slam him back against a chest as hard as one of the sides of beef hanging from a hook in Jack Slade's butcher shop.

Sebastian could hear his own blood surging in his ears, feel the meaty strength of the other man's forearm crushing his windpipe. He tried to pitch forward, but couldn't. With his last strength he lurched backward and felt the big man's feet shoot out from beneath him as his stance shifted on the treacherous, slippery bottom.

They both went under, the impact breaking them apart. Coming up fast, Sebastian staggered back toward the shore. He was about hip-deep in the water when Obadiah broke the surface, sputtering. Swinging around, Sebastian charged into him. Grabbing the lapels of the other man's coat, Sebastian pushed him back and down again, and watched with grim satisfaction as the muddy water closed over the massive, hard-jawed face, the man's eyes open and startled.

From somewhere he heard a shout, the sound of men splashing through mud and rain. Sebastian tightened his hold on Obadiah's coat and held him beneath the cold, muddy surface of the pond.

"Let him go!"

Rough hands closed on Sebastian's shoulders, loosening his grip. A red-bearded man with a wildly disordered neckcloth shoved his face into Sebastian's line of vision. "Wot the 'ell ye doin' there? Ye're gonna kill 'im."

Sebastian felt Obadiah slip from his grasp. Sebastian lurched after him, but two more men had appeared by now to lay hold of Sebastian. They dragged him back toward the shore, where the silent form of the jarvey lay stretched out in the mud beside the hackney.

The rain fell from the sky in a roar that mingled with the droning thunder of the steam engines. Breaking free of the men's hold, Sebastian swung around to look back at the pond. A white mist swirled across the still, empty water.

Obadiah had disappeared.

*   *   *

"The hackney belongs to a man by the name of Miles Buckley," said Sir Henry Lovejoy. He was standing in the doorway of Sebastian's dressing room, watching Sebastian wince as Calhoun applied a clean sticking plaster to the cut above Sebastian's eye. "A small, bandy-legged Liverpudlian of some sixty years of age."

"What does he have to say?" asked Sebastian, stretching to his feet. He was dressed in black evening knee breeches, black silk stockings, and a white silk waistcoat. Outside, the rain had finally begun to clear, the sun peeking from beneath the heavy clouds as it slipped below the horizon.

"Very little. He was found insensible from a blow to the head, in a lane behind the White Horse Inn, in Church Street."

Sebastian reached for a snowy white neckcloth. "Will he recover?"

"Oh, yes. A slight dent in his crown is all. He's a tough old codger."

Sebastian grunted, his chin held aloft as he adjusted the folds of his cravat.

Lovejoy said, "I believe your assailants must have followed you to Chelsea, then availed themselves of Mr. Buckley's hackney, leaving him incapacitated while they shadowed you from Cheyne Walk and waited until you were ready to depart for London."

"A scheme into which I stepped like a regular Johnny Flat."

Lovejoy cleared his throat. "Not exactly. The individual who was driving the hackney won't be waylaying any more fares. You killed him."

"Good."

"A coroner's inquest will be held, of course, but

there's no doubt his death will be found a simple case of self-defense. We've set the local constables to searching the ponds of the waterworks and the riverbank beyond, but Mr. Obidiah Slade appears to have made good his escape."

"He'll be back," said Sebastian, reaching for his coat.

Lovejoy cleared his throat again. "That's what I'm afraid of."

That night, Sebastian prowled the playgrounds of the *haut ton*. Moving purposefully from the theaters of Covent Garden to the glittering ballrooms and drawing rooms of Mayfair, he scanned the throngs of men in black silk and white linen, of women in sparkling jewels and shimmering evening gowns that slipped enticingly from bare shoulders. But the one woman he sought was not to be found.

He was in the flower-decked ballroom of a house on Cavendish Square belonging to the Duke of Isling, his gaze narrowed against the haze of hundreds of beeswax candles, when he heard a woman's familiar voice say, "Good heavens, it is you, Devlin. Bayard swore he'd seen you, but I'd hoped he was simply suffering the effects of too much of Isling's punch."

Sebastian turned to meet his sister's icy blue stare. "Hello, Amanda."

Amanda, Lady Wilcox, was a tall woman, thin and fair like their mother, although she looked too much like Hendon to have ever been pretty, even when she was young. Twelve years Sebastian's senior, she was in her early forties now. Even when they were children, she had never made the least effort to disguise her acute dislike of her youngest brother. Now, watching her lip curl, her nostrils flare with disdain, Sebastian found himself wondering if she had always known—or at least suspected—the ugly secrets swirling around his conception.

"I hear you're at it again," she said, her head turning as she let her gaze scan the crowded dance floor. She could bear to look at him for only a limited amount of time. "Involving yourself in the sordid details of a murder investigation, like some grubby little Bow Street Runner."

Following her gaze, Sebastian watched his niece, Stephanie Wilcox, coming down the set of the country dance on the arm of Lord Smallbone. Just finishing her first London Season at the age of eighteen, Stephanie was everything Amanda had never been: delicate and winsome and breathtakingly beautiful . . . and so much like Sebastian's long-vanished mother, Sophie, that it made his chest ache just to look at her.

Earlier in the Season there'd been talk of a match between the young Miss Wilcox and Smallbone. But no announcement had as yet been forthcoming, and Sebastian knew Amanda was growing anxious. "What's the matter, Amanda?" he said gently. "Worried I'll somehow scuttle my niece's chances of landing a good catch?"

He had the satisfaction of seeing an angry flush touch his sister's cheeks. "Don't be vulgar," she snapped. "Although I don't suppose you can help it."

"Oh? Why's that, Amanda?"

Her lips tightened into a thin line. Rather than answer, she simply turned and left him staring after her, and wondering what she knew, and how she knew it.

"An interesting display of sibling affection," said Miss Hero Jarvis, walking up to him. "Or lack thereof."

She wore a stunning sapphire blue gown of satin

trimmed with velvet ribbons, and was regarding him with her frank, faintly amused gray eyes.

"Definitely a 'lack thereof,'" he said drily. The country dance came to an end with a flourish, disgorging a wave of flushed and perspiring dancers upon them. "Here," he said, cupping a hand beneath her elbow to draw her away from the crush.

"I thought you made it a practice to avoid these functions," she said, gently removing her arm from his grasp.

"Actually, I was looking for you."

"Then you're fortunate to have found me. I'm here only because I was looking for Lord Quillian. The Duchess of Isling is his sister. Or didn't you know?"

"No," said Sebastian, who relied on his aunt Henrietta to remind him of the intricate familial ties that bound one member of the Upper Ten Thousand to the next. "And precisely why, Miss Jarvis, were you searching for Lord Quillian?"

"Did you never find it something of a coincidence that Reverend Earnshaw should have decided to demolish the charnel house on the north side of St. Margaret's and discovered Sir Nigel's body at just this moment?"

"No," Sebastian admitted. "But you're right; it is something of a coincidence that it should all happen now, just when the Bishop was being considered for elevation to the Archbishopric of Canterbury—and preparing to present a Slavery Abolition Act to Parliament."

"You told me once that when it comes to murder, you don't believe in coincidences."

"I did?"

"You did. So I decided to drive out to Tanfield Hill this afternoon, to offer my condolences to Mrs. Earnshaw on the sad loss of her husband."

Sebastian turned to stare at her. "Really? And did she believe you were sincere?"

"She did. You're not the only one who can playact, you know."

"I beg your pardon?"

"You know full well what I mean, *Mr. Taylor*. The woman was upset, obviously, but not disconsolate. I had no difficulty encouraging her to talk about the construction work on the church."

"And?"

"She said the Reverend had been wanting to make the changes for years, only he'd been frustrated by a lack of funds—and by a lack of cooperation from the Bishop himself."

"Interesting. But not exactly damning."

"No, but listen to this: According to Mrs. Earnshaw, the Reverend was very excited because he was able to secure a private donor. After much wrestling with his conscience, he decided to simply go ahead with the construction without informing London House."

"Let me guess. The private donor was Quillian."

Her face fell. "You knew?"

"No. But it was the obvious conclusion, given that you're here looking for him." He studied the dark, full sweep of her lashes, the graceful line of her long neck and bare white shoulders. "Tell me, Miss Jarvis: Why have you involved yourself in the Bishop's death?"

She looked away. "I told you. He was my friend."

"Are you certain that's the only reason?"

She gave a polite laugh. "What other reason could there be?"

"I thought it might have something to do with the

interesting interview I had this afternoon with Dr. Daniel McCain and his wife."

He had the satisfaction of seeing her blanch, although she recovered almost immediately. Miss Jarvis, it seemed, was very good at what she called "playacting." Lifting one eyebrow in an expression that was hauntingly evocative of her father, she said airily, "Dr. McCain? You mean from the Chelsea Royal Hospital? What, pray tell, is your interest in him?"

"I've discovered the Bishop of London called upon Dr. McCain and his wife the afternoon before his death." Sebastian paused, watching her reaction. "Did you know?"

"No," she said smoothly. "Although I'm not surprised, given that it was Bishop Prescott who first encouraged me to look into the dreadful situation at the Royal Hospital—and who introduced me to Dr. McCain."

"Really? That's interesting. Because it seems the good Bishop traveled down to Chelsea last Monday on a different errand entirely."

"Oh?" Her smile was that of someone who was politely puzzled. But there was a shadow of something that looked very much like fear glittering in her eyes. "And what was that, my lord?"

He met her gaze and held it, his voice pitched low. "I think you know, Miss Jarvis."

Chapter 34

*S*he held herself very still, her lips parting as she drew in a quick, steadying breath. But her awe-inspiring composure never slipped. "I can't think what you mean, my lord Devlin."

"Perhaps we should continue this conversation someplace more private," he suggested. "May I escort you down to dinner, Miss Jarvis?"

"I think not." She cast a significant glance about. "We do, however, seem to be attracting an inordinate amount of attention. It might be better if you were to invite me to dance."

"*Dance?*" he repeated in something between shock and horror.

"Why, yes." She gave him an icy smile and extended her hand. "Thank you, my lord."

There was nothing for it but to escort her onto the floor, where two long lines were forming.

They faced each other across a space of perhaps six feet, he in the gentlemen's line, she in the ladies'. She said, "You are entirely wrong in your supposition, you know."

The chamber orchestra struck up, the sweet notes of

the violin barely filtering through the chattering roar that filled the ballroom. The row of gentlemen bowed. The ladies sank into gracious curtsies. Sebastian had to wait until it was their turn to come together in the center of the line to whisper, "I hardly think the dance floor is the place to be having this conversation."

Her smile widened. "Actually, I find the setting quite appropriate, under the circumstances."

They circled each other back-to-back, turning counterclockwise on the jeté. He said, "You know I cannot speak freely."

"Really?" She threw him an evil smile over her shoulder as she swayed away. "And what would you say if you could, my lord?"

He was forced by the movement of the dance to swing away from her, a stout man in exaggerated shirt points hissing in warning when Sebastian would have turned clockwise rather than counterclockwise. He could only glare at her from across the floor until the dance brought them together again.

He said, "You told me there were no repercussions."

She slid her foot daintily to the right, bending and then rising as she drew the other up to it in a graceful glissade *dessous*. "So I did."

He moved behind her in the chassé. "Would you have me believe that your"—he broke off, searching for an appropriate word—"*situation* was not the subject of the Bishop's visit to the McCains?"

They passed, right shoulders together, her brows drawing together in mock confusion. "My 'situation'? Whatever do you mean, my lord Devlin?"

"Do not play the fool with me, Miss Jarvis. I know you are anything but."

She spun around, foot pointing straight down in an elegant *sissone*. "Then you should have known better than to approach me in such a milieu, shouldn't you?"

He needed to be moving on. The stout idiot in the high shirt points was hissing at him again. Sebastian gritted his teeth. "Do you ride in Hyde Park tomorrow morning?"

She swayed away from him. "I think not."

"Then when may we continue this conversation?"

She dipped gracefully, moving sideways. "I see no reason to continue it at any time. Your supposition—if I understand you—is incorrect."

He had to wait until they came together again to growl, "Would you tell me if it were correct?"

She swung around with a curving *ronde de jambe*. "Of course not."

The music ended, Miss Jarvis sinking with the other ladies into a deep curtsy. "Good evening, my lord," she said, and left him there, at the edge of the dance floor, feeling frustrated and angry and deeply disquieted.

Lord Quillian was parting from a group of friends in what was known as the Jerusalem Chamber of Brooks's gentlemen's club when Sebastian came upon him.

"Lord Devlin," said the aging exquisite, resplendent in a silk evening cape and chapeau bras. "If you've come to join in the fleecing of this poor repentant sinner, you're too late. I've decided to retire for the evening while my estates are still unencumbered."

There was a chorus of good-natured ribaldry from his friends. Sebastian said, "Bad round of luck at the tables?"

"Let's just say, not the kind I care to continue." Quillian cast a critical eye toward the night sky. "This dreadful rain has finally ceased, has it?"

"So it seems."

"Good. Walk with me a ways, my lord?"

"You find yourself suddenly inspired by a desire for my company, do you?" said Sebastian as the two men left the club.

Quillian swung his ebony walking stick back and forth between two limp fingers. "Hardly. But I am curious to hear how the investigation into the murder of Bishop Prescott is progressing."

"Really? And what is your interest in the matter?"

Quillian sniffed. "I know perfectly well I have been identified as a suspect. I'm hoping to hear you've begun to focus your inquiries elsewhere."

"Quite the opposite, actually."

Quillian's hand tightened on the silver head of his walking stick, freezing it in midswing. "And what, precisely, is that supposed to mean?"

"It means I've discovered the identity of the mysterious benefactor who was funding Reverend Earnshaw's construction work on the church of St. Margaret's."

"Oh. That." Quillian twirled his walking stick in a graceful arc that set it once more to swinging back and forth.

"Yes. That."

They continued in silence for a moment, their footfalls echoing in the dark, wet street. Sebastian said, "It does rather beg the question: *Why?*"

"I suppose it does, doesn't it?"

Sebastian gave a soft laugh. "I take it you knew Sir Nigel had been murdered in the crypt of St. Margaret's and left there to molder all these years?"

"Knew it? Hardly. But I had developed a theory, yes."

"You think Francis Prescott killed his own brother for

the inheritance? An inheritance he then lost when his nephew was born?"

"It seems the obvious conclusion." Quillian glanced sideways at him. "Wouldn't you agree?"

"I honestly don't know."

Quillian grunted and kept walking.

Sebastian said, "What were you hoping to accomplish?"

"I should think that would be rather obvious. If I were correct—if Sir Nigel's moldering body was lying in that crypt—then suspicion would naturally fall upon the priest responsible for sealing off the crypt in the first place."

"Bishop Prescott."

"Bishop Prescott," agreed the Baron.

"The idea being to keep the Bishop so busy defending himself against the ensuing accusations of fratricide that he would have no time to continue pushing his Slavery Abolition Act through Parliament?"

"Something like that, yes."

"Seems a bit of a long shot."

A tight smile split the aging exquisite's face. "I am a gambler."

Sebastian said, "True. Although it occurs to me that the odds would shorten considerably if you knew for certain that Sir Nigel was indeed moldering down in that crypt."

"I hardly see how I could have known that. Unless, of course, you're suggesting I killed Sir Nigel and left him there myself?" Quillian pulled a face. "It's an interesting theory; I'll give you that." He walked on a few paces, then said, "The thing is, I had no reason to kill Sir Nigel. I barely knew the man. Dreadful bad ton, you know."

"You were both members of the Hellfire Club, were you not?"

The exquisite's eyes narrowed. "My dear lord Devlin, the Hellfire Club was hardly exclusive. It counted *hundreds* of members."

"Not in its inner circle. What were they called?"

"The Apostles," said Quillian. He sighed. "Much as it pains me to admit it, the truth is that I myself was not actually a member of that exclusive inner circle. At the time, I was but a poor second son just a few years down from Oxford and struggling to make my way in the world."

"Really? Doing what?"

Lord Quillian drew up beside a couple of lounging sedan-chair bearers who immediately scrambled to their poles. "Oh, this and that," he said, waving one white-gloved hand through the air in a vague gesture. "Now I fear I find I have exceeded my tolerance for the night air." His walking stick clenched in one fist, he stepped nimbly into the chair. "Good evening to you, my lord."

A cool gust of wind fluttered the lapels of Sebastian's evening coat and buffeted him with the odors of the city, the pungent scents of wet paving and hot lamp oil mixing with a faint, inescapable whiff of sewage. He stood for a moment watching the sedan-chair bearers heft their burden and start off at a trot.

Then he turned toward Brook Street, his solitary footsteps echoing in the stillness of the night.

Tuesday, 14 July 1812

The next morning, Hero was in the library, surrounded by piles of books and papers, when her father walked in the door.

"Good God. At it again, are you?" He picked up a bound copy of dispatches and frowned. "What's this?"

She set aside her pen. "I'm compiling a list of all the men who were in the Foreign Office or close to the King thirty years ago."

Jarvis's eyes narrowed with amusement. "Looking for Alcibiades, are you?"

"Yes."

"Think he murdered your Bishop, as well as the Bishop's brother?"

"I think it's possible."

"Really? I think he's dead."

"Because you never found him?"

"Yes."

"Then why do you think Francis Prescott was murdered in the same crypt as his brother?"

"Maybe someone has a sense of humor."

"I don't see anything the least bit funny about it," said Hero indignantly.

Jarvis frowned. "I know. That's what worries me."

Sebastian was looking over a report from his estate agent when a polite knock sounded at his front door. The day had dawned fine and clear, and he'd thrown open the windows to a warm breeze and the scent of fresh bread baking in the shop down the street. He heard a murmur of voices in the entry, and a moment later Morey ushered Sir Henry Lovejoy into his presence.

"Sir Henry," said Sebastian, rising to his feet. "An unexpected pleasure. Please have a seat."

His round hat gripped tightly in both hands, the little magistrate gave a jerky bow and cleared his throat. "Thank you, but no. I can't stay long."

Sebastian watched Sir Henry reach into an inner pocket and withdraw a packet of worn, yellowing papers. And he knew, from the little magistrate's somber demeanor, that his world was about to change forever.

"I visited the Board of Trade yesterday," said Sir Henry. "No ship named the *Albatross* sailed from Portsmouth in either January or February of 1782. However, an *Albatross* did set forth from London on the twentieth of December, 1781, bound for New York." Lovejoy laid the packet on the edge of Sebastian's desk. The two men's gazes met. Lovejoy looked away first.

A heavy silence fell. Sebastian reached to take up the *Albatross*'s passenger list, the ancient parchment crackling as he spread it open. A quick glance through the names of the passengers was all it took. *Charles, Lord Jarvis. Sir Nigel Prescott. A. St. Cyr, the Earl of Hendon.*

He looked up. "This is the original passenger list."

Lovejoy cleared his throat again. "Yes. I seem to have carried it away with me somehow. I trust I can leave it to you to see that it is kept safe?"

Sebastian nodded, his jaw clenched tight. There was no doubt in his mind that Lovejoy had understood immediately the significance of what he had found. It was a moment before Sebastian managed to say, "Thank you."

The magistrate gave another of his awkward bows. "My lord," he said, and turned away.

He paused at the door to glance back, as if intending to say something more. Then he must have reconsidered, for he merely settled his hat on his baldhead and kept walking.

Chapter 35

*I*n his memories, Sebastian's mother was always laughing. A beautiful woman with silken gold hair and sparkling eyes, she had set out for a few hours' sailing one brilliant summer's day the year Sebastian was eleven. She'd kissed him good-bye and teased him gently, the way she so often did. When her friends' yacht pulled away from the dock, he'd stood and watched her, smiling as the sunlight gleamed for one last moment on the strange bluestone-and-silver necklace she wore so often around her neck.

He had never seen her again.

Drowned, they said. But Sebastian hadn't believed them. Day after day he'd climbed to the cliffs south of town to stare out over the churning waves of the Channel and watch, waiting for her to come back. Not until seventeen years later did he learn he'd been right that summer. Sophia, the Countess of Hendon, hadn't drowned. She'd simply sailed away, leaving a husband, a married daughter, the graves of her two dead sons ... and Sebastian.

For seventeen years he'd lived with the lie of her death. Now he found himself wondering, *How many lies*

can there be? How many lies could obscure the funda-
mental truths of one man's existence?

After Lovejoy left, Sebastian stood for a time fingering the *Albatross*'s passenger list. He poured himself a
drink, raised the glass to his lips. Only, rather than taste
it, he turned and hurled the glass at the cold hearth in
a savage shattering of crystal and pungent, spilled
brandy.

Then he went in search of his mother's husband.

He found the Earl of Hendon in the chambers of the
Chancellor of the Exchequer in Downing Street. He was
standing beside a bookcase, head bowed, a heavy tome
open in his hands as if he were looking something up.

"We need to talk," said Sebastian.

Hendon raised his head, jaw set with annoyance at
the interruption. "Really, Devlin; if you—"

Sebastian sent the *Albatross*'s passenger list spinning
through the air to land with a soft thump on the open
pages of Hendon's book. "Now."

Setting aside the volume he held, Hendon unfolded
the packet, the aged pages crackling in his hands. He
studied it for a moment, then carefully folded the papers
again with a hand that was no longer steady. "I'll get my
hat," he said, and turned away.

Sebastian barely waited until they'd reached the deserted paths and flower beds of the old Privy Garden
before demanding explosively, "*Why?* Why did you do
it?"

He'd been afraid the Earl meant to persist in his
lies. But even Hendon must have realized the time for
denials was past. He walked with his hands clasped be-

hind his back, his chin sunk low between his shoulders. He looked suddenly older than Sebastian remembered him being, and very tired. "You mean, why didn't I repudiate you when you were born? Is that what you're asking?"

"Yes."

"And proclaim myself a cuckold to the world? Not bloody likely." Hendon squinted up at the spreading branches of the ash trees lining the avenue, pale green leaves trembling against a clear blue sky. His jaw hardened. "I was enraged; I won't deny it. What man would not be? But I agreed to raise you as my own. I had two strong, healthy sons. No one ever expected you to be in a position to inherit."

No one ever expected you to inherit.

Sebastian knew a bitter welling of disbelief, fed by rage and a disconcerting sense of being a stranger to himself. "And my real father . . . Who was he?"

"I don't know."

Sebastian stared at the Earl's familiar, craggy profile and wondered if it was a lie. One more lie, piled atop so many others. "What about Amanda? Does she know who he was?"

Hendon threw him a quick, sideways glance. "She may. I don't know. We've never spoken of it. Although it's always been my suspicion she knew far more than a girl her age should of her mother's activities."

"She does know I'm not your son?"

"Yes."

"So the two of you . . . You *both* knew Kat and I were not sister and brother. Yet you let us think—" Sebastian choked, and it was a moment before he could continue. "*In the name of God*, how *could* you?"

Hendon swiped the air with one big hand, his features hardening into a mask of stubborn determination. "I've spent the last twenty-nine years of my life hiding the truth from you. Do you seriously think I would suddenly give it all away? So that you could ruin yourself by contracting a disastrous marriage with a woman of the stage?"

Sebastian threw back his head, his harsh laugh startling a nearby pigeon that rose up with a cry of alarm, wings beating the air in a frantic whirl. "My God, that's rich. Kat is your *daughter*, while I . . . I'm just the illegitimate son of God only knows who. One would think you'd actually *encourage* the match. Then my sons really would be your grandsons—only through Kat, rather than me."

A muscle jumped along Hendon's clenched jaw. "You are my son in the eyes of the world and before the law. I named you that nearly thirty years ago. *Pater est quem nuptiae demonstrant.* Nothing has changed."

"That's where you're wrong," said Sebastian, the shells of the walk crunching beneath his boots as he drew up abruptly. "Everything has changed. Everything."

And he turned and walked off into the trees.

Sebastian sat in one of the high-backed pews that crowded the round nave of the Temple, his eyes half closed as he studied the mail-clad effigy of a medieval knight on the pavement before him. Once, when he was twenty-one and Kat but sixteen, they had come here, to the ancient church of the Knights Templar and pledged their love to each other forever.

He heard the whisper of the door quietly opening and closing, heard her footsteps cross the pavement toward

him, breathed in the sweet scent of her as Kat slipped
into the seat beside him.

He said, "How did you know where to find me?"

A soft smile touched her lips. "I'll admit this isn't the
first place I looked."

The urge to take her into his arms was so overwhelming he had to clench his fists around the back of the pew
before him. He said, "You talked to Hendon?"

"He came to see me." She rested her own hand atop
one of his. "I'm so sorry, Sebastian."

He let his head fall back, his throat stretching tight as
he looked up at the whitewashed plaster ceiling. "I'll not
deny it's a bit of a shock, learning I'm not exactly who
I've always thought I was, but—"

"Sebastian . . . No." She shifted so that she could grip
his right hand between both of hers. "You're still the
same man you have always been. Sebastian St. Cyr, Viscount Devlin. And one day you will be the Earl of Hendon."

"I don't think so," he said evenly.

Her lips parted as she drew in a quick breath. "What
are you saying? You wouldn't— Oh, God, Sebastian . . .
You wouldn't go away?"

"I've thought about it."

"You couldn't do that to Hendon."

He brought his gaze to her face. "Oh, really?"

"He loves you—"

Sebastian made a deprecating gesture with his free
hand.

"No," she said. "You know it's true. I don't think he
wanted to love you. But how many of us can will our affections?"

When he simply continued to stare at her, she said, "You know it's true, Sebastian. Hendon could have told you the truth at any time these last eighteen years. But he didn't, for your sake. He knew what it would do to you."

"What it would do to me?" Sebastian repeated. "How about what his lies did to me—did to us both? If he had told the truth ten months ago, you would never have married Yates and I would never have—" He broke off abruptly.

Her brows drew together in a frown and she shook her head, not understanding. "Never . . . what, Sebastian?"

Freeing his hand from her grip, he brought it up to touch her face, his fingertips sliding across her wet cheek. He hadn't realized she was crying, the silent teardrops falling one after another down her face.

He wanted to say, *Come away with me, Kat. I love you and need you like I have never needed you before. Come away with me to a new land, a land where our pasts do not define us, where we can both be whoever we make ourselves*. Except . . .

Except that nine months ago she had made a promise to Russell Yates, a promise she would not go back on now, simply to grasp at her own happiness. While he had obligations of his own, to Hero Jarvis, and to the child they may have conceived in those moments of terror and impending death beneath the ruined gardens of Somerset House.

He felt it again, that gut-churning surge of despair and rage. "I will never forgive him. Never."

"You must, Sebastian." She brought his hand to her

mouth, pressed a kiss against his palm. "Not just for his sake, but for your own."

He drew her to him, her tears wetting his neck, his fingers tangling in the dark, familiar fall of her hair. "I can't," he whispered. "I can't."

Chapter 36

"*M*y lord?"

Sebastian heard Jules Calhoun's soft voice, and ignored it.

The voice became louder. More insistent. *"My lord."*

Sebastian opened one eye, saw his valet's fresh-scrubbed, cheerful face, and closed both eyes again. "If you value your life," he said evenly, "you will go away."

The valet had the effrontery to laugh. "Sure, then, I could do that. The thing is, you see, I've a suspicion that if I do, the lady's liable to come charging up the stairs and roust you herself."

Sebastian opened both eyes and groaned as the bed hangings swirled dizzily around him. "Lady? What lady?"

"The lady in the drawing room who's here to see you. And it's no use asking me *what* lady," Calhoun added, when Sebastian opened his mouth to do just that, "because she refuses to give her name. She's veiled. Heavily. All I can tell you is she's young, and brown haired, and tall. Very tall. And most imperious in her manner."

"Bloody hell," said Sebastian, who had no difficulty recognizing this description of Lord Jarvis's infuriating daughter.

"Here," said Calhoun, pressing a mug of some hot, foul-smelling liquid into Sebastian's hands. "Drink this."

"What the hell is it?"

"Milk thistle, my lord. To cleanse the lingering toxins from the liver."

"Toxins?"

"Brandy, my lord."

"Oh. That," said Sebastian, and downed the vile brew in one long, shuddering pull.

The tall young woman in an elegant walking gown of slate blue with a matching spencer sat in one of the cane chairs beside the drawing room's front window. By the time Sebastian put in an appearance, she had been sitting there for quite some time and had availed herself of a book to read.

"The Libation Bearers," she said, holding the volume up when he walked in the door. "It seems a strange choice to leave lying about."

"Bishop Prescott was reading it. I thought I'd take the opportunity to reacquaint myself with the tale." He walked to the tea tray Morey had sent up. "Have you no regard for the dictates of propriety, Miss Jarvis?"

It was considered most improper for a young woman to visit the home of an unmarried gentleman. "Of course I do," she said in some annoyance. "I brought my maid. She awaits me in the hall."

"I noticed. And there's the veil, I suppose. I assume you took a hackney?"

"Naturally."

"Naturally," he said, reaching for the pot. "Tea?"

"Please." She pushed back her veil, her eyes narrowing as she studied his face. "You certainly look as if you could use it."

"Thank you," he said drily, adding a measure of cream to two cups before pouring in the tea. "I take it you've come to continue our discourse from the other night?" He held out her tea and, to his chagrin, heard the cup rattle against its saucer.

"Our what?" Taking the cup, she looked puzzled for a moment, then colored lightly as understanding dawned. "Good heavens. Of course not. I've come because I've discovered some interesting new information about Lord Quillian."

"*Quillian?* Again? What has the poor man done to earn your undying enmity?"

"Enmity has nothing to do with it. I have simply come to the conclusion after viewing all of the available evidence that he is the man most likely to have murdered Bishop Prescott."

"Quillian claims he was with the Prince Regent in the Circular Room at Carlton House the night of the murder. He could be lying, of course, but I doubt it. Such a lie would be too easily disproved."

"He was there," she said, taking a dainty sip of her tea. "But he didn't arrive until shortly after ten."

Sebastian reached for his own cup. "You're certain?"

"Yes. My father was also with the Prince that night, and my father is very observant."

When Sebastian said nothing, her eyes narrowed. "Good heavens. Surely you don't suspect my *father* of killing Prescott?"

"Personally? No. Lord Jarvis never does his own dirty work."

"He also favors the subtle over the flamboyant. If someone had slipped arsenic into the Bishop's wine, you might with reason suspect him. But to set someone to bash in the Bishop's head in a crypt full of moldering bodies? I don't think so."

Sebastian raised his tea to his lips and took a deep swallow. "He might have been less than wise in his choice of agents."

"My father is never less than wise."

"We are all less than wise at times," he said, and had the satisfaction of seeing her color.

He went to lean one arm along the marble mantel of the fireplace. "You are aware," he said, "that the decades-old murder victim discovered in the crypt the day of Bishop Prescott's death was actually the Bishop's own brother, Sir Nigel Prescott?"

"Yes."

"So what are you suggesting? That Lord Quillian—having somehow discovered the existence of Sir Nigel's body in the crypt—funded the renovations on the church of St. Margaret's in order to lure the Bishop out to Tanfield Hill and kill him?"

"Not exactly. I am suggesting that Lord Quillian knew Sir Nigel's body was in the crypt because Lord Quillian is the one who put it there."

"You do realize, of course, that Lord Quillian was a young man of some twenty-two or twenty-three years at the time of Sir Nigel's disappearance? What possible reason could Quillian have had for murdering a forty-year-old baronet he barely knew?"

She drained her teacup and set it on the table beside

her with a sharp click. "I assume you are aware of the secret mission sent by the King to the American Colonies?"

She must have obtained that little gem of information from her father. Sebastian studied her face, wondering what else Jarvis had told her. It was a moment before he could trust himself to answer. "Yes."

"You also know that while Sir Nigel was in America, he discovered evidence of a traitor? Someone in a position to pass important information on to our enemies?"

"Yes," said Sebastian in that same noncommittal voice.

She leaned forward impatiently, her hands coming up together. "It seems to me that the traitor must somehow have discovered that Sir Nigel was onto him, and killed the Baronet before he could reveal the traitor's identity."

"That is certainly one possibility."

She sat back, her brows drawing together in a suspicious frown. "What other possibility is there?"

"I'm sorry, but I can't tell you that."

She stared at him in dawning indignation. "You what?"

It was one thing for Sebastian to entertain suspicions regarding Lady Prescott's fidelity to her late husband, and something else again for him to spread such rumors amongst the ton. Pushing away from the hearth, he strolled over to the tea tray and raised the pot invitingly. "May I offer you some more tea, Miss Jarvis?"

"No, thank you," she said, coming to her feet and reaching to retrieve the reticule that had tumbled unnoticed to the floor.

"Miss Jarvis, we must talk," he said, watching her.

"And I don't mean about the murder of the Bishop of London."

She swung to face him, the dusky skirts of her walking dress swirling gracefully about her ankles. "If you are referring to our conversation of the other night, the matter is settled."

"Settled? How is it settled?"

She simply stared back at him in silence, her lips tightly pressed, her gray eyes hard. They had come together, essentially, as strangers; she knew little of him beyond the fact that he was her father's enemy. She had no reason to trust him and every reason not to, and there was nothing he could think of to say that would change that.

He said, "You would have me think the Bishop's visit to the McCains last Monday a . . . what? A coincidence?"

"Yes."

"I don't believe in coincidences, remember?"

"Whether you believe his visit was a coincidence or not is immaterial." She jerked open the strings of her reticule. "You are right; I never should have come here."

"So why did you?"

"A few hours of simple research enabled me to draw up a list of the names of those who were either close to the King or in the Foreign Office at the time of the American revolt." She drew out a sheaf of papers and handed them to him. "Here."

He took the pages from her and glanced through them. "This is quite a list."

"It is. However, thirty years is a long time. I have gone back over the list and eliminated the names of those who are either dead, infirm or otherwise incapacitated, or currently removed from London." She held out another, smaller sheet. "As you can see, the list of those left for consideration is markedly shorter."

There were only some half a dozen names on the second list, three of which immediately leapt out at him: the Earl of Hendon. Charles, Lord Jarvis. And Lord Quillian.

"*Quillian?*" said Sebastian, looking up.

"Quillian. Thirty years ago he was a younger son, just beginning what was to be a career in the Foreign Office. It wasn't until a few years later that his older brother died and he inherited the title and estates."

"You're certain?"

She turned toward the door. "Feel free to duplicate my efforts."

He said, "I still don't understand why you're doing this."

"Bishop Prescott was my friend."

He shook his head. "There's more to it than that."

"What else could there be?" she asked, lowering her veil into place. "Good day, my lord."

Chapter 37

*L*ord Quillian's elegant town house on Curzon Street was a bachelor residence. He had never married, always claiming whenever asked that he simply found households containing women and children too noisy and fatiguing to be endured.

Living in solitary state, he'd had one of the bedchambers on the second floor turned into a massive dressing room, hung with burgundy-and-navy-striped silk and fitted with vast stretches of dark cherry cupboards and drawers. When Sebastian plied the knocker at the barbaric hour of eleven that morning, he was shown up to this vast chamber.

Clothed in fawn-colored breeches, a white shirt open at the neck, and a paisley dressing gown, Lord Quillian had his hands soaking in two bowls of sudsy water. "What an unfashionable hour for a call," he said, not looking up. "I take it therefore I can safely assume you are here for an unfashionable purpose?"

Tossing his hat and gloves on a side table, Sebastian went to lean against the frame of the tall window overlooking the street, his arms crossed at his chest. "You didn't tell me you were in the Foreign Office thirty years ago."

Quillian glanced over at the small, plump valet hovering nearby with a hand towel. "Leave us."

The man bowed, laid the towel beside his master, and withdrew.

Quillian lifted his hands from the water and dried each finger with careful precision. "Didn't I? Perhaps you are right. I do recall I mentioned that my situation as a younger son reduced me to the vulgar necessity of having to earn my own bread. But I may not have identified the exact nature of my"—he made a face at the word—"*employment*. It was not, needless to say, a high point in my life."

"How did your brother die?"

"My brother?" Quillian looked up at that, his eyes narrowing. "If you must know, he died of smallpox. What precisely are you suggesting, my lord? That I was in such dire financial straits as a young man that I sold my country's secrets to the Americans? And then, when an ill-timed peace ended that lucrative venture, I had my brother set upon by footpads so that I might inherit?"

Sebastian studied the toe of his boot. "I don't recall saying anything about a traitor."

Quillian held himself still for a moment, then inclined his head in wry acknowledgment. "Touché, my lord. You are quite right; you did not. Yet you are such an indefatigably inquisitive young man, I've no doubt by now that you have learned of the Alcibiades letters."

"It's my understanding that the existence of the Alcibiades letters was a closely guarded secret."

Quillian reached for a small knife and began paring his nails. "And so it was—thirty years ago. But with the passage of time these things become less critical. Perceval let drop a few choice tidbits about the scandal

within my hearing last April. Needless to say, my ears
pricked up. I mean, the timing was so *curious*. Don't you
agree?"

"Yes."

Lord Quillian sighed dramatically. "In the end, it all
came to naught, of course. Here I was hoping to discover
that Sir Nigel was *himself* Alcibiades, whereas in fact Sir
Nigel was actually the one who discovered the existence
of the traitor. Although not, it seems, the man's identity."

"Not that we know."

Quillian opened his eyes wide in a parody of enlightenment. "So you're suggesting . . . what, precisely? That
Sir Nigel confronted me with evidence of my supposed
traitorous dealings, whereupon I killed him to keep him
silent?" Quillian frowned. "Yes, I can see where such a
scenario has a certain element of logic. There's only one
problem."

"What's that?"

"I'm not a traitor." Quillian pushed to his feet and
threw off his silk dressing gown. "Although I realize
that's an easy thing to say. Not so easy to prove."

"I'm told you didn't arrive at Carlton House before
ten o'clock on the evening of the Tuesday in question,"
said Sebastian. "Where were you before that?"

Quillian looked faintly amused. "Not anyplace I care
to tell about," he said, selecting a freshly starched cravat
from the pile laid out for him.

His attention all for his own image in the mirror,
Quillian carefully wrapped the white Irish linen around
his neck and began the delicate business of tying the
ends. "I take it your attempts to identify the Bishop's
killer have not exactly been crowned with success. Is that
why you've turned your attention to the events of thirty

years ago? Surely you don't think the Bishop and his brother were both killed by the same man?"

"I consider it one possibility, yes."

Quillian leaned forward, his gaze intent as he made a few careful adjustments to the exaggerated knot of his cravat. "I suppose you know what you are doing. But I think you're wrong."

"Really? So what do you think happened to the brothers Prescott?"

"I think Francis Prescott killed his brother thirty years ago for the inheritance. And then, when my helpful interference brought the body of the good Bishop's victim to light, he went rushing back to the scene of his crime—only to fall victim in his turn."

"To whom?"

Turning away from his mirror, the dandy reached for a silk waistcoat of the palest salmon silk backed by fine white linen. "I did give you a little hint the other day. Did you not follow up on it?"

Sebastian frowned. "You mean William Franklin? Would you have me believe the American killed Bishop Prescott over a mere slight involving a couple of schoolboys?"

"Dear me," said Quillian, deftly fastening the row of tiny pearl buttons that ran up the waistcoat's front. "Can it be that you don't know?"

"Don't know . . . what?"

"The depth of the animosity William Franklin held for our good Bishop. You see, as one of the senior Loyalists to take refuge in London, William Franklin worked tirelessly on behalf of his fellow Americans, petitioning Parliament for their relief. Yet when Franklin's own case came before the Parliamentary Commission, he was awarded a mere trifle. The bulk of his claim—amounting to nearly fifty thousand pounds—was disavowed."

"Why?"

"Because Francis Prescott convinced the commission that Franklin's loyalty was suspect, due to the treasonous activities of his well-known father, Benjamin Franklin. It was Prescott's contention that Franklin *père et fils* had deliberately supported opposite sides of the conflict, so that no matter who won, the Franklins would come out on top."

"When was this?"

"The commission's hearings? The late eighties, I believe."

"So you're suggesting that William Franklin waited more than twenty years, until he was old and infirm, before suddenly deciding one night to follow the Bishop out to a rural parish church and bash in his head?"

"*La vengeance est un plat qui se mange froid.* Perhaps now that his wife is dead, Franklin feels he no longer has anything to lose?" Quillian shrugged. "But you are the expert on murder, so I suppose I must bow to your superior knowledge of the subject."

Vengeance is a dish best enjoyed cold. Sebastian watched the Baron slip an intricately engraved gold watch into the pocket of his waistcoat. "I'm curious about one thing," said Sebastian. "How do you come to know so much about Prescott's dealings with William Franklin?"

Quillian added a fob to the end of his watch chain. "What's the saying? 'Keep your friends close and your enemies closer.' Francis Prescott made himself my enemy. Therefore I made it my business to know all the dirty little secrets our good Bishop didn't want anyone else to know." Reaching out, he gave the bell a soft tug. An instant later, the Baron's valet appeared in the doorway.

"Are we ready to put on our coat, my lord?" said the little man with a bow. "Shall I ask James to assist?"

Sebastian pushed away from the windowsill. "It takes the combined efforts of your valet *and* a footman to get you into your coat?"

"I should rather hope so," said Quillian, looking affronted. "Any excess material would lead to unsightly *wrinkles*. And that would never do."

Sebastian reached for his hat and gloves. "I'll show myself out." But he paused in the doorway to look back and say, "One of these days, an abolition act will make it though Parliament, with or without Bishop Prescott. You do know that, don't you?"

"I know it," said the Baron, positioning his cuffs as the valet held a flawlessly tailored a coat of superfine in readiness and the footman waited to assist. "But without Prescott, I can't see it happening for another twenty years or more. And who knows?" The Baron smiled. "By then I may well be dead."

William Franklin stood at one of the open sides of the long, low building that stretched out for hundreds of feet along the edge of Penton Place, near Hanging Field. Known as a ropewalk, the structure had low brick walls that reached only to hip height and a simple shed roof supported by rows of crude posts. Within its shelter, hemp fibers were spun into threads and then twisted into rope. The strands could be twisted together in a straight line only with the strands fully extended, which accounted for the ropewalk's great length.

"Fascinating, is it not?" said Franklin when Sebastian strolled up to him. The old man had to shout to be heard over the *clickety-clack* of spinning metal wheels. "When I was a wee lad, my father used to take me down to the ropewalk near the harbor in Philadelphia. Ellen always enjoys it, too."

Sebastian narrowed his eyes against the cloud of billowing hemp dust. It was messy work, the air heavy with the scent of hemp and tar and the whirl of the spinning fibers. "She's not with you today?"

"She would have come, but she wanted to finish the letter she's writing to her father." The old man's smile slipped slightly at the thought of his wayward son. "He keeps promising to visit her, but he never comes. He has my father's papers, you know. I've been pressing him to publish them; I've even offered to help. But he'll have none of it."

Sebastian studied the American's timeworn face. From what Sebastian had been able to learn, the domestic arrangements of the Franklin males tended to follow a similar, bizarre pattern. An illegitimate son himself, William Franklin had abandoned his own illegitimate son, Temple, to be raised by Benjamin. And Temple Franklin had, in turn, abandoned *his* illegitimate daughter, Ellen, to be raised by William. They were a brilliant but peculiar family. But then, Sebastian thought, perhaps most families were peculiar, each in their own way.

He said, "I'm told Bishop Prescott was largely responsible for the Parliamentary Commission's decision to disavow the majority of your claim."

Franklin cast him a knowing sideways glance. "So that's why you're here, is it? You've heard about the results of the commission." He gave a soft chuckle. "Believe me, Lord Devlin, if I ever felt moved to kill Francis Prescott, it was twenty-four years ago. Not last week."

"Sometimes these things build."

"True," said Franklin. "True." He drew a plain gold pocket watch from his old-fashioned, snuff-stained vest and squinted down at the time. "I promised to take Ellen for an ice at Gunter's. But I've a few minutes yet."

Something about the movement stirred the whisper of a recollection in Sebastian's memory, a thought that was there and then gone before he could capture it.

He lifted his gaze to the ropewalk, where a man with a grooved wooden wedge known as a "top" drew the strands ahead of the twist, keeping it tight. The strands had to be kept under equal tension, without kinking, until the entire fathom of rope was twisted. The standard length of naval rope was a thousand feet.

The length required to hang a man for, say, murder, was considerably shorter.

Sebastian's hands tightened around the top of the brick wall before them as he watched the strands of rope weave in together. "Good God," he said. "Why didn't I think of that before?"

Franklin shook his head, not understanding. "Think of what?"

Sebastian pushed away from the wall. "Thank you for your help, Mr. Franklin."

"Anytime, anytime," Franklin called after him. "And good luck to you, Lord Devlin."

Chapter 38

Stopping by Brook Street, Sebastian slipped a small, loaded double-barreled pistol into his pocket. Then he headed for Bow Street.

He arrived at the Public Office to startle Sir Henry Lovejoy by demanding, "You said you were going to look into the circumstances of Jack Slade's transportation. Did you?"

"Yes," said the magistrate, carefully fitting his spectacles on his face and reaching for a file. "I've my notes right here. But I was under the impression you'd discounted the involvement of Mr. Slade."

"I've changed my mind. Tell me everything you know."

Jack Slade was trimming fat from a leg of lamb when Sebastian entered the butcher shop on Monkwell Street. The butcher had a bloody apron tied around his waist. The hand clutching the thin boning knife was bloody, too, as was the ugly-looking cleaver resting at his elbow. The pungent odor of raw meat filled the air.

Sebastian said, "You didn't tell me it was Francis Prescott's plea for mercy that saved you from the hangman's noose."

Slade glanced up, a smear of blood darkening one cheek, his lantern jaw set hard. "What if it was?"

Sebastian let his gaze rove the small shop, taking in the sides of beef and mutton hung from massive hooks in the walls. A tray of sausages rested on the counter; the battered green shutter that would be used to close the butcher's shop when the day's trading ended stood propped against the wall.

He said, "The thing is, you see, I find myself wondering something. Why would Father Prescott—I assume he was only a priest then, and not a bishop? Anyway, why would Father Prescott intervene to help a man convicted of bludgeoning his wife to death in a drunken brawl? That's right," Sebastian added when Slade's eyes narrowed. "I've discovered you weren't being exactly truthful when you said your wife died while you were in Sydney."

The butcher sliced a ridge of fat and let it drop into the bucket at his feet. "Reckon he felt guilty. 'Cause o' what his brother done to me family."

"That's one explanation," said Sebastian.

"What other explanation is there?"

Sebastian shifted so that he had a clear view of the street, where a costermonger was pushing a barrel up the hill toward the churchyard. "Nice shop you have here. Been in business long?"

"Near on five years. Why ye ask?"

"It's not often a man transported to Botany Bay returns home with the wherewithal to set himself up in business."

Slade's head came up, the handle of his knife clattering against the surface of the butcher block. "What ye suggesting?"

"That you were blackmailing Francis Prescott. That you blackmailed him decades ago to get him to use his influence to keep you from being hanged. And then, when you came back from Botany Bay, you pressed him again to give you the money you needed to set up this shop."

Slade stared at him, forehead furrowed, nostrils flaring with each breath.

Sebastian said, "I suspect he was also periodically slipping you a little sum, was he? Is that why you were arguing with him on the footpath in front of London House on Monday? Because you thought the promise of an archbishopric in his future should increase the price of your continued silence, and he was unwilling to meet your demands?"

Slade swiped the back of his hard forearm across his sun-darkened forehead, leaving another bloody streak. "The Bishop was me friend, see? People know secrets about their friends. People help their friends when they can. Ain't nothin' wrong wit' that."

"And what secret did you know about the Bishop of Lon—"

Sebastian broke off, his preternatural hearing catching the whisper of shifting cloth, the subtle exhalation of a man's breath. Sebastian threw himself sideways just as the giant thighbone of an ox still glistening with fat and gristle whooshed through the space where his head had been.

"Mornin', *Captain* Viscount," said Obadiah, his lips pulling back in a grin, his big body filling the air with the scent of hot, stale sweat as he swung the ox bone again.

Snatching up the tray of sausages, Sebastian slammed the wooden board into the man's face hard enough to send him staggering back against the wall, his face dripping torn sausage casings and ground fat down the front of his leather waistcoat and breeches. With a roar, he pushed away from the wall, head bent like a charging bull.

Sebastian yanked the small flintlock pistol from his pocket and discharged both barrels into the man's face, obliterating it in a spray of blood and bone. The small shop filled with thick blue smoke and the acrid stench of burned powder.

Jack Slade screamed, "*Obadiah!*" Snatching up the cleaver from the butcher block, he clambered over the counter and threw himself at Sebastian.

Instinctively flinging up his right arm, Sebastian only partially deflected the blow, the sharp edge of the blade slicing deep. Then the butcher's massive body slammed into him and the two men went down together.

They careened into the tin pail, tipping it over in a clatter that sent a wash of blood and bits of gore spilling across the floor. Scrambling and sliding in the bloody sawdust, Sebastian managed to roll on top of the butcher. He closed his left fist around Slade's wrist and yanked the hand clutching the cleaver high over the butcher's head. But Sebastian's right arm hung at his side, wet with blood that dripped off his fingertips to mingle with the spilled muck on the floor. He was aware of his vision darkening around the edges. The strength in his grip ebbed.

Slade reared up, the crown of his head butting into Sebastian's forehead. Sebastian reeled back, his blood-slicked fingers losing their grip on the butcher's wrist.

Lurching sideways, Slade swung the cleaver at Sebastian's head. Sebastian jerked out of the way. The heavy blade sank into the wooden frame of the old green shutter beside him, and stuck there.

Face streaked with sweat and blood and sawdust, Slade rocked the cleaver's handle, trying to free it. Sebastian slammed the heel of his boot into the side of the butcher's head, knocking him back. Sebastian closed his own left hand on the cleaver's handle. Levering the blade free of the wood, he swung around just as Jack Slade charged.

The blade made an ugly *thwunk*ing sound as it sank into the butcher's chest. Slade flopped back, jerked, lay still.

His breath soughing in his throat, Sebastian sank back against the blood-spattered wall. He sat for a moment, his heart beating hard against his rib cage, the blood from his sliced arm pooling on the floorboards beside him. Then he yanked the cravat from around his neck and bound it tightly around his arm.

"You're lucky," said Gibson, setting a neat row of stitches along the nasty slash in Sebastian's forearm. "A fraction deeper and he'd have severed an artery. A trifle to the right and you might have lost the use of your hand."

Sebastian had stripped down to his torn, blood-soaked shirt and breeches and was sitting perched on one end of the long, narrow table in the front room of Gibson's surgery. He took a deep pull from the open bottle of brandy he gripped in one white-knuckled fist, and kept his jaw set.

"Hurts, does it?" said Gibson with what sounded suspiciously like malicious satisfaction. He tied off his thread and reached for a roll of bandages. "You think it's true, then? Slade was blackmailing the Bishop?"

"I don't think there's much doubt about it. The question is, what secret was the Bishop paying Slade to keep?"

"That Francis Prescott killed his brother in the crypt of St. Margaret's thirty years ago?" Gibson suggested, wrapping the bandage around his handiwork.

"I don't think so. I keep going back to the way Slade laughed when he heard Sir Nigel had been found down in that crypt."

"If you hadn't killed him, you could have asked him."

"If I hadn't killed him, he would have killed *me.*"

"There is that."

Sebastian took another deep swallow of brandy. "Miss Jarvis knew Prescott was being blackmailed. She just didn't know by whom. But that doesn't mean she doesn't know why."

Gibson tied off the bandage and handed Sebastian the torn, bloody remnant of his coat. "If you're planning on going to see her, you might consider stopping by Brook Street first for a new rig."

Sebastian grunted and eased his arm into what was left of his sleeve.

"And whatever you do, don't drive those chestnuts of yours," said the surgeon, fashioning him a sling. "Or the grays. Either stick to hackneys, or let Tom or Giles drive you. You need to give that arm a rest. Overdo things and you could end up losing the use of that hand after all."

"In case you've forgotten, Tom is nursing an injury of his own."

"I had a look at Tom's shoulder this afternoon. The young heal quickly. If you ask me, this forced inactivity is doing him more harm than good. Besides, it's not like he'll be in any danger. Obadiah's dead."

"And if it wasn't Obadiah who shot at us the other night?"

Gibson picked up the bowl of bloody water and pile of soiled linen. "Somehow I can't imagine William Franklin lurking in some Brook Street area steps waiting to take a shot at you. It was Obadiah."

Sebastian held his own counsel. But he wasn't convinced.

Chapter 39

He found Miss Jarvis surrounded by piles of books and papers, and seated at the dark, heavy table in the library of the house on Berkeley Square.

She wore a simple gown of pale yellow cambric made high at the neck and trimmed with delicate touches of white lace, and she had her head bent over some notes she was making, so that the afternoon sunlight streaming in the tall paned window overlooking the garden fell warmly on her brown hair. At Sebastian's entrance, she looked up and laid aside her quill, her face studied in its calm repose. He searched her even features for some indication that his suspicions might be true. But if she found his presence a cause for concern, she did not show it.

"Lord Devlin," announced the butler, hovering nervously, obviously uncertain of the wisdom of abandoning her to the company of such a dangerous visitor.

"You can tell him I promise not to abduct you," said Sebastian, going to where a carafe of Lord Jarvis's best brandy rested on a tray.

A suggestion of amusement lightened her features. "Thank you, Grisham. That will be all."

Sebastian poured himself a drink and downed it in one long pull.

"Do help yourself to some brandy," she said sardonically.

He refilled his glass. "Thank you."

Her gaze lingered for a moment on his sling. But rather than remark on it, she pushed to her feet and began assembling her papers.

He said, "Embarking on a new project, Miss Jarvis?"

"Actually, it occurs to me that perhaps you are right, that I have focused too single-mindedly on Lord Quillian. So I've decided to pursue several other theories."

He strolled over to study the title of the nearest tome. "*Debrett's Peerage*? So you're . . . what? Expanding your list of suspects to include the entire peerage?"

A malevolent gleam darkened her fine gray eyes. She tweaked the book from his grasp and slipped it back on a shelf. "Did you know that before her marriage to Sir Nigel, Lady Prescott eloped with another man?"

"The unsuitable suitor. My dear Miss Jarvis, have you by chance discovered his identity?"

"Not by chance, my lord. But I have discovered his identity. Lieutenant Marc Hatfield, third son of Lord Bixby."

"Who?"

"Lieutenant Hatfield. He was killed at Yorktown."

Sebastian stared thoughtfully at his brandy. "In other words, he predeceased Sir Nigel by nearly a year."

She nodded. "When I first learned of the elopement, I thought the disappointed suitor might have been responsible for Sir Nigel's death. Obviously, that was impossible."

There was something about the airy way in which this

was said that told Sebastian more than he suspected she'd intended. He took a sip of his brandy and said with quiet amusement, "You thought the unsuitable suitor was Quillian, didn't you?"

A faint hint of color touched her cheeks, but all she said was, "What happened to your arm?"

"An unpleasant encounter with a butcher and his meat cleaver."

"A *butcher*?"

"A man by the name of Jack Slade. Ever hear of him?"

She shook her head. "Should I have?"

"Last Wednesday, you told me you thought someone was blackmailing Bishop Prescott. As it happens, you were correct. Only it wasn't Quillian. It was Jack Slade."

"The butcher."

"The butcher."

"You can't be serious."

"But I am. You see, this particular butcher grew up on the Grange and nursed a powerful grudge against the brothers Prescott. At some point before he got himself transported to Botany Bay for murdering his wife, Mr. Jack Slade came into possession of a powerful secret."

He was aware of her watching him intently. She said, "And do you know the nature of this secret?"

"No." He drained his glass and set it aside. "But you do, don't you?"

"I beg your pardon?"

He walked up to her, close enough that he could smell the faint fragrance of lavender that dusted her shoulders and see the telltale nervous dilation of her pupils. "When you met with the Bishop last Tuesday evening, what precisely did he say that led you to believe he was being blackmailed? And don't even think about quoting me some pious pap about a friend's responsibility to honor a man's confidences even after death. In the past week I've been forced to kill three men. I've been shot at, horsewhipped, attacked with a meat cleaver, and half drowned. My patience is wearing thin."

Two tight white lines had appeared to bracket her mouth.

"Tell me," he said.

She went back to gathering her books, the soft thumps of the bindings slapping together sounding unnaturally loud in the hushed room. He didn't think she meant to answer him. Then she seemed to come to a decision. She said, "When I arrived at London House Tuesday evening, it was obvious something had occurred to trouble him. At first he simply said he'd received disturbing news. But later, after we'd spoken . . ."

"Yes?" he prompted when she hesitated.

"He said it's no pleasant thing to be haunted by the secrets of one's past. And he told me . . . he told me he had fathered a child in his youth."

"Sir Peter?"

Her head came up. "*Sir Peter?* Good heavens. I never thought of that. *Is* Sir Peter his child?"

"I don't know. But I've begun to suspect he might be."

"I wonder if that's why Prescott was reading *The Libation Bearers*?"

"It makes sense, does it not?" He studied her carefully composed features. "What else did the Bishop tell you?"

"Nothing."

Sebastian looked out the window at the neat, high-walled rear garden, at the breeze-ruffled deep green leaves of the shrubbery, at the blueness of the slice of rain-scrubbed sky. He could think of only one reason for Francis Prescott to have shared this painful burden with Miss Hero Jarvis, and for her to have been so reluctant to reveal it.

He had always thought of her as a formidable, intelligent woman of extraordinary courage and fortitude. But now, standing stiff-backed in the afternoon sunlight streaming in the garden window, she looked suddenly vulnerable, and maybe a little afraid.

"This is not a secret you need hide, or bear alone," he said quietly. "We can be wed tomorrow by special license. You must allow me to do this, Miss Jarvis. For your sake, and for the sake of the child."

An angry muscle jumped along her rigid jaw, shattering the image of vulnerability. "You are wrong in your supposition, my lord. There is no child." And then she said it again, her eyes steady and fierce, as if she could compel him to believe her: "There is no child."

She reminded him so much of Hendon, fiercely lying in the face of all evidence to the contrary, that the similarity sent a chill over him. "You said yourself you wouldn't tell me, even if there were."

She swung away, head held high, back rigid, to jerk the bellpull beside the fireplace. The butler must have been hovering nearby, because he appeared almost instantly.

"Viscount Devlin is leaving," she said. "Please show him out."

Sebastian settled his hat on his head. There was just enough uncertainty in his mind to keep him from continuing to press her. But he said, his voice low, "I'm not going to let this go."

"Call again and you will find me not at home," she said, and swept from the room.

Sebastian sat on the tumbledown stone wall of the ruined gardens that had once belonged to the original Somerset House, his gaze on the sun-shimmered waters of the river before him. The air was heavy with the hum of insects and the fecund odor of a long-abandoned garden. Two hundred years ago, a mighty renaissance lord had seized this gently sited strip of land and built here a grand palace with graceful parterred gardens and vine-draped terraces. But the old Somerset House was long gone. All that remained, now, was this deserted, overgrown tangle of broken stones and half-dead roses, and a set of hidden, cracked steps leading down to forgotten cellars prone to flood when the tide rushed in.

He pushed the memories of that day from his mind, his eyes narrowing as he watched a wherryman row his fare toward the opposite shore, oars throwing up a spray of water to sparkle in the sun. He had an uneasy sense that time was running out, although he knew that could simply be a product of his own personal frustration and anger and what Kat had once called his characteristic inability to admit defeat.

He kept coming back to something Sir Peter had said in the Jerusalem Gate on the morning after Francis Prescott's death—something Sebastian had missed, until now. *Says something, don't it*, Sir Peter had said, *when a man needs to make an appointment to see his own bloody uncle.*

Sir Peter claimed last Tuesday's meeting had been just one more installment in an ongoing argument over a certain dark-eyed opera dancer. Except that would imply that Francis Prescott had sought *Sir Peter* out, rather than the other way around.

Sebastian knew it could simply be a coincidence that Sir Peter had met with his uncle the day after the Bishop's angry encounter with Jack Slade on the pavement before London House. But he doubted it.

What would a man like Jack Slade do, Sebastian wondered, if Francis Prescott had refused the butcher's attempts to extort more money? Sebastian could identify three options: Slade could admit defeat. He could proclaim the Bishop's secret to the world in angry revenge. Or . . .

Or he could take his dangerous but valuable secret to a new buyer. Lady Prescott, perhaps.

Or her son. Sir Peter Prescott.

Chapter 40

*M*idway through the afternoon, after her mother had retired to her dressing room for a few hours' rest, Hero ordered her carriage and drove up the river, to Chelsea.

Drawing up in the shade of a spreading chestnut at the end of Cheyne Walk, she sat for a time, her gaze on the neat brick house at Number Eleven. She watched Mrs. McCain venture out to feed the ducks at the river's edge; she watched Dr. McCain come strolling home, his chest puffed out with self-importance, his feet splaying slightly as he walked. They were a kind and worthy couple, and she had no doubt they would someday make a needy child fine parents. But not her child. She could not give these people her child to raise.

Sitting forward, she rapped on the carriage roof and called out sharply, "Drive on."

In deference to Gibson's dire warnings to rest his injured arm, Sebastian allowed himself to be driven out to Tanfield Hill by his tiger. Tom enjoyed the experience hugely, although by the time they reached the village late that afternoon, Sebastian could see a faint shadow in the boy's eyes. Gibson had obviously overestimated Tom's pace of recovery.

Leaving the chestnuts in Tom's care at the Dog and Duck, Sebastian followed the narrow footpath up the millstream. The sun was sinking low toward the western hills, the golden light filtering down through the leafy canopy of the willows and oaks to cast dappled shadows across thick humus still damp from the rain.

Bessie Dunlop, nurse to Sir Peter and his mother before him, sat on a weathered ladder-backed chair drawn up before the open door of her cottage. She was shelling a bowl of peas she held in her lap, and did not look up when Sebastian entered the clearing. But the doe that grazed contentedly near the corner of the cottage froze, muscles tense, ready to run.

"It's all right, girl," Bessie told the deer. "He won't harm you." Only then did she look up. "I expected you yesterday."

"You obviously overestimated my powers of deduction."

She laughed at that, a rich, melodious laugh that could have belonged to a much younger woman.

He went to hunker down beside her, his elbows braced on his spread knees, his gaze hard on her face. "You told me Sir Peter came to visit you last week. What day?"

Gnarled, work-worn fingers snapped another pod, spilling its hard green peas into the bowl. "One evening is much like the next, to me."

"It was the evening the Bishop died, was it?"

"Could have been." She snapped another pod. "He's a good boy, Sir Peter. Never too busy or puffed up in his own conceit to forget to visit his old nurse."

"Yet somehow, I don't think Tuesday's call was in the nature of a social visit, was it?"

When she didn't answer, Sebastian said, "Sir Peter came to ask if what Jack Slade had told him was true, didn't he? That the Bishop was his father."

Her fingers stilled at their task. "Oh, no, he already knew that."

"The Bishop had admitted the truth to him?"

"Yes."

"Then why did Sir Peter come to you?"

"He came to ask if Francis Prescott had killed Sir Nigel."

Sebastian looked across the clearing, to where the millstream flowed lazily past, the trailing leaves of the willows nearly touching its waters. "And what did you tell him?"

"I told him Francis Prescott could never kill any man. Even one as vile as his own brother."

Sebastian pushed to his feet. "And was that the truth?"

She tipped her head to one side, her gaze searching his face. "You have a great regard for the truth, do you not, Lord Devlin? Truth and justice. You have made them your calling. More than that, you have made them your touchstones, perhaps even your gods. But some truths should never be known. And sometimes what men in their righteous ignorance call justice is no justice at all, only one more wrong that can never be made right."

With an ease and grace that belied her years, she rose from her chair, the bowl of peas balanced on her hip. Turning, she walked into her cottage and slammed the door.

He stood for a moment, listening to the warm breeze sigh through the willows, watching a duck paddle across the placid warm waters lit now by the golden light of the westering sun. But the doe had gone, and the peace of the place was broken. He knew he had broken it.

Rather than return to the Dog and Duck, Sebastian walked up the village high street, then cut through the wind-ruffled grass scattered with forget-me-nots and tumbled gray tombstones until he reached the northern side of the old Norman nave. Someone—probably Squire Pyle—had nailed some of the broken boards from the demolished charnel house over the entrance to the crypt. But Sebastian could still smell its rank odor wafting up from below like a cold exhalation of death.

He took a step back, his gaze drifting to the line of willows that marked the millstream. From here he could see two boys in straw hats and bare feet fishing off the arched stone bridge, their lines catching the slanting rays of the setting sun, their joyous laughter carrying to him on the warm breeze. If Sir Peter had visited his old nurse the evening of Tuesday last, he would have passed the church on his way back to London.

The old nurse's words kept echoing in Sebastian's head. Perhaps she was right; perhaps some truths were better left unknown. Thirty years ago, a cruel and vicious man had met a secret death in the depths of this crypt. Perhaps it would have been better if the events of that dark, terrible night had never become known. But the Reverend Earnshaw's innocent destruction of the old charnel house had shed the light of the present on the past. And now Earnshaw and four other men were dead.

He watched a slim blond woman in a shako-style hat

and a riding habit with brass buttons guide a fine blood bay up the high street. At the gate to the churchyard she drew up, the black train of her riding habit trailing over the horse's dark red flanks, the bay throwing its head with a jingle of its bridle as she slid gracefully from her saddle. She paused for a moment, head lifting as she scanned the churchyard. He strolled through the high grass to meet her.

"Lady Prescott," he said, taking her horse's reins.

"Lord Devlin."

They turned to walk together, the mare ambling along behind. She said, "Bessie told me I would find you here."

When he made no comment, she turned to look at him, her gentle blue eyes lit with amusement. "I don't know if she sees things the rest of us don't see, or if she is simply an excellent observer of people. But she can be uncomfortable, at times, to live around."

He said, "Why are you here, Lady Prescott?"

She looked up at the age-blackened stone belfry before them, the light falling full on her face to reveal the smooth skin of her cheeks and a faint scar he now noticed that cut across the lid of her left eye. "Thirty years is a long time to live with a secret."

He waited, and after a moment she said, "Sir Nigel returned from America with a packet of papers—treasonous letters written by someone who styled himself 'Alcibiades.'"

"Yes. I know."

"Do you know who wrote them?"

He shook his head.

She pursed her lips and blew out a long breath. "It was my father. The Marquess of Ripon. He claimed he did it in an outpouring of devotion to republican principles. He was quite the student of the Enlightenment, you know, forever reading the likes of Voltaire and Rousseau."

"But you didn't believe him?"

She huffed a soft laugh devoid of all amusement. "The only thing my father was really devoted to was the gaming table."

"I have heard he was badly dipped."

"They all were. Sandwich. Dashwood. Fox. But they didn't all seek to come about by betraying their country."

"Did you know what he was doing?"

"Not until I saw the letters."

"Sir Nigel showed them to you?"

"Yes. He'd recognized Father's handwriting immediately." She stared off down the hill, to where one of the boys on the bridge was hauling in his line. "In one of the letters, my father revealed some vital information on the Army's plans at Yorktown." She paused. "Someone very dear to me was killed at Yorktown."

Sebastian said, "Why didn't Sir Nigel take the letters to the King?"

"And expose his own wife's father as a traitor?" A tight smile touched her lips. "What do you suppose would have happened then to my husband's ambitions of being named foreign secretary?"

Her hand crept up to her face, her fingertips touching the scar above her eye in an unconscious movement before drifting away. "He had a vicious temper, Sir Nigel. He was furious with Father, and furious with me. He knew he couldn't expose my father without harming his own interests. But he thought the threat of exposure would be enough to force my father to retire from London."

"It wasn't?"

"Father knew my husband's ambitions made him vulnerable. When Nigel threatened him, my father laughed at him. Said he'd retire to his estates if Nigel paid him ten thousand pounds."

"Wily old fox."

"Oh, yes. But my father miscalculated. He underestimated the power of Nigel's fury."

A fly buzzed the bay's ears. The mare shook its head, flicking its mane. Lady Prescott reached out to pat the horse's neck.

"When was this?"

"The day he died. The twenty-fifth of July. He came home from London that evening in a rage. Swore he was going to reveal my father as a traitor and divorce me. I begged him not to do it, but he called for his horse and rode off."

It said something about English marriage laws and the attitudes of their society that a terrified, abused woman would be horrified by her husband's threat to divorce her. Sebastian studied Lady Prescott's half-averted profile. Most women would suffer unimaginable cruelties at the hands of their husbands rather than face the social stigma and financial ruin that were the lot of divorced women. He said, "So you went after him."

She nodded. "I thought he was going to London. But when I rode through Tanfield Hill, the moon was full and I could see his mare—Lady Jane—tied up by the charnel house. My husband and his brothers used to play in the crypt as children. He was always telling me stories, bragging about how he would hide things down there when he was a boy. I realized he must have hidden the Alcibiades letters there. I'd looked for them at the Grange, you see, and hadn't been able to find them."

They'd long ago stopped walking and were standing on the gravel sweep beside the church. From here they could see the piles of rubble left by the demolition of the charnel house. When the wind shifted around, it brought with it an old, old smell.

Sebastian said, "You followed him down into the crypt?"

She stared down at her knotted hands. "I was still hoping I could get him to see reason. But he was drunk on brandy and fury and a lust for revenge. As soon as he saw me, he came at me. I'd never seen him like that before. He'd hurt me in the past, but this time, I swear, he wanted to kill me." Her gaze lifted to where the setting sun baked the golden stones of the bridge over the mill-stream. The boys had gone. "I honestly think he would have."

Sebastian said, "The silver dagger. You brought it with you from the Grange, did you?"

The muscles in her throat worked as she swallowed. "My father had given it to me. He'd brought it back from Rome as a young man, when he was on his grand tour. Sir Nigel had . . . hurt me before he left. When I rode after him, I took the dagger with me. Just . . . just in case.

"When I came down the steps, he was at the back of the crypt. He'd taken a lantern from the sacristy, and I could see the light flickering over the rows of old columns and the stacks of coffins in the bays. He turned when he heard me. I said his name. That was all. Just his name. He started screaming at me, calling me the vilest things. Then he pushed me back against one of the columns and put his big hands around my throat."

She paused for a moment, her gaze on her own hands

twisted together before her. "I could feel his fingers digging into my neck, pressing ever so hard. I couldn't breathe. I tried to beg, to plead with him to stop. But I couldn't speak. And I thought, *He doesn't need to divorce me. He's going to kill me*."

"So you stabbed him."

She nodded, her voice an anguished whisper. "Only he didn't let go. He just opened his mouth and roared and squeezed harder. So I stabbed him again. And again. And then he let me go."

"What did you do?"

"I ran to the vicarage. I was covered in blood. Most of it was my husband's, but not all of it. Francis—Sir Nigel's brother—was the priest in residence at the time. He was a very different sort of man from his brother. While Sir Nigel was away, he and I had become ... close."

She stared off down the hill again. Sebastian waited, and after a moment she continued. "They still burn women who kill their husbands. Did you know? It's considered a form of treason."

"You killed him in self-defense."

The ghost of a smile touched her lips. "And what jury of men do you think would have believed that? I stabbed him *in the back*. In a crypt."

"Francis Prescott believed you?"

"Francis knew his brother."

Sebastian said, "It was Francis Prescott's idea to seal off the crypt?"

She nodded. "He'd been planning to do it anyway. Between the two of us, we managed to drag Nigel farther back into the shadows. Then Francis locked the gate to the crypt, and took the mare and turned it loose on the heath. By dusk of the next day both entrances to the crypt had been bricked up."

She drew in a deep breath that lifted the bodice of her black riding habit. Sebastian looked at the gently fading fair hair that curled against her neck, the soft blue eyes that were so much like her son's, and knew she wasn't telling him everything.

He said, "Did Sir Nigel know you were carrying his brother's child?"

He watched her lips part, her jaw go slack. But she recovered quickly, her chin lifting. "I don't know what you're talking a—"

"Don't," said Sebastian. "Please don't try to play me for a fool, Lady Prescott."

She looked away, her eyes blinking rapidly.

He said, "Did Sir Nigel know?"

She shook her head, her voice a whisper. "I didn't even know at the time. It was . . . It was wrong of us. We knew that. But Francis . . . He was such a good, gentle man. Everything his brother was not. And I was so very lonely."

Sebastian watched a puff of white clouds near the horizon take on a golden hue, and thought about what kind of good, gentle priest comforted his brother's sad, lonely wife with the heat of his own body.

A very human one, he supposed.

"It is forbidden for a man to marry his brother's widow. Besides . . ." She paused, and had to swallow before continuing. "After what happened to Nigel, there was no question of our continuing to see each other. Francis married a young woman several years later, although as Peter's uncle, he was able to play an important role in the boy's life."

Sebastian nodded. What was it the Chaplain had said? *Sir Peter was like a son to him.* Aloud, he said, "How did Jack Slade come to know the truth about Sir Peter?"

He saw the flare of fury and fear in her eyes. "That beastly man. He kept following Francis. Watching us. He heard us talking one day, after Peter was born. It was right before he killed his wife. Francis went to visit him at Newgate, to pray with him, and Slade said if Francis didn't petition the court to have his sentence commuted to transportation, he'd tell everyone my son was a bastard."

"He might not have been believed."

The coloring in her cheeks darkened. "There were already whispers in the village. Not about Francis and me, but about Peter. No one knew Sir Nigel had been in America, but they knew he'd been traveling until the middle of July. I'd given out that the child was due to be born in April, but . . . Well, he didn't look like a seven-months child."

"Did you know the Bishop gave Slade money, after he came back from Botany Bay?"

The light filtering down through the canopy of oaks cast dappled shadows across the planes of her face. She said, "I knew. He did it for Peter. But it troubled him. I think he told Slade he wasn't going to pay anymore, and threatened Slade that if he tried to do anything about it, he'd have him prosecuted for blackmail. That's why Jack Slade killed him."

"I'm not so sure," said Sebastian.

She lifted her blue eyes to his face, and he saw there a mother's deepening fear. "Then who did?"

Rather than answer her, Sebastian said, "Did Francis Prescott know about your father's letters?"

"I told him about them that night. But he never saw them."

"So what happened to them?"

"I don't know. I've always assumed Sir Nigel had them on him when he died."

"You didn't look for them?"

"No. I was . . . I was in such a state. And with the crypt bricked up, what did it matter?"

The mare raised its head, eyes blinking as it swung to nuzzle its mistress. Lady Prescott stroked the horse's velvet nose. "After Sir Nigel's death, I went to my father and told him I knew what he'd been doing, and that if he didn't leave London I would take the Alcibiades letters to the King. He didn't know I no longer had them. He left for Derbyshire the next day. We have never spoken to each other since."

"He's still alive?"

"Yes."

Along the millstream, a mist had begun to form. Sebastian could feel a new chill in the air, smell the tang of wood smoke on the breeze. Lady Prescott gathered her horse's reins and prepared to mount.

"The funeral is the day after tomorrow," she said. "The Church wanted Francis interred at St. Paul's, but Peter thought it only right that he be buried here, in the crypt. He and Sir Nigel both. And then it will be sealed again. Forever, this time."

Sebastian gave her a leg up, watched her settle the velvet train of her riding habit about her.

"Why did you tell me this?" he said.

"I think you know why," she said, and set her heel to her horse's side.

He watched her clatter away, her body bending low over the horse's withers as she wove beneath the oaks, the short veil of her shakolike hat fluttering in the breeze.

Then he turned toward the Dog and Duck.

Chapter 41

"*D*o you believe her?" asked Gibson.

Sebastian sat sprawled in one of the cracked old leather armchairs in Gibson's parlor. He had a brandy cradled in his one usable hand and was watching Gibson stuff a haversack with notebooks, pencils, measuring tapes, and all manner of other paraphernalia.

"I'm not certain," said Sebastian, taking a long drink of his brandy.

"It fits with the wounds on Sir Nigel's body. Two shallow stab wounds, badly placed. And a third that slid home."

"True," said Sebastian. "But she could actually have crept up behind him in the crypt and stabbed him in the back."

"From all that we've heard, I'm not sure I'd blame her if she did." Gibson glanced over at him. "Are you going to tell the authorities?"

Sebastian took another swallow of brandy. "No." He watched Gibson add candles to his rucksack and said, "What the devil are you preparing for?"

Gibson reached for a tinderbox. "Sir Henry tells me they'll be sealing up the crypt of St. Margaret's again after the funeral. I mentioned I'd be interested in taking a wee look around, and he said he'd square it with the proper authorities. I'll be heading out there first thing in the morning. I hear some of those bodies date back to before the Conquest, and I'll not be having much time to study them all."

"To study them for what?"

"Comparative purposes."

Sebastian set his teeth against a new wave of pain rolling up from his arm and took another drink.

Watching him, Gibson said, "Hurting, is it? Aren't you glad you let Tom drive out to Tanfield Hill today? If you had any sense, you'd be in bed."

Sebastian grunted and took another sip of brandy.

Gibson said, "She didn't need to tell you anything. Why tell you a lie?"

It was a moment before Sebastian realized Gibson was still talking about Lady Prescott. He said, "She may think she's protecting her son."

"She thinks Sir Peter killed the Bishop? But ... why? Granted, he may have been a wee bit annoyed with the man for lying to him for the past thirty years. But you don't kill a man for just that."

"Actually, Sir Peter had the same reason to kill Francis Prescott as his mother had to kill Sir Nigel."

Gibson cinched the top of his haversack and looked over at Sebastian with a frown. "He did? What reason?"

"His grandfather's letters."

"But...surely Sir Peter would have no reason to fear the Bishop might betray him now? At this late date?"

"I don't know. From what we've heard, the Bishop's passions ran pretty strong when it came to the American Revolution. And if they quarreled?" Sebastian drained his glass in one long pull and pushed to his feet. "Who's to say what might have happened?"

That night, Sebastian dreamt of bloodstained winding sheets, of ancient, splintered coffins and gleaming skulls. The voices of men long dead whispered to him, their hushed words mingling with the moan of the wind that thrashed the naked branches of dark trees silhouetted against a starless sky.

A row of coffins stood in a misty glen. His throat tight, his footsteps echoing in the stillness, Sebastian approached the open caskets.

In the first lay Sebastian's tiger, Tom, his eyes closed, the sprinkling of freckles across his nose standing out stark against his pallid skin. With dawning horror, Sebastian realized the next casket held Paul Gibson, his hands folded over a rosary at his chest. Beyond him lay a woman, her face hidden by the lace frill of the coffin's satin lining. As Sebastian took a step toward her, he heard the crack of a rifle and awoke with a start, heart pounding, mouth dry.

It was a long time before he slept again.

Thursday, 16 July 1812

Early the next morning, Hero Jarvis climbed the stairs to the old nursery at the top of the house, where she and her brother, David, had passed so many happy hours of their childhood.

The low, narrow beds were draped in Holland covers, the hobbyhorses, tin soldiers, and drums battered and coated in dust. She ran her fingertips across the well-worn surface of the old schoolroom table and found the place where she and David had once carved their names when their governess wasn't looking. She smiled at the memory. Then the smile faded, leaving an ache of want.

She went to stand beside the grimy, cobweb-draped window overlooking the square. As a little girl, she had whiled away many a rainy afternoon curled up here on the window seat, lost between the pages of a book. Her favorites were always tales of adventure and travel. In her imagination, she had followed the Silk Road with Marco Polo, sailed the South Seas with Captain Cook, crossed the desert highlands of Anatolia with Xenophan. *Someday*, she used to tell herself. *Someday, when I am grown, I will hear the warm winds of Arabia whispering in the date palms, watch the rising sun glisten on the snow-covered slopes of the Hindu Kush.*

It had never happened. Lately she'd been thinking that once the child was born, she would have to go away. She could not imagine giving up her child and then simply going on with her life as before, as if none of it had ever happened. And then it occurred to her: Why not go away *now*? Why not bear the child in some distant land and keep it?

She knew a pounding rush of excitement. She could return to England in a few years and simply present the child as an orphan she'd adopted in the course of her travels.

Why not?

That morning, Sebastian revolted his tiger by once again summoning a hackney carriage.

"Ye don't like the way I 'andled the chestnuts on the

way to Tanfield 'Ill?" said the boy, his street urchin's face pinched tight with suppressed emotion.

"It's not that," said Sebastian. "It's—" He broke off, unwilling to vocalize the faint wisps of unease left by the previous night's dreams. He slipped his dagger into its sheath in his Hessians and said simply, "I know how much yesterday's drive hurt my arm, and I know it must have pained you as well. I want you to rest another day. That's all."

The boy's face cleared a little, but he still looked mulish. "My shoulder's fine."

"It'll be even better after another day's rest. Now go find me a hackney."

Sir Peter kept his opera dancer in Camden Town, in a small house just off Brompton Road. It was a respectable if unfashionable street of tidy houses with shiny, freshly painted doors and window boxes spilling pelargoniums and heartsease against carefully pointed redbrick walls.

Sebastian's knock was answered by a flat-chested, sharp-chinned lass of perhaps thirteen who wore a starched white cap and a startled expression. This was obviously a household that received few visitors. "Gor," she whispered, expelling her breath in wonder.

"Amy," called a woman's voice from inside the house. "Is that the— *Oh.*"

Sir Peter's opera dancer appeared behind her young maid, one tiny hand flying up to her lips in consternation when she saw Sebastian. She had thick, dark ringlets and twinkling eyes and a Devonshire-cream complexion that must have made her the darling of the opera once. Now, from the looks of the bulge beneath the high waist of her simple sprigged muslin gown, she was at least six months heavy with child.

"I beg your pardon for the intrusion, madam," said Sebastian, removing his hat. "I was looking for Sir Peter."

"He's taken Francis down to Whitehall, to watch the Changing of the Guard."

"Francis?"

"Our son." She smoothed her left hand over her swelling stomach in a self-conscious gesture, and Sebastian saw the morning sun glimmer on the gold of the simple band on her third finger.

"She's not my mistress," said Sir Peter. "She's my wife. She has been for nearly four years now, since before Francis was born."

They stood together at the edge of the Horse Guards parade, where a flaxen-haired lad of about three clambered over the barrel of a Turkish cannon captured a decade earlier in Egypt. "She's lovely," said Sebastian.

A soft smile lit the other man's features as he watched his son. It faded slowly. "Her lineage is respectable. Her father was a physician. But when he died, the family was left penniless. She came to London looking for work." He paused. "You know how that goes."

Sebastian stared off across the parade, toward the Hyde Park Barracks. A warm sun bathed the park in a golden light, but he could see the threat of dark clouds building again on the horizon.

"Of course," Sir Peter was saying, "her birth makes no difference now. Not after she's trod the boards. What kind of a man marries his mistress?"

"The kind of man with the courage to follow his heart," suggested Sebastian.

"Courage?" Sir Peter gave a harsh laugh. "If I had courage, Arabella would be living openly with me as my wife at the Grange, rather than being hidden away in Camden Town."

They could see the new guard now, dark horses advancing in majestic solemnity, sun shining on the red-coated men's helmets and white plumes. "The Bishop knew of your marriage, did he?" said Sebastian. "Is that why you quarreled?"

Prescott narrowed his eyes against the sun. "Initially, yes."

The little boy, Francis, slid off the cannon and ran toward them. "They're coming, Papa!"

Sebastian said, "I know Jack Slade paid you a visit last Monday night, and I know why."

Sir Peter kept his face half turned away, his gaze on the approaching Life Guards, their dark mounts moving in flawless precision. "It's no easy thing discovering that your entire life has been a lie."

Sebastian stared off across the field and said nothing.

After a moment, Prescott continued. "Slade wanted me to give him money. Two thousand pounds."

"Did you oblige him?"

"I told him I needed time to gather such a sum."

"Would you have given it to him?"

"I don't know." He glanced sideways at Sebastian. "I hear you killed him. I must say, I'm glad."

Sebastian watched the royal standard snap in the breeze. "He had no proof of anything. Only his word."

Prescott huffed a soft, humorless laugh. "That, and the fact that my uncle had been paying to keep him silent for years."

Sebastian watched the trumpeter lift his instrument

for the royal salute. "You told me you were here, in Camden Town, the night Francis Prescott died. But that's not true. You rode out to Tanfield Hill that evening to see Bessie Dunlop."

Prescott turned to face him. "What the devil are you suggesting, Devlin? That I saw the Bishop in St. Margaret's churchyard when I was riding through the village and decided to follow him down into the crypt and bash in his brains? What the bloody hell would I do that for? Because he cuckolded my mother's husband? Because he didn't like my own marriage?"

"Ever hear of the Alcibiades letters?"

"No."

Sebastian studied his old schoolmate's flushed, angry face, the soft blue eyes and disheveled fair curls that fell across his brow. If it was an act, it was a good one.

The notes of the salute drifted across the parade. "*Toot-toot*," said Master Francis, marching in place, hand raised as he blew into an imaginary trumpet.

Sebastian watched the sun glint on the boy's flaxen curls and finely featured face. "Your son looks amazingly like you," he said. "And your mother." For a moment, the shrill notes of the trumpet and the shouts of the small crowd faded. He was thinking of another man with fair curls and soft blue eyes and the delicate bone structure of a scholar.

Or a priest.

As if from a long way off, he heard Sir Peter say, "The Ashleys always breed true."

Sebastian swung to face him. "*Ashley* is your mother's family name?"

Sir Peter's brow wrinkled in confusion. "Yes. Why?"

"And Dr. Simon Ashley—the Bishop's chaplain—is what? Your mother's brother?"

"Yes."

"Bloody hell," whispered Sebastian.

"Why didn't Uncle Simon come with us to watch the Changing of the Guard?" demanded Master Francis, following the drift of their conversation in that disconcerting way of children.

"He had someplace else he was supposed to be," said Sir Peter.

Sebastian knew a sudden chill. "You saw him today?"

"It was rather curious, actually. He said he'd heard tales of the Prescott brothers playing in the crypt of St. Margaret's as children, and he wanted to know if Uncle Francis ever told me the secret hiding place they'd had there."

"Had he?"

Sir Peter nodded. "There's supposed to be a small altar niche in the western wall of the crypt. One of the stones at the base of the niche is loose."

"When was this?"

"That we saw him? Shortly before Francis and I left the house. Perhaps half an hour ago. Why?"

Sebastian thought about Paul Gibson, shoving notebooks and candles into a haversack last night in gleeful anticipation of a day to be spent inspecting and analyzing the moldering remains of centuries of his fellow men. An ambitious churchman who had already killed twice in his attempt to secure the evidence of his father's treason would not hesitate to kill a one-legged Irish surgeon with an abiding fascination with the human body.

"Papa!" said Master Francis, tugging at his father's

coattails. "Do you see—" The boy let out a whoop as Sebastian scooped him up and took off at a run across the parade grounds.

"Quickly," he shouted over his shoulder to Sir Peter. "I need to borrow your horse."

Prescott struggled to keep up with him. "But I don't understand—"

"I don't have time to go back to Brook Street. And I'll need you to take a note to Bow Street. It is very important that you deliver it personally into the hands of Sir Henry Lovejoy. Can you do that?"

"Yes, but— Hell and the devil confound it, Devlin! What the devil is going on?"

"Simon Ashley murdered your father. Your *real* father. And if I don't make it out to Tanfield Hill in time, he could very well kill a friend of mine. Paul Gibson."

Chapter 42

Sebastian spurred Sir Peter's neat chestnut gelding hard, his left hand sweaty on the reins, his injured right arm hugged in tight to his body. A stiff wind scurried the growing banks of clouds overhead, hiding the sun and thrashing the limbs of the oaks and elms that shadowed the road to Tanfield Hill. By the time he reached Hounslow Heath, the pain in his sliced arm was a searing, white-hot agony that kept his breathing quick and shallow and dulled his thoughts. He pushed on.

The first drops of rain began to fall as he clattered over the millstream's bridge and spurred the gelding up the hill. Rain streaked the quiet tombstones with splashes of wet and pattered softly in the long grass of the churchyard. Reining in beneath the ancient bell tower, Sebastian slipped from the saddle, one hand coming up to cup the gelding's nose when it would have whickered softly. The churchyard was deserted. If either Gibson or Simon Ashley were here, they had stabled their horses at the Dog and Duck before descending into the crypt.

Cradling his aching arm close to his body, Sebastian worked his way around the church. At the gaping entrance to the crypt's stair vault, he slowed, alert to any sound of movement. Someone had torn away the weathered boards from the broken opening and thrown them aside. He could see the narrow, steep steps plunging down into a dark void faintly lit as if by a distant flickering flame.

Chill, dank air wafted up from below, bringing him the smell of old, old earth and death. Painfully conscious of the soft crunch of debris beneath the soles of his boots, Sebastian crept down the worn stairs. His feet found the last step, then the sunken, uneven paving of the crypt's floor. Flattening his back against the coursed, rough stones of the wall, he drew in a deep, steadying breath.

The flame of a single candle glowed at the far western end of the crypt, sending the long, distorted shadow of a man stretching out across the worn paving and rows of crude columns. Then the shadow moved, and Sebastian saw Simon Ashley, the hem of his black cassock brushing the dusty floor. He had his back turned, his shoulders working as he used an iron bar to pry up the stones at the base of a crude niche in the back wall.

Gibson was nowhere to be seen.

Sebastian reached down with his left hand to slip the dagger from his boot. Moving cautiously, he crept past shadowy bays stuffed with dusty, cobweb-draped caskets stacked five and six high, some banded with iron in an attempt to foil grave robbers, others pitifully small and painted white, as denoted a child. As his eyes adjusted to the sepulchral gloom, more details began to emerge: the ruched frill of a coffin lining peeking through split wood, its lace edging threaded with tattered ribbon; a casket handle shaped like a cherub; the tarnished brass of a lozenge-shaped end plate that read, *Mary Alice Mills, died 1725, aged 16 years* ...

The toe of his boot bumped against something lumpy and yielding. Looking down, Sebastian saw Gibson's haversack, a jumble of notebooks and tape measures and calipers spilling across the worn paving stones.

Paul Gibson lay just beyond it, sprawled facedown at the base of a towering wall of ancient coffins warped and crushed by the weight of the ages. Crouching beside him, Sebastian pressed his fingertips to his friend's neck. Gibson's pulse was faint, but there. At Sebastian's touch, he let out a soft moan.

The Chaplain jerked around, his fist clenched on a yellowing packet of letters, his eyes widening at the sight of Sebastian. "*Devlin.* What the bloody hell are you doing here?"

Sebastian pushed to his feet, the dagger held low at his side. "Give it up, Ashley," he said evenly. "A Bow Street magistrate and half a dozen runners are already on their way here."

The Chaplain shook his head, the flickering light from the candle he'd wedged atop a nearby casket dancing over his pale face and the stark white of his ecclesiastical collar. He slipped the letters inside his coat and wrapped both fists around the iron bar. "I'm sorry, but I don't believe that."

Sebastian was hideously aware of his right arm hanging useless in its sling, of Gibson lying unconscious beside him, of the time it must have taken Sir Peter to find Lovejoy. How long, he wondered, would it take Lovejoy and his constables to make the journey out to Tanfield Hill? An hour? More?

Too long.

He said, "I know about your father and the Alcibiades letters. What I don't understand is how you came to hear of them. You must have been a child at the time this all happened."

"Rosamond told me. Years ago, when I was taking her to task for never visiting Father. She said Sir Nigel had the letters on him when he died. So when I heard the crypt had been opened and his body found, I thought I needed to act quickly, before the letters could be brought to light."

"So Prescott did tell you about the crypt."

Ashley nodded. "Right after Earnshaw left. I thought I had more than enough time to get here, retrieve the letters, and be gone long before the Bishop arrived. But my horse picked up a stone in its shoe and went lame. By the time I came down the steps, he was already crouched over his brother's body. He had some papers in his hands. I assumed they were the Alcibiades letters. I'd picked up an iron bar the workmen had left at the top of the steps, and when he turned, I just . . . hit him. I didn't want to kill him. I swear I didn't. But I had to get those letters." The Chaplain's jaw sagged, and he swallowed. "Only, it wasn't the letters. Just some old estate papers."

"But . . . Francis Prescott was your friend; your sister was once married to his brother. You don't think he would have kept quiet about your father's treason? For Lady Prescott's sake, if not yours?"

Ashley frowned. "For Rosamond's sake? Why would he?"

Sebastian studied the other man's puzzled features. Lady Prescott might have told her priestly little brother about their father's treason, but she'd obviously kept quiet about her own infidelity.

Ashley said, "You think I should have taken that chance? Risked seeing my father tried and hanged for *treason*?"

"Rather than kill a man? Yes."

Ashley's lips twisted. "My father's *life* depended on my acting quickly. His life, and my future. It's easy for you to stand there, secure in your position as your father's heir, and judge me. You have no idea what it's like to be a younger son, to have to make your own way in the world. *No idea.* These letters would destroy any chance I ever had for advancement in the Church. Believe me, sons of traitors don't rise very far in the ecclesiastical hierarchy."

Sebastian was aware of Gibson stirring at his feet. "And Earnshaw?"

The Chaplain tightened his grip on the iron bar and raised it like a cricket bat. "He saw me in the churchyard. He didn't get a good look at me, but he saw enough that something could have later jogged his memory. The shape of my silhouette, perhaps, or something distinctive about the way I move. I couldn't take the—" Ashley broke off as Gibson let out another groan and fought to push himself up onto his elbows.

For one disastrous moment, Sebastian's attention jerked back to his friend. He heard the whoosh of Ashley's iron bar slicing through the air and dropped to his hands and knees an instant before the curved end of the bar smashed into the big, velvet-draped casket beside where his head had been.

The ancient coffin shattered, raining down splintered wood and the stained horsehair stuffing of its old lining and the gleaming shards of a broken skull. Ashley staggered with the impact, struggling to free the tip of the iron bar from the wood. Sebastian kicked up at him, hitting the Chaplain in the knee just as the iron bar popped free of the coffin.

Ashley spun around to slam back, hard, into the stack of coffins crammed into the last bay. The dry, ancient wood shattered and buckled, the coffins shifting ominously. Then the entire stack collapsed in a roaring cascade of broken wood, unfurling brown-stained shrouds, and disjointed, desiccated body parts.

Sebastian threw himself across Gibson's prone body, his one good arm coming up to protect his head as bits of wood and bone rained down around them. A grinning skull still covered with leatherlike skin and stuck to its frilled pillow by a mass of matted dark hair crashed into his upraised arm and sent his knife spinning into the rubble. The candle Ashley had balanced atop a nearby coffin toppled.

The crypt plunged into a suffocating blackness.

Sebastian's eyes adapted quickly to the lack of light. But like most men, the Chaplain was hopelessly blind in the dark. He stumbled about, coughing in the dust, his iron bar whistling through the air as he swung like a madman in first one direction, then another, the tip clanging against a stone column, whacking into another stack of coffins.

Quietly searching the rubble around him, Sebastian found what looked like someone's kneecap and hurled the bit of bone against the back wall of the crypt. It hit the stones and fell with a clatter.

"Devlin?" Ashley swung around, trying frantically to peer into the murky gloom. "We can make a deal. You keep quiet about my secret, and I'll keep quiet about yours."

Moving stealthily, Sebastian slipped his good arm beneath his friend's unconscious body.

"I know about Miss Jarvis," said Ashley, his voice echoing about the dark vaults. "I overheard her talking to the Bishop a couple of weeks ago."

Sebastian froze.

Ashley shouted, "I know you can hear me, Devlin. You try to pin these murders on me, and everyone in London will know about the bastard you planted in Lord Jarvis's oh-so-proper daughter."

His heart pounding in his chest, Sebastian struggled, one-handed, to lift his friend. "*Gibson,*" he whispered, then froze as a faint glow illuminated the dusty scene.

Ashley's candle had not, obviously, gone out. Falling into one of the collapsing caskets, it must have sputtered, only to catch again. Now, fed by ancient cloth and wood, it flared up to fill the crypt with a growing light and the smell of burning hair and wool.

"Bloody hell," swore Sebastian, struggling to haul Gibson up with him.

But he'd already lost the brief moment of advantage offered by the darkness. With a hiss that sounded like burning pitch, the mummified body in a nearby coffin blazed up as if it were a giant torch, filling the crypt with a surge of light and the stench of burning flesh.

"Devlin!" roared Ashley, the iron bar raised over his head as he charged.

Closing his hand over a mound of debris, Sebastian scooped up a fistful of grit and smashed bone and threw it in the Chaplain's face. The Chaplain flung up one crooked arm to protect his eyes, his step momentarily faltering.

Letting go of Gibson, Sebastian rammed into the

Chaplain headfirst, barreling the man across the aisle to crash into the cobweb-draped pile of coffins in the opposite bay.

The wall of caskets collapsed around them in a dusty crescendo of bones and wood and broken iron bands. The two men went down together, rolling over and over. A jagged piece of wood tore a gash down Sebastian's leg. His injured arm whacked into the base of a stone column and a whiplash of pain exploded in his head, stealing his breath and dimming his sight.

He was aware of Ashley rearing up, that damned iron bar still gripped in his fists.

"You bastard," swore Sebastian. Pivoting, he slammed the heel of his boot into Ashley's forearm. The bar went spinning out of sight.

He heard a roar, and realized the glow in the crypt had brightened. With an ugly whoosh, the flames raced from one bay to the next, fed by the massive piles of dried wood and corpses and ancient textiles stiffened with congealed body fluids.

Ashley scrambled up, eyes wild. Sebastian drove his good fist into the cleric's face, knocking him back in a crash of breaking wood and clattering, bouncing bones.

The fire was all around them now, filling the air with a foul, oily smoke that stole Sebastian's breath and stung his eyes. "Gibson!" he shouted. Coughing badly, he lurched back to where the surgeon was trying to push himself up onto his one good knee.

"Put your arm around my neck," Sebastian shouted over the roar of the fire.

Sebastian surged up, dragging Gibson with him. Together they staggered toward the stair vault through a tunnel of flames. The bays of coffins had turned into giant banks of fire that filled the air with flaming wisps of ancient winding sheets and burning pieces of wood that rained down everywhere.

Then the stack of coffins nearest the stair vault collapsed in a fiery avalanche that sent flaming debris skittering across the central aisle. A smoking slab of wood fell on Sebastian's head, slamming him to his knees. He tried to get up and felt something heavy clobber him in the back, knocking the breath from his lungs. He pitched forward, losing his grip on Gibson.

"Gibson!" he shouted, reaching for him. A violent fit of coughing racked his body, stealing the last of his strength.

He knew a terrible rage: for the unborn child who would never know its father, for the woman who would face the birth of that child alone. Gritting his teeth, he fought to push himself up, and heard a shout from somewhere up ahead.

Looking up, he saw the dark shadows of men moving purposefully through the smoke and curling flames. Hands reached out, lifting Gibson from Sebastian's grasp, carrying him toward the stairs. Sebastian heard a familiar, high-pitched voice, saw the gleam of fire reflected in the lenses of Sir Henry Lovejoy's glasses.

"We must hurry, my lord," said the magistrate, his fists closing on Sebastian's coat. "Can you get up?"

Sebastian nodded. He was coughing too badly now to talk. Leaning heavily on the little magistrate, he staggered up the worn, narrow steps.

At the top of the stairs, he tripped over the remnant of the old brick wall and went down. Rolling onto his back, he blinked up at heavy gray clouds. Rain splashed in his face, and he dragged the sweet air of the countryside into his lungs.

"*Gibson?*" he asked, the effort of turning his head in search of his friend bringing on another bout of coughing. "How is he?"

"He has a nasty gash on the side of his head, but he looks to be all right. Better, in fact, than you, my lord."

"And Ashley?"

"We couldn't reach him."

Sebastian coughed again and gave up trying to sit up. For the moment it felt good simply to lie here on his back in the cool grass, letting the rain wash the dust and cobwebs and the smell of old death from his face.

He said, "I didn't think you'd make it in time. Sir Peter must have found you far quicker than I'd anticipated."

"Sir Peter?" Lovejoy frowned. "I haven't seen Sir Peter."

Sebastian raised his head to look at the magistrate. Lovejoy's hat was gone. The sleeve of his coat was singed, and there was a rakish-looking black smear above one eye. "Then what the devil are you doing here?"

"Miss Jarvis looked up the surname of the Marquess of Ripon in *Debrett's Peerage* and made the connection to the Bishop's chaplain. When she discovered it was Dr. Ashley's intention to drive out here this morning, she insisted we come after him. I personally thought she was overreacting. Obviously, I was mistaken."

Sebastian let his head fall back against the wet grass and started to laugh.

Chapter 43

Friday, 17 July 1812

Clad in a navy silk dressing gown, white linen shirt, and doeskin breeches, Sebastian descended to his breakfast parlor the next morning to find his aunt Henrietta seated at the table, awaiting him.

She was dressed in a splendid carriage gown of a fine mauve satin, with frog closures down the front and a towering turban of mauve and lemon silk perched on her head. As he paused on the threshold in surprise, she said, "I told your man not to announce me." When he continued to stare at her, she added, "I've spoken to Hendon."

"Ah." He went to splash ale into a tankard and drank deeply. "Did you think I'd refuse to see you?"

"I thought you might."

He reached for a plate and held it up in inquiry. "May I fix you something?"

She gave a genteel shudder. "It's bad enough to be abroad at this hour. To actually consume sustenance would be barbaric."

He gave a laugh and moved to the sideboard, where an array of dishes awaited his selection.

"I wanted to thank you for your assistance with this recent unpleasantness," she said. "The Archbishop tells me you've solved the murders of both Francis Prescott and that reverend from Tanfield Hill. He also tells me you believe the murderer of Sir Nigel will never be found and is in all likelihood dead." She paused. "He believed you, of course."

Sebastian looked over at her. "You don't?"

She met his gaze and held it. "I know you."

He came to sit at the table. "Sometimes it's better that the truth never be known."

"Well, I certainly wouldn't argue with that. Although it's not a sentiment I ever expected to hear coming from you."

He picked up his fork and then paused, his gaze on her plump, shrewd face. "Have you always known?" he asked. There was no need to say more; one never knew when servants were listening.

"From the beginning, yes," she said quietly. "My affections for you have nothing to do with the particulars of your birth. Your brother Richard was a fine young man, and his death grieved me as if I'd lost one of my own." She sniffed. "I never cared much for Cecil. He was too much like his mother."

"I rather liked my mother," said Sebastian. "And Cecil."

"I know you did. Hendon tells me you have agents in France, seeking news of her. Any success yet?"

"Not yet."

She was silent for a moment, watching him. "I suppose you think the earldom should by rights go to that idiot cousin of yours up north?"

Like Hendon, Henrietta had never had anything except contempt for Delwin St. Cyr, the oafish, slow-witted distant cousin who lived in Yorkshire and stood next in line, behind Sebastian, to the earldom. Sebastian raised one eyebrow. "You don't?"

"Hardly. Delwin's grandfather—my father's cousin—was impotent. His son was fathered by the local vicar."

"You can't know that."

"Oh, but I can. So you see, if you think you are depriving Delwin of his 'rightful' inheritance, you're wrong. Delwin is no more a St. Cyr than you are. Less so, in fact. Your mother had St. Cyr blood in her, after all, through her grandmother."

Sebastian gave a wry smile. He should have known. *The St. Cyr bloodline. The St. Cyr name. The St. Cyr legacy.* As long as Sebastian could remember, nothing had mattered more to Hendon than preserving and continuing the St. Cyr heritage. Nothing.

She watched him struggle to eat with his left hand, his right resting carefully in his lap. "I am told you've injured your arm. Is it serious?"

"It will mend."

She nodded. "Hendon will be pleased to hear," she said, and he knew this was why she had come, to let his father—to let *the Earl*, he mentally corrected himself—know how he fared.

She heaved herself to her feet with a mighty grunt. "He's the only father you have, Sebastian. And you are as dear to him as any son could be. The estrangement that arose between you this past winter grieved him seriously. Don't let what Sophia did thirty years ago come between you now."

"There's far more to this than what Sophia did, as well you know."

She sniffed again. "If you mean Kat Boleyn, I've never thought she was the wife for you. You can look daggers at me all you want, Sebastian, but it's true—and I mean that quite apart from the less-than-desirable facts of her birth or her profession. You need someone to keep you in line."

"The way Claiborne kept you in line?"

"Good heavens," she said, affronted. "He never did any such thing."

"My point exactly."

"I'm not you." She turned toward the door.

He stopped her by saying, "As a member of the King's mission to the Colonies, Lord Jarvis . . ." Sebastian paused, choosing his words carefully. "Jarvis would have known the truth. Yet as much as he and Hendon have locked horns over the years, he has never used this knowledge to his advantage. Why?"

"Jarvis and Hendon are old, old adversaries. They each know secrets that the other would prefer be kept buried."

"Meaning?"

"Meaning it's often better that the truth never be known."

He came upon Miss Jarvis in the sun-warmed gardens of Berkeley Square, as she strolled with her maid along carefully manicured paths of crushed shell. She had not attended the funeral of the Bishop and his brother, for burials were considered dangerous occasions from which women were excluded for health reasons.

She was so obviously lost in her own troubled thoughts that she did not see him, and he paused for a moment in the shadows of a clipped yew hedge to study her. She wore a very fetching sprigged muslin gown and a straw hat tied beneath her chin with a jaunty red ribbon. But her cheeks were unnaturally pale, her features strained. He knew why.

She was confronting with grace and courage what must be for any gentlewoman the most unimaginably catastrophic of developments. He remembered with bemusement those moments beneath the ruined gardens of old Somerset House, when they'd believed they faced death and had instead created a new life. The thought of a future with Miss Hero Jarvis as his wife—and Charles, Lord Jarvis, as his father-in-law—scared the hell out of Sebastian and tore at his gut. But as a man of honor, he could not allow her to suffer the consequences of that day alone. He took a deep breath and walked toward her.

At the sound of his footsteps, she looked around and froze. He said teasingly, "You've forgotten your parasol."

She didn't smile. "I was just going inside. Good day, my lord."

"Oh, no, you don't," he said, falling into step beside her when she would have turned away. "I'm not going to be a gentleman and let you run off. First of all, you must allow me to thank you for saving my life."

"You're welcome. Now I really must be—"

"No. I know the truth," he said bluntly. "You can deny it all you want. Simon Ashley told me."

"Ashley? But how did he—" She drew up sharply to throw a speaking glance at her maid. The woman dropped back out of earshot.

Miss Jarvis continued up the path, her arms crossed at her chest, her voice lowered. "What precisely are you saying, Lord Devlin?"

"I'm saying that in the midst of trying to kill me, Dr. Ashley made a rather interesting proposal. He suggested that if I agreed to remain silent about his recent murderous activities, then he would be willing to keep quiet about my unborn child."

The air was heavy with the scent of damp earth and sun-baked stone and a faint breath of lavender. She had the grace not to continue her denials. She simply walked on, her back held straight, her lips pressed into a tight line. But he could see her throat work as she swallowed.

He said, "I have in my pocket a special license. We can be wed this—"

"No."

"Miss Jarvis—"

She swung to face him, her eyes dark with fear and anger and something else he couldn't identify. "No. You know my opinion of the institution of marriage in England today."

He was startled into giving a soft, shaky laugh. "Miss Jarvis, I can assure you that I will neither beat you nor force my unwelcome attentions upon you, nor risk whatever wealth you might bring to our union on the turn of a card. And I'm not asking you to take my word for it. I can have a marriage settlement drawn up guaranteeing—"

"No." She brought one splayed hand to her forehead, shading her eyes. "What you are suggesting is madness. It's madness for you, and it's madness for me, and I won't do it."

"If you won't do it for your sake, then think about the child."

"I am thinking about the child."

He cast a quick glance back at the maid, then leaned toward Miss Jarvis, his voice low and earnest. "You cannot mean to give this child to the likes of Dr. McCain to raise."

"What's wrong with Dr. McCain?"

In truth, there wasn't anything wrong with the man except that he wanted to adopt Sebastian's child. Sebastian said, "I suppose his wife's harmless enough, but Mc-Cain himself is a stuffy, narrow-minded bore."

"There are worse things than being a stuffy, narrow-minded bore."

"That's debatable. If you remain adamant in your opposition to marriage, then give me the child. I will raise it."

Her nostrils flared on a quick breath. "No."

"Why not?" He knew a powerful welling of frustration and anger, tinged with fear. "You must allow me to do *something*—"

"Believe me, Lord Devlin, there is no need. I have decided I shall simply go away to have the child. Travel for some years, to Arabia, or perhaps to the land of the Hindu Kush."

"You mean have the child *in Arabia*? Are you mad?"

"No, I am not mad. Merely determined to keep both my child and my independence. When I return in a few years' time, the exact age of the infant will be easily obscured. I can present the child as one I adopted during the course of my journeys, and no one will be any the wiser. Oh, there might be whispers, but so what?"

He searched her pale, strong face. "You would do that? Have him grow up believing he's someone he's not?" The thought of it tore at Sebastian, a painful rending of a raw wound he knew was never going to heal.

"There is no alternative."

"Of course there is an alternative. You can marry me."

"I will write," she said. "Let you know the child is well. Now, you must excuse me, my lord. I have much to do."

She made as if to brush past him, but he grabbed her arm, stopping her. "I can't let you do this."

She carefully withdrew her arm from his grasp. "And how, pray, do you intend to stop me?"

"I don't know. Kidnap you, perhaps?"

"Don't be ridiculous," she said, and left him there, to the sun and the soft wind and the faint, lingering scent of lavender.

That night, Jarvis put in a rare appearance at his own dinner table.

He talked to Hero for a time of the war in the Peninsula, and the bellicose posturings of the young United States. As usual, Annabelle contributed little beyond the typical stray, inane remark.

They were just finishing up a nice cream of asparagus soup when Hero drew in a deep breath and said bluntly, "I've been thinking I might hire a companion and travel for a while."

Annabelle dropped her spoon with a clatter. "Travel? But . . . travel where, Hero?"

"Arabia. India. Who knows?"

"Good God," said Jarvis. "What put this idea in your head?"

She looked over at him, her face set in oddly stiff lines. "You know I've always wanted to see the world. I think I've finally reached the age that I can do so without exciting too much comment."

"But . . ." Her mother groped for her wineglass. "Whatever will I do without you?"

"End your days in Bedlam, where you belong, no doubt," suggested Jarvis maliciously.

"Papa," said Hero in a low, tense voice. "You shouldn't say that, even in jest."

Jarvis raised one eyebrow. "What makes you think I'm jesting? Do you seriously expect me to put up with her nonsense without you here to coax and wheedle her into a semblance of normality?"

Jarvis considered himself a master at reading both men and women, but what he saw in his daughter's drawn, troubled face confused him. She reminded him of a hunted fox backed into a corner.

"Hero?" said Annabelle in a weak, pleading voice.

Hero reached out to grip her mother's hand, tightly, in her own. "It's all right, Mama." She forced her lips into an unconvincing smile that didn't reach her eyes. "It was just a thought. Don't worry. I won't go."

"If you're that bored," snapped Jarvis, "what you need to do is to find a husband and start having babies."

Hero glanced over at him. He expected her to make one of her usual provocative remarks on the inequities of modern English marriage laws. Instead, she gave a strange, soft laugh and said, "Perhaps I shall."

Author's Note

*W*hile the church of St. Margaret's and the village of Tanfield Hill are fictional, the crypt of St. Margaret's was inspired in both its design and the details of its rediscovery by the very real crypt of St. Wystan's in Repton, England.

For nineteenth-century burial customs and the condition of burials in crypts, see the fascinating material published both in print and on the Internet on the archaeological excavations of Christ Church, Spitalfields, London; of St. Pancras Church, Euston Road; and the recently rediscovered crypt of the former Dominican church in Vác, Hungary.

As surprising as it may seem, the incredibly long delay in the funeral of Bishop Prescott was quite common at the time, with the average being ten to twelve days; English gentlewomen did not attend funerals until Victorian times.

The fire that forms the climax of this tale is inspired by a real event: A fire in the crypt of St. Clements in London burned for days at the end of the nineteenth century, fueled solely by its jam-packed coffins and their contents.

The person of Bishop Francis Prescott is based,

loosely, on the very real Bishop Beilby Porteus, who was for many years Bishop of London. An ardent reformer and abolitionist, Porteus was one of the leading supporters of the Slave Trade Act that passed Parliament in 1807. While a vocal opponent of both the French Revolution and the republican doctrines of Thomas Paine, he also penned the antiwar, antiempire poem quoted, in part, by Lord Jarvis. He died (peacefully) at the Bishop of London's summer residence of Fulham Palace in 1809. John Moore was the Archbishop of Canterbury from 1783 to 1805, when he was succeeded by the rather colorless Charles Manners-Sutton. My thanks to Ms. Janet Laws, personal secretary and assistant to the current Bishop of London, for answering some of my research queries on the bishops' former London residence.

Numerous sites and buildings referred to in this series, such as the first church of St. Pancras and the Temple, have been renovated or rebuilt in the past two hundred years and therefore appear differently now than they would have in 1812. I have described them as Sebastian would have seen them.

The life of William Franklin, son of Benjamin Franklin, was much as I have portrayed it, although he actually sailed from New York in September of 1782, rather than at the beginning of June, as I have it here. Most of the comments my characters make about the American Revolution and the young United States are taken from actual letters, journals, and speeches made at the time. While they might strike some as having a modern, slightly satirical ring, they are actually very true to the period, with most gentlemen of the Regency era viewing the new American state and its radical new form of government as a serious threat to civilization.

Wednesday, 22 July 1812

$\mathcal{A}$ cool wind gusted up, rattling the branches of the trees overhead and bringing with it the unmistakable clatter of wooden wheels approaching over cobblestones. Standing just outside the open gate to the alley, Paul Gibson doused his lantern, his eyes straining as he peered into the fog-swirled darkness. Thick clouds bunched overhead, obscuring the moon and stars, and promising more rain. He could see nothing but the high, rough stone walls of the yards around him and the refuse-choked mud of the lane that curved away into the mist.

A dog barked somewhere in the night. In spite of himself, Gibson shivered. It was a dirty business, this. But until the government revised its laws on human dissection, anatomists like Gibson could either resign themselves to ignorance or meet the resurrection men in the darkest hours before dawn.

Paul Gibson was not fond of ignorance.

He was a slim, dark-haired man of medium height,

Irish born and in his thirty-second year. Trained as a surgeon, he'd honed his skills on the battlefields of Europe until a French cannonball had shattered the lower part of one leg and left him with a weakness for the sweet relief to be found in poppies. Now he divided his time between sharing his knowledge of anatomy at hospitals like St. Thomas's and St. Bartholomew's, and working from his small surgery here, at the base of Tower Hill.

The dog barked again, followed this time by a man's low curse. A two-wheeled cart loomed out of the mist, the rawboned mule between the poles snorting and jibing at the bit when the driver drew up with a guttural "Whoa there, ye bloomin' idiot. Where ye think yer goin'? We got one more delivery t' make before ye can head home to yer barn."

A tall, skeletally thin man in striped trousers and a natty coat jumped from the cart and tipped his top hat in a flourishing bow. As he straightened, a waft of gin underlain with the sweet scent of decay carried on the wind. "We got him fer ye, Doctor," said Jumpin' Jack Cockran with a broad wink. "Mind ye, he's not as fresh as I like me merchandise to be, but ye did say ye wanted this particular gentleman."

Gibson peered over the cart's side at the bulky, man-sized burlap sack that lay within. Another name for the resurrection men was the sack-'em-up boys. "You're certain you've got the right one?"

"It's him, all right." Cockran motioned at the sturdy lad who accompanied him. "Grab the other end there, Ben."

Grunting softly, the two men slung the burlap-wrapped merchandise off the back of the cart. It landed heavily in the rank grass beside the gate.

"Careful," said Gibson.

Cockran grinned, displaying long, tobacco-stained teeth. "I can guarantee he didn't feel a thing, Doctor."

Hefting the heavy sack between them, the two men carried the merchandise into the stone outbuilding at the base of Gibson's overgrown garden and heaved it up onto the granite-slab table that stood in the center of the room. Working quickly, they peeled away the mud-encrusted sack to reveal the limp body of a young man, his dark hair fashionably cut, his hands soft and well manicured, as befitted a gentleman. His pale, naked flesh was liberally streaked with dirt, for the body snatchers had stripped off his shroud and grave clothes, and stuffed them back into his coffin before refilling the tomb. There was no law against carting a dead body through the streets of London. But stealing a cadaver *and* its grave clothes could earn a man seven years in Botany Bay.

"Sorry about the mud," said Cockran. "We've had a mite o' rain today."

"I understand. Thank you, gentlemen," said Gibson. "Here are your twenty guineas."

It was the going price for an adult male; adult females generally went for fifteen, with children being sold by the foot. Cockran shook his head and hawked up a mouthful of phlegm he shot out the door. "Nah. Make it eighteen. I got me professional pride, and he's not as fresh as I like 'em to be. But ye would have this one."

Gibson stared at the pallid, handsome face of the body lying on his dissection table. "It's not often a healthy young man succumbs to a weak heart. This gentleman's body has much to teach us about diseases of the circulation system."

"Weery interestin', I'm sure," said Cockran, scooping

up his muddy sack. "Thank ye kindly fer the business, and a weery good night to ye, sir."

After the men had left, Gibson relit his lantern and hung it from the chain suspended over the table. The lantern swayed gently back and forth, the golden light playing over the pale flesh of the body below. In life, his name had been Alexander Ross. A well-formed gentleman of twenty-eight years, he'd had long, leanly muscled arms and legs, and a broad chest tapering to a slim waist and hips. He looked as if he should have been the epitome of health. Yet, four days before, his heart had stopped as he slept peacefully in his own bed.

The delicate dissection of the defective heart would need to wait until daylight. But Gibson set to work with a bowl of warm water and a cloth, sponging off the mud of the graveyard and casting a preliminary practiced eye over the corpse.

It was when he was washing the soil from the back of the man's neck that he found it: a short purple slit at the base of the skull. Frowning, Gibson reached for a probe and watched in horror as it slid in four inches, easily following the path previously cut through living flesh by a stiletto.

Taking a step back, he set aside the probe with a soft clatter, his teeth sinking into his lower lip as he brought his gaze back to the young man's alabaster face. "Bloody hell," he whispered. "You didn't die of a defective heart. You were murdered."

The first rays of the rising sun caught the heavy mist off the river and turned it into shimmering wisps of gold and pink that hugged the soot-stained chimneys, church spires, and rooftops of the city. Standing beside his bedroom window, Sebastian St. Cyr, Viscount Devlin, cradled a glass of brandy in one hand. Behind him lay the tangled, abandoned ruin of his bed. He had not slept.

He was a tall man, leanly built. Not yet thirty years of age, he had dark hair and strange yellow eyes with an unnatural ability to see clearly at great distances or at night, when, for most men, the world was reduced to vague shadows of gray. Now, as the world outside the window brightened, he brought the brandy to his lips only to hesitate and set it aside untasted.

There were times when memories of the past tormented his sleep and drove him from his bed, times when his dreams echoed with the crash of cannonballs and the screams of mangled men, when the cloying scent of death haunted him and would not go away. But not this night. This night, he was troubled more by the present than the past. By a life-altering truth revealed too late, and a future he did not want but was honor-bound to embrace.

He reached again for his brandy, only to pause as the sound of frantic knocking reverberated through the house. Jerking up the sash, he leaned out, the cool air of morning biting his bare flesh as he shouted down at the figure on the steps below, "What the bloody hell do you want?"

The man's head fell back, revealing familiar features. "That you, Devlin?"

"Gibson?" Sebastian was suddenly painfully sober. "I'll be right down."

Pausing only to throw on a silk dressing gown, he hurried downstairs to find his majordomo, Morey, dressed in a paisley gown of astonishingly lurid reds and blues, and clutching a flickering candle that tipped dangerously as he worked at drawing back the bolts on the front door.

"Go back to bed, Morey," said Sebastian. "I'll deal with this."

"Yes, my lord." A former gunnery sergeant, the majordomo gave a dignified bow and withdrew.

Sebastian yanked open the front door. His friend practically fell into the marble-floored entrance hall. "What the devil's happened, Gibson? What is it?"

Gibson leaned against the wall. He was breathing heavily, his normally jaunty face haggard and streaked with sweat. From the looks of things, he hadn't been able to find a hackney and had simply hurried the distance from the Tower to Mayfair on foot—not an easy journey for a man with a wooden leg.

He swallowed hard and said, "I have a wee bit of a problem."

Sebastian stared down at the pale body stretched out on his friend's granite slab and tried to avoid breathing too deeply.

The sun was up by now. The wind had blown away the clouds and the last of the mist to leave the sky scrubbed blue and empty. Already, the day promised to be warm. From the corpse before him rose a sickly-sweet odor of decay.

"You know," said Sebastian, rubbing his nose, "if you'd left the man in his grave where he belonged, you wouldn't have a problem."

Gibson stood on the far side of the table, his arms folded at his chest. "It's a little late now."

Sebastian grunted. To some, they might seem unlikely friends, the Earl's heir and the Irish surgeon with a passion for unraveling the secrets of the human body. But there had been a time when both had worn the King's colors, when they'd fought together from the West Indies and Italy to the mountains of Portugal. Theirs was a friendship forged in all the horrors of blood and mud and looming death. Now they shared a dedication to truth and a passionate anger at the wanton, selfish destruction of one human being by another.

Gibson scrubbed a hand across the lower part of his face. "It's not like I can walk into Bow Street and say, 'By the way, mates, I thought you might be interested to know that I bought a body filched from St. George's churchyard last night. Yes, I know it's illegal, but here's the thing: it appears this gentleman whose friends all think died in his sleep was actually murdered.'"

Sebastian huffed a soft, humorless laugh. "Not if you value your life."

The authorities tended to turn a blind eye to the activities of body snatchers, unless they were caught redhanded. But the inhabitants of London were considerably less sanguine about the unauthorized dissection of their nearest and dearest. When word spread of a body snatching, hordes of hysterical relatives had a nasty habit of descending on the city's churchyards to dig up the remains of their loved ones. Since they frequently discovered only empty coffins and torn grave clothes, the resultant mobs then turned their fury on the city's hospitals and the homes of known anatomists, smashing and burning, and savaging any medical men unlucky enough to fall into their clutches.

Gibson was well-known as an anatomist.

Sebastian said, "Perhaps Jumpin' Jack dug up the wrong body."

Gibson shook his head. "I plan to check the rolls of mortality later today to make certain, but my money's on Jumpin' Jack. If he says this is Alexander Ross, then this is Alexander Ross."

Sebastian walked around the table, his gaze on the pale corpse.

Gibson said, "Do you recognize him?"

"No. But then, to my knowledge, I've never met anyone named Alexander Ross."

"I'm told he had lodgings in St. James's Street, above the *Je Reviens* Coffeehouse."

St. James's was a popular locale for young gentlemen. "Who told you he died of a defective heart?"

"A colleague of mine at St. Thomas's—Dr. Anthony Cooper. He was called in to examine the body. Swore there were no signs of any violence or illness; the man was simply lying dead in his bed when his valet came to rouse him that morning. Cooper was convinced he must have had a weak heart. That's why I was so anxious to dissect the body—to observe whatever malformation or damage might be present."

Sebastian hunkered down to study the telltale slit at the base of the man's skull. "Your Dr. Cooper obviously didn't think to look at the back of his patient's neck."

"Obviously not. But surely there would have been traces of blood on the pillow and sheets?"

"If Mr. Ross was killed in his bed, yes. I suspect he was not." Sebastian straightened and went to stand in the open doorway overlooking the unkempt garden that stretched from the stone outbuilding to the surgery beyond.

Gibson came to stand beside him. After a moment, the Irishman said, "Looks like a professional's work, doesn't it?"

"It does."

"I can't just pretend I didn't see this."

Sebastian blew out a long breath. "It's not going to be easy, investigating a murder no one knows occurred."

"But you'll do it?"

Sebastian glanced back at the pallid corpse on Gibson's dissection table.

The man looked to be much the same age as Sebastian. He should have had decades of rewarding life ahead of him. Instead he was reduced to this, a murdered cadaver on a surgeon's slab. And Sebastian knew a deep and abiding fury directed toward whoever had brought Ross to this end.

"I'll do it."

Sebastian St. Cyr investigates a murder
connected to an ancient legend in

WHEN MAIDENS MOURN,

the seventh Sebastian St. Cyr Mystery.
Available in hardcover from Obsidian in
March 2012.

Camlet Moat, Trent Place, England,
Sunday, 2 August 1812

Camlet Moat, Trent Place, England,
Sunday, 2 August 1812

*T*essa Sawyer hummed a soft, breathless tune to herself as she pushed through the tangled brush and bracken that edged the black waters of the ancient moat. She was very young—just sixteen at her next birthday. And though she tried to tell herself she was brave, she knew she wasn't. She could feel her heart pounding in her narrow chest, her hands tingling as if she'd been sitting on them. When she'd left the village, the night sky above had been clear and bright with stars. But here, deep in the wood, all was darkness and shadow. From the murky stagnant water beside her rose an eerie mist, thick and clammy.

It should have wafted cool against her cheek. Instead, she felt as if the heavy dampness were stealing her breath, suffocating her with an unnatural heat and a sick dread of the forbidden. She paused to swipe a shaky hand across her sweaty face and heard a rustling in the distance, the soft plop of something hitting the water.

Choking back a whimper, she spun about, ready to run. But today was Lammas, a time sacred to the ancient goddess. They said that at midnight on this night, if a maiden dipped a cloth into the holy well that lay on the northern edge of the isle of Camlet Moat and then tied her offering to a branch of the rag tree that overhung the well, her prayer would be answered. Not only that, but maybe, just maybe, the White Lady herself would appear, to bless the maid and offer her the wisdom and guidance that a motherless girl like Tessa yearned for with all her being.

No one knew exactly who the White Lady was. Father Clark insisted that if the lady existed at all—which he doubted—she could only have been the Virgin Mary. But there were those who claimed the White Lady was one of the Grail Maidens of old, a chaste virgin who'd guarded the sacred well since before the time of Arthur and Guinevere and the knights of the Roundtable. Some even whispered that the lady was Guinevere, ever young, ever beautiful, ever glorious.

Forcing herself to go on, Tessa clenched her fist around the strip of white cloth she was bringing as an offering. She could see the prow of the small dinghy kept at the moat by Sir Stanley Winthrop, on whose land she was trespassing. Its timbers old and cracked, its aged pale blue paint worn and faded, it rocked lightly at the water's edge as if touched by an unseen current.

It was not empty.

Tessa drew up short. A lady lay crumpled against the stern, her hair a dark cascade of curls around a pale, motionless face. She was young yet and slim, her gown an elegant flowing confection of gossamer muslin sashed with peach satin. She had her head tipped back, her neck arched; her eyes were open but sightless, her skin waxen.

And from a jagged rent high across her pale breast flowed a rivulet of darkness, showing where her life-blood had long since drained away.

ABOUT THE AUTHOR

C. S. Harris is a historian who lives in New Orleans. Writing as Candice Proctor, she is the author of seven award-winning historical romances. Under the name C. S. Graham, she coauthors contemporary thrillers with her husband, former intelligence officer Steven Harris. She has two daughters. Visit the author at www.csharris.net and http://csharris.blogspot.com.

AVAILABLE NOW

C.S. Harris

WHY MERMAIDS SING

A Sebastian St. Cyr Mystery

Murder has jarred London's elite. The sons of prominent families have been found at dawn in public places, their bodies brutally mutilated. With the help of his loyal friends and lover Kat Boleyn, high-born ex-spy Sebastian St. Cyr realizes that the key to finding the killer may lie in the enigmatic stanzas of a haunting poem...and in understanding an assassin with truly diabolical intentions.

"St. Cyr is a charismatic hero."
—*Kirkus Reviews* (starred review)

Available wherever books are sold or at
penguin.com

OM0033

AVAILABLE NOW

C.S. Harris

WHERE SERPENTS SLEEP

A Sebastian St. Cyr Mystery

London, 1812. The slaughter of eight young
prostitutes leaves one survivor—and one witness:
Hero Jarvis. When her Machiavellian father quashes
any official inquiry that might reveal his daughter's
unorthodox presence, Hero launches an investigation
of her own and turns to Sebastian St. Cyr for help.

Working in an uneasy alliance, Hero and Sebastian
follow a trail of clues leading from the seedy brothels
of London's East End to a noble family's Mayfair
mansion. Risking both their lives and their
reputations, the two must race against time to
stop a killer whose ominous plot threatens to shake
the nation to its very core.

OM0049